BLOODBORNE

OTHER BOOKS AND AUDIO BOOKS
BY GREGG LUKE

Altered States

Do No Harm

The Survivors

Blink of an Eye

BLOODBORNE

a novel

GREGG LUKE

Covenant Communications, Inc.

Cover image *Abstract Aged Paper* by Sx70 © iStockphotography.com, and *Mosquito isolated on white background* © iStockphotography.com

Cover design copyright © 2011 by Covenant Communications, Inc.

Published by Covenant Communications, Inc.
American Fork, Utah

Copyright © 2011 by Gregg Luke
All rights reserved. No part of this book may be reproduced in any format or in any medium without the written permission of the publisher, Covenant Communications, Inc., P.O. Box 416, American Fork, UT 84003. This work is not an official publication of The Church of Jesus Christ of Latter-day Saints. The views expressed within this work are the sole responsibility of the author and do not necessarily reflect the position of The Church of Jesus Christ of Latter-day Saints, Covenant Communications, Inc., or any other entity.

This is a work of fiction. The characters, names, incidents, places, and dialogue are either products of the author's imagination, and are not to be construed as real, or are used fictitiously.

Printed in the United States of America
First Printing: August 2011

17 16 15 14 13 12 11   10 9 8 7 6 5 4 3 2 1

ISBN: 978-1-60861-366-3

To Clifford Perkins
Teacher, father-in-law, spiritual giant, mosquito abatement worker, and good friend

Acknowledgments

The list of people who help me on my novels—either directly or indirectly—is endless. I am always bouncing ideas off coworkers, family, friends, and other health professionals—incorporating their suggestions into my writing. I would especially like to thank my daughters Brooke and Erika, and my lead technician Melissa Duce for offering wonderful critiques of the novel, and fellow authors Josi Kilpack and Erin Klingler who gave valuable suggestions to improve scenes and characters. In particular, I would like to thank my brother Lemar Luke for his incredible help on the technical details throughout the novel. If any tech errors slipped through, they are my fault, not his. I would also like to thank the staff at Covenant for continuing to support my mindless wanderings, and my amazing editor, Kirk Shaw, for his insights and brutal honesty.

FRIDAY
NOVEMBER 4, 2011

Chapter 1

Erin Cross's phone plinged and vibrated, indicating the receipt of a text message. The incoming number was a string of zeros; no name was attached. She pressed view.

You are about to die.

She palmed her phone and glanced around. Giamboli's sandwich deli looked like it usually did at this hour: Estelle Giamboli, an old Italian woman seemingly fresh off the boat, stood at the cash register near the entrance, chatting with whoever would give her an ear; a young man and woman, both in company aprons with their names embroidered as Sam and KrisAn, assembled sandwich orders behind a half-wall divider. The people she didn't recognize were the other patrons: an older couple sitting at a table across from the register, a quintet of high school–aged girls clucking and squealing around a table near the back, and a dark-haired man sitting alone two booths down from Erin's small table. The man looked to be in his early forties. He was reading from a notebook and was smiling. He was kinda cute but probably full of himself. Most of the good-looking ones were. A corner of sandwich and an untouched pickle were all that remained on his plate. His cell phone sat next to his crumpled napkin.

Erin pressed an app on her phone to access the caller info.

information unlisted

She toggled to call sender.

number out of service.

Out of service? Then how could they send a text? Figuring it was simply a glitch in her phone service or just a wrong number, Erin closed her phone and took another bite of her turkey and avocado croissant. Her phone plinged and vibrated again.

Say good-bye, Dr. Cross.

She frowned at the message for a time before realizing she was holding her breath. Perhaps whoever knew her name and cell number was playing a joke—albeit a sick one. Looking up, she noticed the man in the booth was now pressing keys on his cell phone. Was he the one sending her the messages? She didn't recognize him—

Pling-buzz.

You're dead in 60 seconds.

This was ridiculous. Not wanting to prolong this stupidity—but unable to completely ignore it—she focused on each patron in the deli. None of them looked like a would-be killer or a sick practical joker—at least not the kind you always saw in the movies.

Just then the man in the booth looked up with a serious expression. He glanced at Erin then at the high-school girls across from him then back at his phone.

It *was* him—it had to be. Erin pushed away from the table and marched over to the man. "I don't know who you are, but I don't appreciate your sick jokes," she snapped.

The man flinched. "Excuse me?"

"Don't play ignorant. The texting? I *saw* you do it!"

Taking a hesitant look around, the man appeared sincerely confused. "Is texting not allowed in here?"

"Don't get smart, jerk face." Erin tapped her phone. "Text me again and I'll call the police."

The man slid from the booth and held out his phone. "Look, I didn't text you, I promise. I'll show you my last transmission. See? From me, Sean Flannery, to Britt Flannery, my daughter. Unless your name is also Britt Flan—"

A loud crash stopped him mid-sentence. A man wearing a black ski mask and black clothing had burst through the glass front door, causing it to crack. In his gloved hand was a small metallic box with a short tube sticking out the front, a long and narrow box jutting from the bottom of the grip, and a trigger. The man quickly scanned the deli then raised the box, pointed it at the staff behind the counter, and pulled the trigger. The loud, metallic buzzing of machine-gun fire fractured the air. Estelle Giamboli screamed and fell. The younger employees dove for cover.

The high-school girls screeched and fled to an empty booth.

Sean grabbed Erin and shoved her into the booth.

"Stay down," he ordered.

Still in a fit of anger, Erin hated being told what to do. In spite of the danger, she sat up and watched Sean grab a chair and dash toward the gunman. Still firing at the employees behind the counter, the gunman saw Sean too late. One leg of the chair slammed into his face while another one struck his ribs. The momentum of the assault knocked both men to the floor. The machine gun clattered just out of reach.

As Sean scrambled for the gun, the masked assailant quickly regained his footing and vaulted over the counter.

"Stand up slowly where I can see you!" Sean yelled at the now gunless man, pointing the weapon in his direction. "You, call 911!" he shouted at Erin.

The masked man slowly rose and faced Sean. The assailant now gripped a large butcher knife in one fist.

"Drop the knife," Sean ordered.

The gunman pulled off his mask. Erin saw only his profile: light complexion, cropped dark hair, early thirties. In a steady, monotone voice, Erin heard the attacker say, *Pro novus ordo seclorum.* He then raised the knife and pointed it at the base of his throat.

"I said drop it!" Sean growled.

An eerie smile spread across the gunman's face. "It has begun," he said calmly. And with that, he quickly plunged the blade into his neck, gurgled for breath, then fell to the floor.

The intensity of the whole event finally slammed into Erin, and her adrenaline-charged anger evaporated. Her entire body began to tremble as her mind whirled. Exiting the booth, she dropped her phone.

"Did you get through?" Sean barked.

Erin stared numbly at her phone on the floor, trying to remember if she had made the call. She could not focus her thoughts, could not rein in her emotions. The room began to swim, and she felt her knees weaken.

"Did you call 911?" Sean shouted brusquely.

She stared at him but could not speak.

One of the high-school girls stepped from her booth and held up her cell phone. "I did. Police are on the way." The young woman's voice was staccato, shaky—exactly the way Erin felt.

Sean nodded then moved behind the counter.

In spite of her determination to be stoic, Erin's knees faltered. Losing the last vestiges of willpower, she collapsed back into the booth and forced herself not to cry.

Chapter 2

SEAN CHECKED OUT THE GUNMAN, confirming he was dead. Unfortunately, so were the old Italian woman and the young woman. The young man was alive but critically injured. Sean called one of the high-school girls over and had her put pressure on an oozing hole in the injured boy's shoulder. The others looked too shocked to help, one having passed out. The older couple remained seated, holding each other tightly, staring slack-jawed at the mess.

The gunman was middle-aged, Caucasian, in good shape but not athletic, with short hair. Physically, nothing about him screamed serial killer or fanatical terrorist. Sean thought it best to leave his cursory examination at that. He'd let the police search the guy for ID and other clues. He didn't want to become more involved than he had to.

Carrying a can of Sprite from the fridge behind the register, Sean returned to Erin and asked if she was hurt.

"No, I'm fine," she replied in a fluttery voice.

He sat down across from her, looking very serious. "Fine. Now tell me what *that* was all about."

She blinked hard a few times, as if appalled at the question. "The shooting? I have no idea. Why would you think I know anything abou—"

"Because you came up to me accusing me of sending sick messages," he interrupted harshly. "Then some psychopath comes in shooting up the place, and—" Sean stopped, realizing he was yelling at her. He leaned forward and took a breath. "Look, I didn't say you *were* involved. But there's got to be some connection between your accusations toward me and what just happened—don't you think?"

Erin considered him with steely eyes—like she suspected *him* of somehow being involved. "Like I said, I have no idea. I was just eating my lunch when I started getting these creepy texts."

"What did they say?"

She hesitated. "They were . . . threatening."

"Have you checked the return number?"

"Of course I have!" she huffed. "It was just zeros. When I hit CALL BACK, it rejected it as an invalid number."

"An invalid number, and you still got texts from it?"

"Hey, I'm not an idiot." Her look and tone radiated offense. "I *know* that's not possible, but it *is* what happened."

The strained wail of sirens peeled into the deli as two police cars screeched to a stop just outside. Sean shot a glance toward them then snapped open the can of soda.

"Fine. Stay right here and sip this. It'll help prevent you from going into shock. I'll be right back."

"What makes you think I'm going into shock?" she forced through a thin, shaky voice.

"Just do it," he said with zero compassion before heading back to the front of the deli to check on the injured boy.

* * *

Erin didn't want to sip his stupid soda. She *was* shaky, true, but she wasn't going into shock. And she didn't want to *stay right there* either, as he had insisted. Who did he think he was, anyway? She wanted to get out of that place. The air was rank with gunpowder and the scent of drying blood.

Even though Erin considered herself a strong person, the suddenness of the incident *had* left her light-headed and nauseous. She stood, took a step, then dropped back onto her seat as a wave of vertigo overwhelmed her. Maybe she *was* in shock. Maybe. But how could *he* tell?

She scowled and pinched the bridge of her nose. It didn't matter.

The fact that she was being so weak infuriated her. She refused to be one of *those* women.

The five high-school girls stood at the rear of the deli, all chatting anxiously on cell phones. *As if they needed more fodder for their bubble-headed gossip sessions,* Erin thought caustically. The unconscious one had awakened a few minutes earlier and was now sobbing into her phone. Having almost fainted herself, Erin actually felt for the girl—a little. At least Erin wasn't blubbering like a ninny. The old man and his wife still held each other tightly, their pale skin all the more pasty from fright. Erin wondered how long they'd been together. She was surprised neither had died from a heart attack.

Erin sipped her soda but found it hard to swallow. Her throat felt constricted, gummy. The police entered the next moment with guns drawn. An ambulance chirped to a halt just outside. The dark-haired hero identified himself and began speaking to the officers. She heard some of their words, but none of their conversation registered in her head. The officers began asking questions of the old couple. She heard garbled muttering, but her thoughts were too disjointed to allow comprehension. She sipped her soda again and tried to focus.

A bulky officer with a shaved head and deep-set eyes approached her.

"Ma'am? Are you okay?" The gentleness in his voice surprised her.

She nodded. "I'm fine, thank you." The soda's sugar was kicking in, and her tremors were subsiding.

The officer wrote down her demographics then asked her several questions related to the incident. She answered with concise, clipped responses and showed him the threatening texts. She tried to be helpful, but she had little useful information to offer.

"Ma'am, I need you to identify the gunman," he said almost as an apology.

Erin was instantly defensive. "Identify him? How am *I* supposed to know who he is?"

"That's what we need to determine," the officer said. "You mentioned you only saw his profile from a distance. Please. It'll only take a second."

The officer helped Erin to her feet and escorted her around the counter. The man's face was covered with a dish towel, which formed a teepee where the knife still stood. She took a breath and nodded. An EMT drew back the cloth just enough to see the gunman's face. Erin's brows pulled together. The guy looked fairly average: no piercings or tattoos she could see, a short conservative haircut, and a lightly tanned and pleasant face—had he not been dead. Still, she had no idea who he was.

"I've never seen him before," she whispered.

The EMT replaced the towel. The officer escorted Erin back to her seat, thanked her, and left. She took another sip of the Sprite and fixated on the condensation beading on the cold aluminum can.

"How're you holding up?"

Erin looked up to see that the dark-haired man had rejoined her. "Okay, I guess."

"Look, we kinda got off on a bad foot. My name is Sean Flannery." He smiled and tilted his head to one side. "Yes, the ancestry is Irish, but I was born right here in the USA, so I don't have the charming accent."

"Erin Cross," she said, allowing herself a slight smile. "Sorry for biting your head off earlier."

Sean nodded in acceptance. He had a few strands of gray at his temples and a smattering of crow's-feet when he smiled. It was a lopsided, almost boyish smile. He had remarkably pale blue eyes, which made for a disarming contrast with his dark hair. There was a warm, rich timbre to his voice, making some of his words felt as well as heard. He was about six feet tall and in very good shape—which meant he was probably obsessed with exercise.

"Well, truth be told, I came across pretty gruff myself," he said. He looked back to the commotion at the front of the deli. They were placing the dead man on a stretcher. "So, any thoughts on whether or not your creepy text messages and the psychopath are connected?"

She shook her head.

"Did you mention them to the police?"

"Yes. The officer even checked my call log to verify the texts and that the incoming number was inoperable."

Sean paused, thinking. "Well, all's well that ends well. I guess we both came off pretty lucky." He pulled out his cell phone and began texting a message.

Lucky? Erin frowned. Still dizzy and on edge, his words came across as glib. True, she wasn't dead. But witnessing a murder-suicide was certainly not her idea of luck. Nor did she believe this madness had fully ended. She didn't know why she felt that way. If the gunman had sent the messages, then that was that. But who was he? And why did he want *her* dead?

And then there was this Rambo-wanna-be. Although Erin was very grateful for his intervention, he was just as big a mystery. "Where did you learn to move like that?" she asked, nodding toward the front of the deli.

"Marines. Special Ops," he said in a noncommittal tone.

"Oh."

The conversation abruptly ended at that point. Sean turned to watch the police and EMTs do their work.

Erin felt nausea inching up her throat. The longer she sat there, the more intense the odor of clotting blood and spent gunpowder became. The deli's normally fragrant cold cuts now reeked as if putrefied; the fresh-baked bread smelled fetid, moldering. The noises around her congealed into a disorienting tumult. The walls began to close in. She needed fresh air.

"Excuse me," she mumbled. "I have to go."

Erin stood and staggered to the door. Sean tried to help, but she shooed him away.

The angle of the setting sun blinded her as she exited the sandwich shop. A crowd had gathered outside, and the myriad sounds, flashing lights, and jumbled conversations added to her delirium. Doing her best to ignore them, Erin headed down the sidewalk at a brisk pace. The meager exercise helped. She breathed deeply through her nose and rolled her shoulders to relax them.

Just as she started her car, her cell phone plinged and vibrated.

A line of zeros. She cringed and flipped it open.

It's not over.

Chapter 3

Erin sat in her black Nissan 350Z with her eyes closed. The unseasonably warm afternoon was gone, and even though the evening had cooled considerably, she cranked up her AC to help clear her head. The disturbing sights and sounds she'd experienced a few hours earlier still harried her mind. She had no idea who was trying to kill her or why. And who the heck was Sean Flannery?

Erin shook her head and took several deep breaths. She glanced up and down the street. The Friday evening traffic was already thick. She shifted into first gear and launched into a narrow gap in traffic. Instead of going straight home, she headed toward her office. Once there, she'd call the police and inform them of the text she'd just received. Because she'd missed the last half-day of work, she was concerned about not having everything secure before leaving for the weekend. Not that she had any big weekend plans. She rarely did.

At a red light, Erin looked in her rearview mirror. A dark sedan, two cars behind her, looked like the same one she'd seen several blocks back. But there was only one man inside. Usually there were two: one to drive, one to shoot. She snorted then laughed.

"This is nonsense," she said out loud. "You're not in a stupid spy movie. Stop being so paranoid."

But was she? She'd just witnessed a double murder and a suicide, where someone claimed *she* had been the intended target.

A honking horn signified the traffic light had turned green. She took off and again looked in her mirror. Erin swore under her breath as the car behind her turned left, leaving the black sedan directly behind her. The man wore dark glasses and held a deadpan expression. Perhaps he was simply a bored businessman heading home for a much-needed weekend. Then again . . .

Because of her delayed start, there was a generous gap in the traffic in front of her. Erin floored her Z, creating a cloud of tire smoke as she peeled away. Reaching the next intersection in a matter of seconds, she turned right and hit the accelerator again. At the next intersection she turned left, and found herself entering a large used-car dealership. She pulled between two F-150 pickups and put her car in park. Stepping out, she peered over the hood of the truck at the dealership entrance. Willing her heart rate and respiration to slow did no good. She sucked in each breath as if she'd just finished a hundred-yard dash.

But the dark sedan was nowhere to be seen. Had she really outrun him? Or had he been following her in the first place?

Erin slumped against the hood of her Z and chastised herself. She was better than this. *Flighty* was not a word anyone would use to describe her, she was certain. So why was she acting that way now? Her gaze drifted up to the darkly bruised sky and marveled at how closely it resembled her current angst. She groaned with regret. She had a pretty good guess why she was acting this way: something close to this had happened before.

Dr. Erin Cross was a brilliant, twenty-nine-year-old recluse. Having grown up in a male-dominated, athletics-obsessed household, Erin spent a lot of time hiding in the background. Back then, her father was the head football coach at Timpanogos High; her five older brothers were all into football, wrestling, and a few additional sports when they could find the time. Erin's mother had been a volleyball star at BYU and at sixty-five still competed in half-marathons. While the boys were very popular in school, church, and in the community, Erin had been just the opposite. She kept to herself and stayed indoors most of the time. Many people didn't even know her brothers had a little sister. She simply never got into the Utah Valley social scene. In fact, her mom was more concerned about Erin's social life than she was.

Much to her family's chagrin, Erin had not inherited any of the athletic traits the rest of them possessed. Although she was decidedly pretty, at five foot four and 161 pounds, Erin was statistically overweight but not obese. She claimed she was "well-rounded" in more ways than one. Actually, she didn't give a hoot what others thought about her proportions. She was comfortable with who she was. She had taken a course in self-defense at the behest of her mother but really didn't need it to boost her self-confidence. Erin's passion was science, not activities that involved sweat, social obligations, or potential damage to her body or ego.

In spite of that, Erin rarely felt lonely. She delved into the what-ifs of science to the point that the thrill of discovery became her adrenaline rush. She read everything that was required and then some. If a teacher mentioned a book as *suggested* reading, she'd pick up a copy that day. If a book annotated a text that looked intriguing, she'd read that book too. Her rigorous study habits led to the development of a near-photographic memory, or, as she claimed, an eidetic memory. After three quick years, she graduated valedictorian of Timp High with a full-ride scholarship to the University of Utah. There, she devoured college with a singularity of appetite. At twenty-one, she'd finished her bachelor's in biochemistry; at twenty-four, her PhD in epidemiology. Her thesis, "Viral Antigenic Shift in Pandemic Diseases," was heralded as groundbreaking—perhaps even Nobel-worthy. But she wasn't interested in accolades or notoriety. Her desires focused on eliminating the horrific diseases that plagued most third-world countries.

Two weeks before her undergraduate commencement, Erin's parents had moved to the Midwest, where her dad was offered an assistant coaching position at Ohio State. Her brothers had long since married and moved away to start their own careers. No one in her family made it back to watch her accept either of her university degrees. Even with a number of friends at school and church, receiving her Baccalaureate without family present made her feel alone; receiving her PhD alone made her feel abandoned.

Erin was offered several prestigious jobs across the country, but she ended up accepting a position at Timpanogos Research Industries—TRI for short—a designer biochemical and genetics lab in Lehi, Utah. The company slogan was, "We do more than try at TRI." Corny, but accurate. They were recognized as a global player in genetic research and biochemical engineering. They had even contracted with the

Department of Homeland Security to model proactive bioterrorism scenarios. Erin quickly became one of their most highly regarded researchers.

Her most recent discovery could literally change the mortality rate of the world. To drug manufacturers, it could mean billions in profits.

Erin's cell phone rang, startling her. It was TRI's private line.

"Hello?"

"Erin, it's Tom. I just heard the news. Are you okay?" His voice was urgent, filled with concern. Tom Jenkins was CEO of Timpanogos Research and a very good friend.

"Just a little shaken up, Tom. I wasn't hit."

"Oh, thank goodness." He expelled a burst of air, as if he'd been holding his breath for hours. "I tried reaching you at home, but I just got your machine. That's why I'm calling your cell. Where are you?"

"Just out for a drive," she said, feeling comfort just hearing his voice.

"Really? Okay, listen, it's almost eight. Please tell me you don't have any ridiculous notions about coming back to work until Monday."

She smiled. "*You're* still at work."

She heard him chuckle lightly. "Yeah, but I'm just leaving. Julie and I are gonna spend some time with the grandkids. After hearing what you've been through, I bet you want some time off, too."

Erin looked at the stream of lights flowing along I-15 and sighed. Time off. Why would she need time off? She never did anything. "Thanks, Tom. I'll think about it. But I do need to close things down for the weekend, so I'll be there in a few."

Tom's response was not immediate. "Um . . . okay, Erin . . . if that's . . . what you think is important. I'll see you sometime next week, then. If you decide to take some time off, that's fine, too, but call me first, okay?"

"Sure, Tom. Thanks. Have fun with the grandkids."

Erin closed her phone and allowed herself another smile. Tom Jenkins was the father she never had. Even though her bio-dad had been loving and kind, Erin never felt a true bond with him. She knew it was from her lack of interest in sports. In spite of what he said, she always felt he was disappointed—perhaps even embarrassed—by her lack of athleticism. His actions spoke louder than his words. But she didn't hold it against him. After all, his lack of interest in science was about the same.

When Erin had hired on with TRI, Tom had immediately taken her under his wing. Tom Jenkins and a financial wizard named Luther Mendenhall had started the company nineteen years earlier. While Luther ran the business end of things, Tom focused on R&D. The small lab took some time gaining a foothold in the fiercely competitive bio-research market, but before long they were holding their own.

Erin had met Luther only once or twice at company parties and such. He was arrogant and aloof—a stuffy billionaire whose egocentric nature bordered on narcissism. Tom, on the other hand, she saw almost daily. Tom was kind and encouraging and subtly brilliant. He had a beautiful wife and four amazingly successful sons. Just as he'd become Erin's surrogate father, she'd become his surrogate daughter. She'd even accompanied the Jenkinses on family outings a time or two. She knew she could ask anything of Tom at any time—which gave her a good deal of comfort.

Erin had just dropped her phone in her purse when it plinged and vibrated. Text received. Tom must have forgotten something. She pulled the phone back out. It wasn't his number.

A string of zeros.

Normally, she never sent or read texts while driving, but this instance was unique. She pressed VIEW.

You can run, but you can't hide.

Chapter 4

Dr. Jacob Krantz looked like your average Joe Businessman: five ten, narrow-framed (except for a well-formed paunch), thinning hair neatly trimmed, dark crescents under his eyes, and an indolent smile. He wore a loose Utah Jazz necktie against a starched white shirt, Dockers, and Rockports. He had a windbreaker draped over one arm and his medium-sized carry-on slung over his shoulder.

Waiting in the Delta Airlines queue at Salt Lake International, he appeared patient but bored. Most people in the line were frantically checking and rechecking everything, making sure nothing would hinder their departures.

The security steward compared his boarding pass with his passport and driver's license, smiled curtly, and mumbled a disingenuous, "Have a nice flight." Jacob said thanks, moved to the security check, placed his satchel on the conveyor belt, removed the requisite clothing, and stepped into the scanner. Green light.

The TSA officer at the conveyor belt opened his carry-on and examined its contents. Jacob stood by and watched as impassively as he could. He had five 100-mL bottles in a ziplock baggie inside the satchel: two marked SHAMPOO, two marked SOFT SOAP, and one marked CONDITIONER. Each bottle was made of opaque plastic that allowed quite a bit of light to penetrate so one could see the liquid sloshing inside. They all had tops with a hinged nipple that allowed easy dispensing of the contents. The officer pulled a bottle from the baggie, flipped up the nipple, and sniffed it. It smelled like soap. He returned the bottle to the baggie, rummaged through a few other items in the satchel, then handed it back to Jacob with a curt expression of thanks.

"No problem," Jacob said.

He retrieved his other belongings and moved to a bench to don his belt and shoes. A chubby man in a gaudy Hawaiian-print shirt and cargo shorts plopped next to him. The man's shorts rode several inches higher than his pinkish tan line. In a voice twice the volume needed for a private conversation, the man declared, "Next thing you know, they'll require a full body-cavity search."

Jacob smiled politely. "Actually, the technology already exists where they can do an instantaneous X-ray of your internal and external body parts and even read the manufacturer's label on your underwear—no stripping required."

The big man paused mid-buckling of his Birkenstock sandals over his argyle socks. "You mean it?"

Jacob nodded. "You bet. From your hair plugs down to your toenail fungus. They can even reveal that embarrassing tattoo you hope no one ever sees."

The man swallowed hard, finished buckling his sandals, and tugged on a ball cap advertising REVYVE. "Hey, honey," he called to a hefty woman the next bench over. "You gotta hear this," he said, moving toward her.

Knowing he would soon be a focal point as the man shared what he'd just learned, he slipped a Bluetooth phone over his ear and headed toward the departure gate.

Finding a seat away from anyone else, he took out a blank 5×8 index card and a fountain pen from his carry-on. Using a clipboard, he stood the pen in a suction-cup stand and placed the index card in front of it. Depressing a small button, a small red laser dot emanated from a pore near the top of the pen, centering on the card. After a five-second wait, the laser projected a QWERTY keyboard on the card in the same red light. Using the virtual keys, he typed, *No problems getting past security.*

Pressing ALT and S, two soft beeps sounded in his Bluetooth earpiece. Sending an encoded message was a lot more secure than making a phone call, especially in an airport that monitored every electronic device. Using a device like his computer pen was just plain fun.

After a moment's pause, the keyboard morphed into a single cursor that blinked three times then typed out, *Proceed as planned.*

"Hey, buddy," a familiar voice said in greeting. "You headin' to the islands, too?"

Jacob clicked off the computer pen and looked up. It was Hawaiian Shirt and his wife. Jacob smiled and raised a hand to the unit on his ear and held up an index finger with the other, requesting a moment.

The man placed his beefy hand over his mouth and gave an exaggerated grimace in way of apology.

"Yeah, that's okay with me," Jacob said aloud to no one, as if talking on his Bluetooth phone. "I love you, too, sweetheart. I'll call you as soon as I get in. Bye-bye." He tapped the earpiece and slid the blank index card into his satchel.

"Sorry about that," Hawaiian Shirt said. "I can't get used to people using those ear things. I guess I'm hopelessly lost in technological denial."

"That's okay. I always feel weird using it because it looks like I'm talking to myself," Jacob said with a halfhearted chuckle.

"Chattin' with the wife?"

"Daughter. She's nine. I wish I could bring her along, but school, you know."

"Great age, nine," the man said as he made himself comfortable in the seat across from Jacob. "Still haven't developed an attitude yet, and you're still a hero. Give it two or three years and suddenly you're a mean, heartless taskmaster who doesn't understand anything. You can take my word on that," he said, followed by an exasperated expulsion of air.

"All the more reason I wish she was with me," Jacob said.

"So is your wife with you?" Hawaiian Shirt's better half asked, sitting next to him. She wore a matching Polynesian-print shirt that strained against her generous bosom and girth.

"She passed away two years ago," Jacob said, pretending to unsuccessfully hide a quaver in his voice. "My daughter stays with my sister when I'm away on business."

The woman's hand quickly settled on her breastbone as she drew a short gasp. "Oh, I'm so sorry."

Jacob rubbed the back of his neck and said, "Life goes on, right?"

"What business you in?" Hawaiian Shirt asked.

"Clothing. I have a small distributorship that sells off-label brands to local retailers."

"Make any money?"

"Barely keeps me one step ahead of the bill collectors."

"Right," the man said skeptically. "That's why you're heading to the islands tonight."

"Trust me, this *is* a business trip. I want to market Kauai's Red Dirt Shirts in the Intermountain area." Jacob smirked and tugged on his tie. "You think I'd be heading to Hawaii in a shirt and tie if I didn't have to?"

The man guffawed and leaned forward, extending his meaty hand. "Okay, you got me. Gordon Talley."

Jacob's hand almost disappeared in the man's gorilla-sized fist. "Dan Brown. Not the author."

Gordon pulled an enormous bag of red licorice from his carry-on and opened it to Jacob. "Licorice, Dan? It's fat free."

Jacob shook his head. "No thanks. I'm strictly a black licorice man. I consider it one of the four basic food groups."

"We're into ReVyve, Dan," Mrs. Talley said. "You ever heard of it?"

Jacob nodded. ReVyve was the latest craze in the multilevel-marketing circus of wonder products guaranteed to cure every ailment known to man while boosting vitality, virility, veracity, and vivaciousness.

Having earned a PhD in Infectious Disease, Jacob was always interested in new "scientific" discoveries. But everything he'd read on ReVyve products was the same old hype derived from minimal research and tons of extrapolation and speculation. ReVyve was a new extract from the Tibetan goji, a red, pod-shaped fruit containing tiny yellow seeds. But it wasn't really all that new. It'd been used for centuries throughout Northern Asia and Europe. It was supposed to be the next big "super fruit," with antioxidant levels off the charts.

He scoffed inwardly. Even if that was true, it didn't mean it would perform miracles. ReVyve's marketing spin was typical of MLM health product promoters. Their claims—based largely on anecdotal evidence and small population studies—were also off the charts. They always were. First there was aloe vera, then Tahitian noni, then sea buckthorn, then acai, now goji. Ugh! He braced himself, knowing an overzealous MLM, get-rich-quick pitch was imminent. Perhaps stating he knew all about it would circumvent the forthcoming diatribe.

"It's a super fruit from Northern China," Jacob said. "But I don't—"

"It's a miracle is what it is," Mrs. Talley exclaimed, cutting him off. "It's been around for thousands of years, too, but the big drug companies have kept a lid on it because they can't patent it, which means they can't get rich off it. Such greed is downright immoral. But the secret's out now. And we're in on the ground floor. We won this trip to Hawaii by becoming gold-leaf distributors. Even if you're not good at sales, you can be a millionaire before you know it because this stuff sells itself. Since I've been on it, I've lost twenty pounds and my irritable bowel issues have—"

"Oops," Jacob interrupted, raising a finger to his earpiece. "Excuse me a sec." He tapped the earpiece once. "Hello, this is Dan. Oh, hello, sir. Yes, I'm at the airport now. My plane leaves in about an hour. Yes." Jacob stood and moved to a more private area. The Talleys didn't seem to mind.

Pretending he was talking to someone was his only means of escape. Normally he didn't mind chatting up people at the airport. It took his mind off flying. He hated flying. Air travel was just . . . wrong. But in this instance, he didn't have much choice. The test site he and his superior had agreed on was ideal, pristine. And time was of the essence. The larvae teeming in the five plastic bottles in his carry-on would hatch into adults within forty-eight hours.

Chapter 5

Erin walked through the sour whitewash of mercury vapor lamps in Timpanogos Research's parking lot. The lot was occupied by about a dozen vehicles belonging to the night staff, many of whom she knew because she spent so much time at work. Erin entered the main entrance with a determined stride.

"Hey, Harry," she greeted the night watchman.

"Hey, Dr. C. Y'all okay?"

Harry Harriman was a large black man from Baton Rouge who started at TRI long before Erin joined the firm. His face was one of those elastic kind that could go from the friendliest, twinkling-eyed smile just begging for a hug to a hard, brow-furrowed scowl that would intimidate a grizzly with a toothache. His face unfailingly belied his mood. Luckily, his smile was broad and toothy this evening.

"Yeah. Just had an extended lunch and I want to shut things down for the weekend."

"An 'extended lunch?'" he scoffed in his flagrant Cajun accent. "Y'all made da evenin' news, girl. Shoot, it's lucky y'all ain't dirt-nappin' in da morgue."

"Wait—I'm on the news already?"

"Jus' your name, cher'. You was listed wid a bunch'a others in dat Italian deli. Why? What's da matta' wid bein' on da news?"

"Oh, no reason," she said. Then, stopping just past his semicircular reception desk, she asked, "Hey, you haven't seen anyone . . . *strange* around here lately, have you?"

Harry's smile dropped a notch. "Strange?"

"Yeah, you know. Someone who doesn't work here or seems to be loitering, or is asking a bunch of questions for no apparent reason?"

The smile slipped another notch. "No, ma'am, not really. Dere be dat bunch from Japan who come in wid Dr. Moran da otha' evenin'. Den dere dat mess o' rug bugs from Eagle Mount'n Element'ry las week. I still can't reckon what a bunch o' kids would fine interestin' 'bout a place like dis."

"No, I mean someone acting alone."

"*Actin'* alone?" he questioned.

Erin bit her lower lip, frustrated at her inability to voice exactly what she was thinking. It would help if *she* knew what she was thinking. "Never mind, Harry. Just . . . well, let me know if anyone you don't recognize asks for me, okay?"

The smile was totally gone now. "Is someone botherin' you, cher'? You want I should call da police?"

She shook her head. "No. But thanks. I've just had some prank phone calls, that's all."

The big man folded his thick arms across his equally thick chest. "Y'all not just smokin' blowfish now, are ya, suga'?"

Erin grinned. "I don't even know what that means, but I'm going to answer no."

Harry leaned forward. "You need me, you call, ya hea'?"

"Thanks, Harry."

Erin headed for the twin elevators. Ascending to her sixth-floor office, she couldn't help but feel anxious. The more she thought about the gunman in the café, the more a connection formed between what she had discovered a few years back and why her death would protect others. Her reasoning bordered on paranoia, but it was still viable.

The door to her office was locked—just as she'd left it that afternoon. After swiping her key card, she punched in her access code. A bright red light flashed, accompanied by a harsh buzz. ACCESS DENIED. Huh? She tried it again and got the same result. She punched the intercom button, which connected to the front desk.

"Hey, Harry, it's Erin. I can't seem to get my office unlocked. Can you have security open it from your end?"

The guard did not answer.

She held the down button. "Harry? Can you hear me?"
Still no answer.
Bathroom break, she thought.

Returning to the elevators, she waited for the car, watching the numbers indicate its ascent to her floor. Just after the first car started to rise, the second one did, too.

Perhaps Tom had secured her office to help protect her research. He was the only one who understood her desire for secrecy. *Yeah, that had to be it. Good ol' Tom.*

Erin was the lead scientist on her current project. There were several others privy to her research, but the details still remained secured in her computer. Good thing, too. From past experiences, she insisted on that modality. Her new drug—a vaccine, really—could save millions of lives worldwide. But it had yet to be perfected. An early release could spell disaster. Just like last time.

The elevator arrived with a subtle pling that reminded Erin of her cell phone. She stepped into the car and pushed the button for the first floor. Pulling out her phone, she accessed the incoming text files.

You are about to die.
Say good-bye, Dr. Cross.
You're dead in 60 seconds.
It's not over.
You can run, but you can't hide.

The deli gunman clearly had not sent the messages, because they continued after his demise. So who else would want her dead?

Sean Flannery claimed that the gunman had said something in Latin. She had heard only a portion of it: something about a new world order. Maybe that was a clue. Hopefully he'd remember what the psycho had said. Thanks to Erin's incredible memory, she knew the number to Sean's cell phone from just a glance. She started to dial it but then realized it was now almost eleven at night. It would be rude to awaken him at this hour. Well, that is assuming he was already asleep. Someone with his looks was probably out on a date or at a singles event hunting for his next conquest. By tomorrow morning he probably wouldn't remember her anyway. Most men didn't look twice at her.

The elevator doors opened on the main floor with a soft *whoosh*.

Erin exited and headed toward the reception counter. Harry was not there. Nor was his BE RIGHT BACK placard. That was not right. Harry took his job very seriously. Even if he'd taken a bathroom break, he would have left the placard on the counter.

"Harry?" she called.

No answer.

Drawing closer to the reception desk, she smelled something like smoke—but it was harsher, sharper than cigarettes or matches. Then she saw Harry's shoes extending out from behind the desk. Rounding the reception counter, she put her hand to her mouth to stifle a scream.

Harry Harriman lay on his back, halfway under his desk. A bright red stain spread from the center of his chest, where a dark hole sat in stark contrast to his white shirt. His eyes stared blankly at the underside of the desk. His mouth was partially open, as if wanting to make one final utterance.

Harry's been shot! Why would someone kill Harry?

Down the hall, a second elevator dinged its arrival. Erin froze, not knowing what to do. She heard the doors begin to slide open. Was it *him*—the guy who had killed Harry? Was it the same guy who wanted *her* dead? Was she next?

Fearing what those answers might bring, Erin bolted for the front doors and fled into the chilly, shadow-strewn parking lot.

Chapter 6

Back in his Orem apartment, Sean Flannery sat on his sofa, staring at a football game on his plasma screen TV but not really seeing it. The images of that afternoon kept playing through his mind. He had been eating a leisurely lunch at Giamboli's deli; he got a text from his daughter about a class she was taking; a short blonde lady came up to him accusing him of sending sick text messages; a masked gunman came in and starting shooting up the place; he intervened; the gunman said something in Latin before killing himself; the police came, questioned everyone; and everyone left.

It was the first time Sean had eaten there. He wasn't sure why he'd picked it. He liked trying new places, and he had been craving Italian food. Perhaps it was just curious timing.

He tugged at his lower lip as he focused on the woman. She said her name was Erin Cross. She had no idea who the gunman was—but neither did Sean.

Erin Cross. He knew they'd never met before, but her name had a certain ring . . .

So did the Latin phrase the gunman quoted . . . but Sean couldn't remember from where.

He shook his head and decided to get some writing done. He first went to the fridge for a diet soda, swallowed an ibuprofen, then moved to his computer and logged in. He always took an ibuprofen before a stint at the computer because he was prone to headaches from the flat screen's artificial light. His latest project was a sequel to a children's story he'd published three years earlier.

How the Snail Got Its Slimy Trail, by Sean Flannery.

Sean had promised his daughter he'd write the sequel when she entered high school. Now that she'd gone back east to college, he figured he'd better get to it before she lost interest. It amazed him how fast time flew.

Sean smiled at the memories surrounding the story. He'd made it up on the spot while teaching Britt about the negative consequences of lying. It was a clear day in early spring. He had poured Britt the cereal and milk and asked her to eat it in the kitchen. After just a few minutes of writing, he left his computer to grab a soda. Heading to the kitchen, he found a pile of soggy Froot Loops surrounded by a purple-tinted milk stain on their beige living room carpet. Sean set about cleaning up the mess and called to Britt. She shuffled in with eyes lowered and a doll held tightly to her chest.

"Sweetie, I asked you to eat this in the kitchen, didn't I?"

Six-year-old Britt shifted from one foot to the other but didn't answer.

"Why didn't you clean up this cereal when it spilled?" Sean asked.

She continued shifting but wouldn't meet his eyes.

"Honey, I asked you a question. Please answer me."

The little girl stopped shifting and hugged her doll tighter.

"I sure hope this doesn't stain permanently. It sure would have been a lot easier to clean up if we'd done it right after you spilled."

"I didn't spill," Britt said softly.

Sean stopped sponging the floor and gave her a stern look. "Britt, the only thing worse than not cleaning up a mess is lying about making one."

Tears balanced on her lashes and her chin began to quiver. "But I didn't."

Sean's voice remained calm. "Britt, listen to me, sweetheart. It's bad that you didn't clean this up right away or didn't ask for help to clean it up. I'm sure it was an accident, and that's okay. Accidents happen. But you and I are the only ones home right now. And I know *I* haven't had any Froot Loops today. So that means either an evil troll named Snotdrop intentionally made this mess, or perhaps a little girl who I love very much had an accident, and she was afraid to say anything.

Now, which story is probably the true one?"

Britt sniffled and used her doll to wipe her tears. "The little girl."

Sean smiled. "I agree. Now, can you get me some more paper towels, please, so we can clean this up before Mommy gets home? Then we'll both have a bowl of Froot Loops *in the kitchen*, okay?"

"Okay," she said as she peeled off to the kitchen.

Later, as they ate their cereal, Britt asked whether or not the carpet would be stained forever. She was afraid everyone would know she had fibbed because of the stain. The comment sparked something in Sean's mind and he created the snail story on the spot. It flowed so naturally it was almost as if he was reciting something already written. He jotted it down, polished it a bit, and sent it to a freelance agent a week later.

Three weeks after that, his wife left him and took Britt with her.

Sean shook his head to prevent his mind from visiting such unhappy memories. The trouble was both good and bad memories were so closely entwined. The bad times haunted him—along with many experiences from his stint in Special Ops. But he had so many reasons to be happy, too. He had his daughter—his sole purpose for living. He was in good health, physically and mentally—well, as much as could be expected after such military service. And he was a mildly successful writer—a dream of his since childhood.

Sean stretched his neck to one side and huffed at his blank computer screen. He simply could not get into the mood of the tale. Sometimes that happened—especially when his memories haunted him. It also was an indication it was time for his meds. His desk clock read 10:49 PM. Oops. He was almost an hour late. He hurried to the kitchen to swallow his nightly regimen of pills. He hated taking them but knew they were necessary. He simply was not the same man without them. In fact, he hated the man he became without them. Apparently, Valerie had too. Perhaps that's why she left him. Well, one of the reasons, anyway.

He went to shut down his computer then remembered he hadn't checked his e-mail. Britt usually tried to shoot him off a message if her school schedule wasn't too demanding. He pulled up his account and saw only one message. Opening it, he read:

Don't forget to take your meds. I'm so proud of you, Daddy!

He smiled as a penetrating warmth filled his chest. He typed that he was proud of her, too. He then shut off his computer, brushed his teeth, said his prayers, crawled into bed, and fumbled into a tenuous sleep.

Chapter 7

Jacob Krantz, PhD, had managed to board the plane while avoiding further conversation with the Talleys. But he almost wished they'd been there to distract him. Entering the fuselage, he'd kept his eyes fixated on the seat numbers. He refused to look down the length of the large, overcrowded aluminum cylinder he'd soon be strapped in. He reclined as far back as his business class seat would go, swallowed a Valium, donned his headphones, and tried to relax. As soon as he could, he'd ask the flight attendant for anything with alcohol. It just never felt right traveling 35,000 feet in the air in a metal tube that weighed roughly 190,000 pounds. That's 95 tons! He shuddered. People should not trust their lives inside something that heavy, held that high in the air, on the simple principles of a vacuum and air pressure. He shuddered again and gripped the arm rests to keep his hands from trembling. When they began to taxi, his grip turned viselike. He could have popped an M&M for all the good his Valium was doing him.

If Jacob had any positive feeling, it was being fortunate to have found this nonstop evening flight. If his luck held, he could sleep the full seven hours it took to get to Oahu. He might have to take another Valium to do so . . . but so be it. From there, he'd have to endure a two-hour layover then one more flight on an island hopper to Kauai. His boat to Ni'ihau wasn't scheduled to leave until noon tomorrow, so he'd have another hour or so to kill. He'd probably spend that time recuperating his post-flight nerves. They offered a helicopter shuttle to the small island, but the thought of flying in an aircraft without wings was even more panic-inducing than flying in a 95-ton jet. If he could have taken a boat the entire way, he would have.

His shuddering began to border on convulsions as the whine of the engines increased. Better not to think about such things. He had to focus on his bugs. And on the bugs within his bugs. The larvae suspended in his plastic bottles carried a virus—a lethal one. He called it the Armageddon virus.

Jacob had developed it after studying the human immunodeficiency virus, the elusive bug that caused AIDS. Like HIV, the Armageddon virus entered the body's immune system cell nuclei, and, after using special enzymes to become double stranded, joined itself to the host's DNA. Then, whenever the host cell replicated, so would the virus, significantly multiplying the opportunity for spreading its disease. From there the virus would infect every major organ system in the body, causing devastating results.

Jacob's original idea was to create a drug that blocked the virus's ability to become a double strand, thus inhibiting its ability to splice into the host DNA. Because HIV uses a specific enzyme to perform this function, all he needed to do was develop an enzyme deactivator for that stage of the virus's life.

But something strange had happened. Rather than blocking the enzyme, his drug potentiated it, causing it to double in length, sometimes multiple times, making it the dominant base sequence in the host DNA. In doing so, the immuno-defense cells became immuno-killer cells. The overall projected effect was to turn the body's immune system against itself.

Where HIV merely weakened the human immune system, making the carrier more prone to infection, Jacob postulated his virus would obliterate it, making the carrier fatally susceptible to every infective agent they encountered. A mote of pollen could close an infected person's windpipes. A tiny sliver could cause flesh to rot off the bone. A neighbor's sneeze could fill the lungs with fluid. The common cold would be fatal in under thirty hours; a flu bug in under eighteen. If the newly contaminated person was already fighting an infection, the following day would arrive without them. It was so powerful that even the strongest modern antiviral drugs couldn't touch it. It was more dangerous than Ebola, the deadliest virus known. That's why Jacob named it Armageddon.

The brutal nature of the bug fascinated Jacob, emboldened him—and scared him. He immediately set about developing an antidote . . . just in case. Following his premise of enzyme inactivation, he was able to synthesize a polymer that did exactly that. Being the creator of the original virus, he easily followed the biochemical markers and pinpointed precisely where the mutation began. In a few short months he had synthesized a vaccine against Armageddon. Unfortunately, it didn't work against HIV. But the destructive, unstoppable nature of his virus brought to mind other possibilities, none of which were humane. Armageddon was so virulent that Jacob theorized it could wipe out whole armies, entire countries.

But how to weaponize it?

Like HIV, his virus had to have a carrier. HIV used specific fluids in the human body. That eliminated the possibility for a dirty bomb. The virus would die before it reached its target. It had to have a live host to survive.

Through his superior, Jacob learned of Dr. Erin Cross's research on the swine flu. The man suggested her inroads on viral mutations might be the missing puzzle piece. Jacob arranged to work with her and had immediately tried to befriend her to become more involved in her studies. But their relationship never quite got off the ground—personally or professionally. She hated his flirty little sayings and habits—or so she said. He thought those traits came across as adorable. Guess not. Too bad. She could have shared in his glory—and in his immunity to Armageddon. Then their research hit a snag. A major snag. He opted out of the project to work on his virus, leaving Erin to clean up the mess.

Jacob shook his head and bit back his anger. He didn't want to dwell on that. The memory of it always made him bitter. No—more than that. It made him seethe with hatred, with betrayal and vengeance. She had tried to pin the mess on him, but he knew the real score. She shouldered as much blame as he did. And yet, it was her research that had given him what he'd been searching for. Funny how fate played such games.

Yeah, it was all really too bad. Dr. Cross could have helped him rule the world. He freely admitted to having a boyish crush on her. They could have been a modern-day Adam and Eve. She could have ascended with him all the way to the top. Even Jacob's arrogant benefactor would have to treat them with respect. No more taking orders. No more cowing to another's demands. *He* would write the rules. *He* would determine . . . well, everything. But Cross was so elusive, so cold and standoffish. Well, that was years ago. It *really* was too bad. For her.

Jacob opened his eyes and realized they were already in the air. Good. The takeoffs and landings were the worst part of air travel. He sighed and held up one of his small, plastic bottles. The opaque plastic prevented him from seeing the hundreds of tiny, wormlike organisms teeming near the surface. *No matter,* he thought, smiling. They were there. In fact, he could almost imagine the larvae smiling back at him.

Chapter 8

The drive to Erin's Provo townhouse usually took twenty minutes. She did it in ten. She spent as much time looking into her rearview mirror as she did out the windshield. Little good it did. All she saw at that late hour were headlights. She considered calling 911 to report Harry's shooting but she knew the dispatcher would ask why she was no longer at the scene of the crime, and they'd probably want her to come to the police station. She couldn't make the call anonymously from her cell phone. Panic slithered up her back. No question she was someone's target. No—more than someone. A group of someones. She'd received a text after the gunman was dead. That proved he wasn't acting alone. Which meant *any* stranger could be her assassin.

Parking in the dark cast of a huge willow around the corner from her townhouse, Erin kept to the shadows as she darted inside. Leaning against the door frame, she struggled to control her erratic breathing and trembling hands. She reached for the light switch then hesitated, fearing the illumination would confirm her whereabouts to whoever was after her. They had already compromised her workplace; had they done the same here? Assuming the worst, Erin knew she had to gather her private research notes before it was too late. In the pit of her stomach she sensed *too late* had already come.

Moving more by memory than by sight, she inched her way into the gloomy living room. A misty pall of moonlight penetrated the semi-sheer drapes covering the sliding patio door, giving the room a tomblike feel. She paused and held her breath to listen, but she could hear nothing over the pounding of her heart. Still, she felt something wasn't right. The room was somehow . . . different. Instead of a safe harbor, her townhouse now felt like a death trap.

Move, Erin, she silently commanded herself. Rummaging through her purse, she located the small penlight and clicked it on. The weak, narrow beam revealed a slight variance in the positioning of her furniture, and a cluttered disarray of volumes in her bookcase. Normally, her place was neat and orderly to the point of fastidiousness.

Someone's been here—or perhaps still is.

Forcing herself into action, Erin moved quickly to her bedroom and stopped short. The place was a shambles. Her penlight revealed the contents of her dresser drawers strewn across the floor, her mattress upended, and her personal belongings razed and violated. Her office nook was worse. Her filing cabinets were emptied, and the contents of her document shredder littered the floor like confetti. Worse, her computer had been completely gutted. Upon closer inspection, Erin saw the hard drive was missing, as were all her SD cards and USB drives.

Moving quickly to her open closet, she slid a shoe rack to one side and pulled up a corner of carpet. A small lockbox embedded in the subfloor looked undisturbed. Holding her breath, she dialed the combination and opened it. Inside was a 32GB thumb drive and an envelope filled with ten 100-dollar bills. Pocketing the jump drive and emergency cash, Erin grabbed her purse, reentered her living room—and froze.

The sliding door to her patio was open. She knew for certain it had been closed only moments before. The room was still milky-dark, but her sheer drapes now moved with a languid night breeze. With her penlight extinguished, she scanned the living room and adjoining kitchen as best she could. As far as she could tell, whoever had entered was no longer there.

It's not over.

You can run but you can't hide.

As she slowly made her way toward the front door, a muffled noise came from her garage. Peering intently into the dark kitchen, she realized the entrance to the garage was slightly ajar. Someone was in there.

Stepping quickly to the front door, Erin opened it as quietly as possible. Other than a ghostly breeze disturbing the trees and shrubs, the night was eerily quiet. Remaining in the shadow of her porch, she scanned the area, looking for any potential threat. Across the street sat a dark gray sedan she did not recognize; but being a recluse, she wasn't sure who owned what in this neighborhood.

Forcing her legs to move, she eased toward the edge of the porch for a better look. She was certain the dark sedan had not been there when she had come home. But she couldn't be sure.

Just as she was about to dash to her car, a white spark flashed from the sedan coinciding with a section of stucco exploding inches from her head. Before she could react, a second shot left the sedan, shattering the unlit porch lamp directly behind her.

Sprinting toward her car, Erin heard her garage door opening. From the corner of her eye, she saw a man step out of the sedan, gun in hand. A sharp whistle of air passing her ear was followed by a harsh pop. She dove into her car and struggled getting the key into the ignition. From her rearview mirror she saw another flash and heard a bullet careen off her roof with a frenetic whir. She cursed at the man—not for trying to kill her but for dinging her 350Z. *Jerk face!*

A second man, also with a gun drawn, ran from the garage and joined the first.

As the Z's engine roared to life, Erin slammed her foot on the accelerator and popped the clutch. Her tires generated a plume of blue smoke as her sports car screeched from the curb and fishtailed into the night. From her mirror she saw the two men sprint toward their car.

Erin knew the men were after the information on her USB drive. That's why they had ransacked her townhouse. There was no doubt now—they were willing to kill her for it.

Chapter 9

THE PRAEFECTUS MAGNUS STUDIED THE information extracted from the woman's computer and compared it with the documents from Timpanogos Research. It was evident she knew too much.

He'd been following the young researcher's progress for years. She was brilliant. She would be a perfect candidate to adopt into his Order—a unique invitation indeed. The secret society rarely admitted female members. But times were different now. And Dr. Cross was . . . *exceptional.*

Yet it wasn't to be. The woman's rise to greatness could have been as great as his . . . if only she had embraced the vision of the Order. Regrettably, the subordinate he'd sent to make initial inquiries had been less than enthusiastically received. It may have been the approach the man used, or it may have been the words he chose. When presenting a concept of this magnitude, words were like a drug; they could enliven or debilitate depending on how they were used. But the woman had rejected everything the subordinate had tried. At least that was his report.

That shouldn't matter, the Praefectus Magnus reasoned. Anyone with true enlightenment would have seen past the subordinate's inept delivery and would have focused on the amazing potential of the Order. Perhaps she wasn't that exceptional after all. Not as exceptional as he was, anyway. He had a grander vision, an enlightened understanding. That's why he could see what had to be done before anyone else could. That's also why he had ordered her extermination.

The luminary went by the name Magnus. It wasn't his real name, but that was typical of men of his standing. All high-ranking members of the Grand Order took on pseudonyms. In Latin, Magnus meant "great." In many northern European countries the name broadened to mean "house of power and might." It was a perfect moniker considering his ambitions.

Magnus's rise to greatness *was* exceptional . . . in many ways. In the real world, he had completed his doctorate thesis in economics but never presented or defended it. He had walked away from Yale saying he was "bored with academia." He never received the advanced diploma, because "he didn't need it." His natural intelligence came from a genetically superior mind. *Intelligence* was such a subjective measurement anyway. One man's intelligence was another man's common knowledge; therefore, how could a piece of paper from an overinflated university *prove* intelligence? All it showed was that you could jump through a regimen of academic hoops. No—*true* intelligence was measured by the transcendence of mediocrity. And that path often took a lifetime to traverse. Magnus, however, had done it in just a few seasons.

The mighty Praefectus Magnus came from a family swimming in money and notoriety. Magnus went to Yale because it was his father's alma mater. He'd completed his bachelor's degree in accounting with exceptionally high marks. During work on his doctorate degree, he'd met up with other ambitious young men from elite families in New England. They were part of a highly selective fraternity called Benjamin's Blood—named after founding father Ben Franklin. Franklin was a known student of Adam Weishaupt, the father of the infamous Illuminati. The Benjamin's Blood fraternity claimed to be a direct line of Weishaupt's intellectual order through Franklin himself. Many considered it a splinter group, a mere faction of the original Illuminati, but that didn't matter to its pledges. Throughout the ages, countless monumental achievements had risen from dead ideals. And the Grand Order of the original Illuminati was all but dead.

Each member of Benjamin's Blood hailed from mega-wealthy or mega-powerful bloodlines. Not many knew the fraternity existed; it was one of only a handful of selective clubs believed to maintain total internal secrecy for more than 200 years.

The fraternity brothers would talk into all hours of the night about what their families had done to accumulate their wealth, what they wanted to do with their individual riches, and flirted with what they *could* do with their amassed wealth. Their great-grandfather's fathers had begun a process of establishing a secret, unified Order of Power. *Perseverantia per patientia* was the mantra for the Order of Benjamin's Blood. "Persistence with patience." When everything was in line, world enlightenment would begin.

Magnus felt the Grand Illuminate of the original Order had lost sight of Weishaupt's ideals, as had the founding fathers of Benjamin's Blood. That's why he had fought to become Praefectus Magnus of the Order. World enlightenment *would* come to pass. And it would be Magnus that heralded the new age of illumination.

Swinging his feet onto his mahogany desk and lacing his fingers behind his head, Magnus stretched out and reminisced about his beginnings with the Order. In a chamber deep underground, Magnus was asked to drink from a gold chalice while standing over a ten-inch disk inset in the floor. The disk covered a cylinder carved into a one-ton block of solid granite. The cylinder housed a bronze urn said to be cast by Aegean metallurgists long before America was its own nation. A relief embossing on the disk showed the image of a single eye atop an unfinished pyramid, surrounded by flames and rays of light. According to Order legend, the urn held the cremated remains of Benjamin Franklin. Although most people believed Ben Franklin is interred next to his wife and son in Christ's Church cemetery, Philadelphia, the Benjamin's Blood fraternity had "verifiable" information that his remains had been exhumed in the cause of "further enlightenment." After a complete dissection, Franklin's bones were sequestered by a sect of the Illuminati, and through one misplacement followed by another they eventually became the property of the Benjamin's Blood Fraternity.

Dressed in gnostic robes festooned with Egyptian, Macedonian, and Druidic symbols, Magnus lifted the chalice, admiring the dance of torches reflected in the polished gold surface. He raised it above his head three times in slow, ritualistic motions. With each thrust he chanted a different phrase: "*Meus cruor pro specialis. Meus corpus pro obsequium. Meus vita pro novus ordo seclorum.*"

After each chant, the circle of brothers surrounding Magnus would chant, "*Novus ordo seclorum,*" while raising red candles into the air.

Magnus drained the cup in three loud swallows. He gagged on the thick, warm, saline liquid. Wiping a few dribbles from the corners of his mouth, he got his first glance of what he'd consumed. It was blood. He wondered what kind of blood. Then he wondered if he should be asking *whose* blood. Steeling himself, he finished the ritual and became a full-fledged member of the secret order, committing his life to the Order of the New Age. That night he received the first of five possible gnostic symbols tattooed over the first knuckle of his right hand, signifying his covenant to the Order. He also received his ring—a heavy gold band with a polished onyx stone engraved with the single heavily lidded eye gazing out from the center of a triangle.

He never did find out about the blood. It changed with each ritual.

Blood. Magnus pondered on the uniqueness of the word in his life. He was born of superior *blood*lines, his initiation dealt in *blood,* the name of his order used the word *blood,* and Dr. Cross's research and Dr. Krantz's weapon of Armageddon were directly linked to *blood.* A mere curiosity? A lucky coincidence? No—it was more than curious. More than coincidence.

It was illumination born of blood.

And it was a pity Dr. Erin Cross did not share the same illumination.

Chapter 10

The autumn night was cool and dry. Yet in spite of a lack of ambient humidity, Erin drove through a self-made mist of tears. She was not a woman prone to flighty emotions, nor was she one to let uncontrollable circumstances predicate her actions. Still, the terrible quandary that began that afternoon was almost more than she could bear.

Erin had been weaned on a generous work ethic and nurtured by a hunger for achievement. Letting her emotions rule her mind was not in her nature. "Emotions are something you must learn to master, or they will master you," her father used to say. "If something goes wrong, look at it as a lesson of what not to repeat—not as something at which you failed." For a football coach, it was a very Edisonian way of thinking.

When the famous inventor was asked how he felt about failing 6,000 times before discovering the right filament for the electric light bulb, Thomas Edison was said to have replied, "I didn't fail 6,000 times. I simply found 6,000 ways *not* to make a light bulb."

And that's often easier said than done, she scoffed inwardly.

Constantly checking the thin line of headlights in her rearview mirror, Erin sped south along I-15. She didn't know why she chose that direction. She hoped it was opposite of what they would expect. But then, not knowing who *they* were, she could be heading right into *their* grasp.

Glancing at the thumb drive now attached to her key ring, she thought about everything it contained. Much of it was investigational information: random notes, outlines, references. All of it was worth billions in the R&D sector—and, depending on how it was used, perhaps in the military sector too. It also contained all the data from previous experiments, both successes and non-successes. More importantly, it contained all her research on her new vaccine—the one that would save millions of lives. It was an inspired discovery.

She felt the seed for all her discoveries was sent from above. Sure, she put in her share of the work, but she knew better than to claim all the credit. Another favorite Edison quote was, "Genius is one percent inspiration and ninety-nine percent perspiration," although she felt the ratio was more fifty-fifty. The USB drive was filled with her "perspiration." Heavenly Father had blessed her with inspiration more times than she could count.

So why wasn't He *inspiring* her now?

She pressed against the bags under her eyes. At just after midnight the highway was lightly trafficked. Her 350Z purred at ninety miles per hour as it weaved around the big rigs struggling to climb the Fillmore grade. Her car didn't even notice the incline. The Z seemed happier going fast, as did she. And although Erin knew this stretch of I-15 was an infamous speed trap, she was more afraid of those chasing her than of a traffic citation.

Erin lowered the driver's window and felt the cool air sting her face with icy fingers. Winter was hard upon Northern Utah, and the tops of the mountains were blanketed with a sheet of snow that looked strangely luminescent at night. She inhaled deeply through her nostrils in an attempt to clear her head. It was silly to try and run anywhere; they surely knew what car she drove. Who's to say they couldn't tap into the satellite monitoring her car's GPS feature and simply head her off?

A moving roadblock of two refrigerator rigs forced Erin to slow to fifty mph and concentrate on driving. She swore under her breath. It seemed like she could walk faster than the lumbering, brightly lit semis crawled. In her rearview mirror, a widely spaced string of headlights snaked its way back toward Utah Valley. Were the men who shot at her one of those pairs of lights? Probably.

Downshifting into second gear, she passed the big rigs on the paved shoulder to the right, eliciting an angry air-horn blast from both truckers. The maneuver took all of seven seconds, but it helped to clear her head. Breaching the summit increased her speed to 100 mph.

Less than two hours later, and with no speeding ticket, Erin saw the hazy lights of Cedar City through the grime on her windshield. Just in time, too. She was physically and emotionally drained.

Pulling into the Wal-Mart parking lot in Cedar, she coasted into the darkened area on the south side of the store near the receiving dock. She rubbed her fatigued eyes and pressed her fingers against the headache forming a drum line just behind her temples. She needed to figure out who was behind all this. It was ridiculous to assume *everyone* was against her.

Because it had been hours since her last contact with the mysterious someones who seemed bent on her demise, Erin allowed a brief flood of satisfaction to soothe her nerves. Perhaps she *had* outrun them and now had some time to—

Pling-buzz!

Erin flinched. She pulled her cell phone from her purse and stared at the string of zeros on the readout. With fresh tears burning the backs of her eyes, she flipped it open.

Are you enjoying Cedar City?

SATURDAY
NOVEMBER 5, 2011

Chapter 11

Sean tossed and turned, trying to reenter the elusive doorway to sleep. His meds sometimes kept him from true restfulness, plaguing him with disturbing dreams and night sweats. Mostly, he'd learned to sleep through them. Sometimes he'd have to take an extra pill. But tonight the images of the deli incident would not go away. Neither would the image of a very distraught, but undeniably pretty, face.

At just after three he rolled out of bed and flipped on his TV. He tuned to the local news channel for a weather update in hopes of a weekend hike in the mountains. That was what he really needed, to get away and clear his head. Instead, what he saw made him scoot to the edge of his couch and turn up the volume.

A press photo of Erin Cross hovered in the upper-right corner of the screen. The late night anchorwoman had a concerned expression on her brow as she described the shooting death of a security guard at Timpanogos Research, Inc.

"Cross was seen fleeing the scene of the crime about ten o'clock this evening, which the county coroner estimates as the approximate time of death of security guard Harold Harriman. Authorities say parking lot surveillance recordings show Cross entering and exiting the research complex; however, the security recordings of the foyer have been deleted. Company officials aren't sure if Cross had access to the security office where the DVRs are kept, but someone with knowledge of the system has erased any evidence of the actual murder. For now, investigators say Cross is considered a person of interest in the death of Harriman."

The background image switched to an exterior shot of Giamboli's deli.

"Cross was also at the scene of a fatal shooting at Giamboli's deli in Lehi around two o'clock this afternoon. Even though she appeared to be a victim at the time, police are now investigating the possibility of a connection between the two shootings. If anyone has information on the whereabouts of Dr. Erin Cross, please notify the Lehi police at the number on the screen."

That's ridiculous, Sean thought. A murderer? No. Not even an accomplice to murder. The woman was frightened out of her gourd. It was all she could do to stay on her feet. Plus, she'd claimed someone was harassing her with—*wait.* What did the newswoman just say? *Doctor* Erin Cross? Doctor of what?

Sean booted up his computer and did a name search. There were hundreds of Erin Crosses nationwide. He narrowed the search to those in Utah: twenty-seven listings. He narrowed it again to Utah County: three listings. One woman was eighty-three and lived in Payson. Her biggest achievement was as Onion Queen in 1967. The second one was an eight-year-old in Pleasant Grove who had just been baptized. The third listed a woman residing in Provo: no picture, no phone, no street address, no birth date. She wasn't on Facebook, Twitter, or LinkedIn. The White Pages posted her demographics as unlisted.

Sean was baffled. If she was a medical doctor, she'd certainly be listed with an office or an affiliation with a hospital. If she was a professor, then some school would list her as a faculty member. But there was nothing. The newscast said something about TRI, right there in Utah County. He looked up her name on the TRI website. *There!* Dr. Erin Cross, head of R&D in new compounds. She'd been with the company for almost five years. Her list of accolades, patents, and awards was impressive. Sean felt intimidated just reading her credentials.

The news story replayed again in his mind. Dr. Erin Cross . . . a person of interest in a murder . . . perhaps even a murder and a terrorist act? No way.

Sean logged onto the Provo police blotter to see if they'd posted that day's events. No such luck. He scratched his head and stared at the uninformative screen. When nothing came to him, he returned to the newscast, but it had moved onto entertainment news. He had little interest in that. It was now 3:22. He had to get some sleep, or he'd be worthless tomorrow.

Swallowing half an Ambien, Sean returned to bed . . . but with little hope of having calmer dreams.

Chapter 12

THE INTERSTATE TRAFFIC WAS JUST beginning to thicken as the rising sun turned the early morning sky a brassy turquoise and fringed the cirrus clouds with fuchsia piping. The heavenly beauty was in direct contrast to the feeling of angst the two subordinates felt churning in them as they listened to the speaker phone. The men were refueling their car at a Chevron Minimart in Parowan as they spoke to their superior.

"Where does she think she can run to?" the Prefect asked.

"I don't know, sir. We almost had her," subordinate Adams said. "We fired a couple of shots, but it was very dark, and I don't think we hit her."

"Your guns were silenced?"

"Of course."

"How'd she get away?"

"She entered her house without us knowing."

"How could you not know? You were watching, weren't you?"

"Yes, sir. She parked around the corner and must have kept to the shadows as she entered. We first saw her as she was leaving."

"Did you pursue?"

"Yes, sir, but she drove like a maniac," subordinate Jefferson chimed in. "Per our mandate, we followed as fast as possible but tried not to draw undue attention. She lives in a quiet neighborhood, and a car chase at that hour would've ruined our stealth."

Initially they had tried to keep up with Erin without making too much noise. But their four-door Taurus was no match for Erin's 350Z, in horsepower, handling . . . or looks. They had pursued her about five miles before they gave up. They knew she was heading south on I-15. They had immediately called their field support and asked for GPS acquisition. The woman was still heading south on I-15. She was just outside of Beaver. *Already? She must be flying!*

Stopping just before they ran out of gas, Adams and Jefferson called their superior to update their progress.

"But she *did* go inside her house. You're sure of that."

"Yes, sir," Adams said. "I saw the beam of a small flashlight through her living room window. I went in the back to try and corner her. Since she didn't drive up, I thought maybe she was going to open the garage door from the inside. When I went in there, she snuck out the front door."

A burst of exasperation sounded like static on the speaker phone. The anxious churning both men were experiencing doubled in intensity.

"Did the advance team find anything in her home?" Jefferson asked in a hopeful tone.

"Possibly," the Prefect said. "We have her hard drive and a number of files we're analyzing as we speak. The advance team fulfilled their assignment. Unfortunately, you did not."

"Yes, sir," both men agreed flatly.

"I will have to inform the Grand Council of your failure."

There was a brief silence. Jefferson drew a breath as if to speak, but Adams gave him a warning glare. They had said enough already. Making excuses would only emphasize their inability to complete an assignment.

When the Prefect spoke again, his voice was hard. "The consequences of your failure may be very serious."

"We accept that, sir. It is part of the Order," Adams confirmed.

"Good. We triangulate her current position in a Wal-Mart parking lot in Cedar City, about twenty miles south of your present location."

"Thank you, sir. Should we pursue?"

"Yes, but be extra cautious in remaining anonymous. An adept will meet you in Cedar City to help coordinate Dr. Cross's elimination. Your standing rides on this one task. Do you understand?"

"Yes, sir," both men said in unison.

"*Pro novus ordo seclorum.*"

"*Pro novus ordo seclorum,*" the subordinates echoed.

The Prefect disconnected the line.

The two subordinates exited the gas station and headed south. They rode in silence, jaws clenched, mouths pursed in hard lines. Each wore a silver ring with a single onyx stone mounted in the apex. Etched into the black stone in silver scrimshaw was the image of a heavily lidded right eye gazing out from the center of a triangle. Tattooed above the first two knuckles of each man's right hand were gnostic symbols signifying their level in the Order.

Just as the first rays of sunlight spilled over the mountains, illuminating the valley in which they drove, the two men kissed their rings with deep reverence, and whispered, "*Meus vita pro novus ordo seclorum.*"

Chapter 13

A honking horn woke Erin with a start. Confusion swept over her, constricting her chest. She was parked somewhere in her car. She was very cold. Her windows were streaked with condensation. *What had—* oh, yeah.

Erin crawled out of her Z and stretched and groaned in the brisk morning air. Her body ached from head to toe. Around 4:00 that morning she had moved her car behind a semi that had entered the lot to offload. She hadn't planned on falling asleep—it just happened. Glancing at her watch, it was presently 7:46.

She shook out her legs and moved to the front of the semi. From there she scanned the parking lot as best she could. Being a Saturday, the stalls were filling up quickly. It helped that the store was having a Thanksgiving case lot sale. It was only a moment before she saw a dark gray sedan with tinted windows enter the parking lot and begin to cruise up and down the aisles. She wasn't one-hundred-percent sure the sedan was filled with bad guys. But the car looked exactly like the one in front of her home the night before. And it was exactly the kind a secret government agency would drive while searching for their next target. Erin pinched the bridge of her nose. Normally, she'd laugh at herself for having such paranoid thoughts. Presently, it didn't seem so funny.

She briefly considered returning to her Z and making a run for it. But if they had found her this easily once, they could do it again. It must be the GPS in her car's integral navigation system. She decided to abandon the Z for a while. She hoped they'd think she found another form of transportation and had escaped.

She waited until the sedan was heading away from her before sprinting toward the store. As she entered, she heard the revving of an engine and the squeal of tires some distance behind her. Once inside the vestibule, she watched the dark sedan lurch into the handicap stall. Two men in dark suits quickly exited the vehicle and headed toward the entrance. They'd seen her!

Turning, she walk-ran into the store.

"Welcome to Wal-Mart," growled a woman who looked like she was on work-release from a detox clinic. Her clothes reeked of stale cigarettes, and her skin had the texture of a pig's ear dog treat.

"Women's clothing?" Erin asked breathlessly.

"Somewhere over there," the parolee rasped, pointing over her shoulder.

Erin hurried in that direction and quickly found the fitting booths. Looking back, she saw the men talking to the door greeter and watched as she pointed toward the women's wear department. Ducking behind a display on the end of the aisle, Erin tried the first dressing room door. It was locked—as was the second and the third.

"Can I help you?" a wide, no-nonsense-looking black woman asked.

"I need to get in one of these rooms," Erin said, somewhat shakily.

"You tryin' something on, honey?"

Erin peeked toward the store front. The one man had closed half the distance, the other was nowhere to be seen. The man heading her way had a shaved head and shoulders wider than most doorways. She turned back to the woman. "Please, I just need to hide for a minute."

The woman scowled then leaned to one side to follow Erin's previous line-of-sight. "You hiding from Mr. Clean on steroids?" she asked, jutting her chin toward the man.

Erin nodded fervently. "Yes."

"He government?"

"No." She honestly didn't know.

"An ex?"

Erin made a snap decision to lie and nodded again. "With an ego as big as he is."

The woman produced a key and unlocked the door nearest them. "He looks it. Don't you worry 'bout a thing, honey. You just keep quiet, you hear?"

Glancing at the woman's name tag, Erin said, "Thanks, Shaniqua." She scooted into the small room, closed the door, and rammed the dead bolt in place.

"Hey, you," she heard a man's brusque voice call out.

"You talkin' to me?" Associate Shaniqua asked.

"You seen a young woman come through here, blonde, about five four?"

"Are you blind?" she replied in sardonic hyperbole. "This is the *women's* fitting area and we are in *Utah*. All I see is blonde women comin' through here."

"Great. How about within the last couple minutes?" he retorted with an equally sarcastic tone.

"Why—you a cop?"

"Look, lady, a simple yes or no will do—unless you're incapable of such advanced communication."

Shaniqua's tone sharpened. "If I wasn't on the clock, you'd hear some advanced communication, Conan."

The man growled a few curse words and stormed off. After a few moments, Erin heard the associate whisper, "You just stay there, honey. I'll let you know when baldy is gone."

Erin slumped onto the tiny bench and put her head between her fists. What in the world was happening? Now that she'd gotten a good look at them, these guys had government written all over them. But her current research had nothing to do with any secret government projects. Nor was it anything organized crime members would care about or anything religious fanatics would deem unholy. She was simply trying to save lives. They wouldn't want her dead because she was trying to save lives, would they? That was preposterous. Perhaps it was something altogether different. But what?

She clenched her jaw in defiant anger. She should just go confront the men chasing her to find out what was going on. This was the United States of America, for heaven's sake. This was Utah! Things like this weren't supposed to happen here. *Stop being such a ninny,* she scolded herself. *They won't do anything to you in the middle of a Wal-Mart.*

Deciding enough was enough, Erin stood, determined to get to the bottom of this.

Pling-buzz.

She stifled a startled cry and braced her hands against the walls of the dressing booth to support her suddenly weak knees. She took a breath and retrieved her phone from her pocket. She switched the settings to "mute all call and message tones." The display showed a string of zeros. Nervously, she opened her phone.

We know where you are.

She clamped her phone shut. Panic crept up her throat, threatening to strangle her. She forced herself to take long, steadying breaths, but it didn't help much. With resignation, she admitted she was in deeper than she could handle. She needed help. But who could she turn to? Everyone within her limited circle of friends was affiliated with Timpanogos Research. After the death of Harry Harriman, there was no telling who was involved there. The police might help. But they'd already taken her statement about the threatening texts, and when the interviewing officer saw the call number, it was all he could do not to laugh. A string of zeros? Not possible.

She knew Tom Jenkins was out of the state visiting his grandkids, but she pulled up his number and sent him a text anyway.

Tom. I need your help. Someone is trying to kill me. This is no joke. Please call as soon as you can.

Along with the text, she sent a fervent prayer.

She stared into the dressing booth mirror and forced her mind to focus. She was a grown woman. She had a PhD, for heaven's sake. She could figure this out. The trouble was "this" was something she'd never had to figure out before. What she needed was an expert in criminal procedures. Or covert espionage. Or military special ops. *As if someone like that lives around here,* she scoffed.

Wait—

Chapter 14

SEAN SAT AT HIS COMPUTER again staring at a blank screen, willing his mind to fill with fanciful characters and whimsical environs. He closed his eyes and exhaled slow and long. Forcing his muse never worked before—why should it work now?

Leaving his work station, he donned his jogging shoes and sweats and began stretching. He often resorted to a good jog when his imagination was stuck. It had something to do with the increase in circulation and the release of endorphins . . . or something like that. He wasn't a doctor, so he wasn't sure. It was something he'd seen on Discovery Health or learned in Special Ops . . . maybe.

Looking at his watch, he saw it was just before nine. He usually ran a lot earlier, but he hadn't slept much the night before and had awakened later than usual. Oh well. He loved any form of exercise but especially morning exercise. It invigorated him.

The deep azure sky was already fading behind long wisps of cloud. He hoped the sun would burn off the haze. He could use a nice bright day. The air was clear and crisp, perfect for a run. It would be a good warm-up to his hike. He walked to the end of his block and looked across the valley toward Utah Lake. To the south, dark thunder clouds were building, threatening to curtail any chance of a sunny day. Well . . . there went his hike.

Sean followed a familiar route that led him from his residential neighborhood to a park near the center of Orem, a distance of about a mile. There was a nice jogging trail there, and several people were out in running shoes and sweats, giving their hearts a good beating.

After an hour and a half, he had covered nine miles. He jogged back to his neighborhood apartment and went right to his refrigerator. He kept a large pitcher of purified water chilled at all times. Drinking three large glassfuls, he headed to his shower but stopped when he noticed his cell phone was blinking on his dresser. Who would be calling him on the weekend?

Pressing PLAY VOICE MAIL, he listened to a breathy, panicked whisper: "Mr. Flannery, this is Erin Cross. I'm the woman from the café yesterday. I know you don't know me, but I need your help, and I don't know where else to turn. My life's still in danger."

The urgency in her voice convinced him she was being serious. Erin gave her cell number, said "please" again, then disconnected.

Sean stood staring at his cell phone a full minute before his mind started spinning in high gear. He replayed the deli incident in his mind for the hundredth time. He'd acted purely on impulse and training. Although the police had officially deemed the incident a random act of violence, Sean was still plagued with a few oddities. If Erin Cross was the intended target, why did the gunman spray the entire deli? Or was she actually an accomplice as the news anchor had hinted last night, and the whole thing was an act to paint her as an innocent bystander? And why did the assailant utter that phrase in Latin before killing himself? *Novus ordo* . . . something. Then there was the incident at Timpanogos Research with the night watchman. Now this same woman makes a frantic call asking for his help. It was all too crazy to be a hoax.

Sean dialed her number and let it ring eight times before hanging up. Why didn't she answer? She hadn't called that long ago. He played the message again. The phone log said the message was forty-nine minutes old. He was going to try once more then decided to send a text instead.

Dr. Cross. I just got your call. I tried to call back. I am available now. Please call again. I'll help if I can. Sean.

If she was away from her phone, it might be a while before she'd call or text back. Deciding to clean up while waiting, he jumped in the shower. He had just rinsed the shampoo from his hair when he heard his cell phone chirping like a canary. Someone was calling. He quickly left the shower and wrapped a towel around his waist. Just as he exited the bathroom, his phone went silent. Moving to it, he saw NEW MESSAGE flashing on the phone's LCD display. Again, he toggled to PLAY VOICE MAIL.

"Mr. Flannery, I just got your text." Erin's voice was more urgent than before, as if she were trying her best to remain unheard by everyone except Sean. "My phone is on silent mode. They're after me. Please, help me! I'm in Cedar City in—oh no, I—I can't talk anymo—"

Click.

Chapter 15

Standing on a dock in Hanapepe Bay, Kauai, Jacob Krantz stared in complete dismay at the rusty fishing boat awaiting him. This *couldn't* be the "transport" his superior had secured. Over the past two years, his superior had provided more than a billion dollars to fund Jacob's research. He had paved the way for Jacob to glean key knowledge from the brightest minds in the field. And he had arranged Jacob's visit to the island of Ni'ihau—which was an accomplishment many considered impossible.

Privately owned since 1864, Ni'ihau had been completely closed to outsiders for decades to preserve its native Hawaiian heritage, earning it the nickname "the Forbidden Isle." Yet Jacob had been granted a two-week stay on the tiny isle to do field research. So why then couldn't his superior have secured him a decent boat on which to get over there?

Jacob looked out over the generous expanse of ocean at the long blue smudge that was Ni'ihau. He had personally suggested it as a test site for two main reasons.

One, its social and geographic isolation were perfect. Located some seventeen miles southwest of Kauai, Ni'ihau was the smallest inhabited island in the Hawaiian chain—barely seventy square miles of land mass. The Forbidden Isle had no tourist trade, no abundant natural resource, and no regularly scheduled trips to and from its shores. The main settlement of Pu'uwai boasted barely 100 residents. The island was so primitive, in fact, that there were no paved roads, no airport, no public electricity or plumbing, and no telephones. Such factors almost guaranteed zero outside influences that could skew Jacob's results.

Two, despite its small size, Ni'ihau had the distinction of being home to Hawaii's largest landlocked body of water, Halali'i Lake. That feature played right into his guise. Jacob was allowed access to Ni'ihau because the islanders thought he was a World Health Organization expert studying the incidence of West Nile virus in the Hawaiian archipelago. West Nile virus had plagued the island for years. Unbeknownst to the inhabitants of Ni'ihau, Jacob had no interest in the West Nile virus. His Armageddon virus would prove a hundred times worse than anything the entire Hawaiian archipelago had ever seen. After Jacob was finished, the name "Forbidden Isle" would take on a whole new meaning.

Pulling his gaze back to the small craft bobbing in the reserved slip, Jacob grimaced, wishing his luck would take a turn for the better. He glanced around the harbor, desperately hoping he'd come to the wrong pier. He double-checked his manifest: Hanapepe harbor, slip forty-one, noon, Pacific Time. The *Little Kahuna*. This was the right place, the right time, and—diappointingly—the right boat. He ground his teeth reflexively.

The boat in question looked like it was on loan from the Old Man and the Sea. On closer inspection, he noticed some water sloshing in the bottom of the craft. *Great.* Survive two white-knuckle flights over vast expanses of ocean only to sink within sight of his destination.

Jacob sighed heavily and examined his collection of bottles. His larvae were in need of fresh water and oxygen. He could add fresh water from a drinking fountain, but he didn't want to risk accidentally killing them with water chlorinated for public use. He shoved the baggie of bottles back in his satchel and looked for a place to sit down. His head pounded with a lingering migraine, and the early-afternoon glare burned his retina. His hands quivered with fatigue. In spite of choosing an overnight flight from Salt Lake International, he had slept very little. Plus, his body was still on Mountain Time.

Ninety-five tons at 35,000 feet; 2,551 miles over open ocean. With his luck, shark-infested *ocean.* Those are the kind of details that would keep any *sane* person awake, gripping the armrests with such force as to permanently leave fingerprints embedded in the plastic.

"Docta' Brown?" a voice called.

Jacob turned to see a stocky young man in a loose Hawaiian shirt and shorts, no shoes, walking down the dock toward him.

"Yes?" Jacob said, almost forgetting he was traveling under a pseudonym.

"*Aloha auina la*. I be Kapono Kahuleula. I be sailin' you ta Ni'ihau. Welcome 'board my tub, brah," he said, holding out his hand in greeting.

Jacob shook it. "Hi. Thanks. So is *this* your boat?" he asked, nodding toward the craft.

"She be my beauty," the young man said, taking Jacob's bags and stepping into the leaky fishing boat. "My *Little Kahuna*."

"Great. So how long's this gonna take?"

"Nah but da blink of an eye, brah." Kapono's accent was decidedly islander—a horrendous amalgamation of Pidgin English and Hawaiian, with a generous helping of surfer slang on the side. "Da waves go bumpy an' hard ta'day. Hope you don' get da queasy heaves, cha?"

"I'll be all right. It's just that it's important I get to Ni'ihau as soon as possible."

"No bodda, brah. We gon' fly."

"Fly?"

"Cha. Fast as a tub can go an' stay in da wadda."

Jacob boarded the small motor craft with serious trepidation. It was a standard fishing trawler—a raised cabin, open back deck, two swivel chairs with sconces for fishing poles, inboard motor—but it still seemed disturbingly small to him. And there was the water sloshing in the bottom. Jacob plopped into a seat with a heavy grunt, tipped his head back, and stretched through an enormous yawn. He then placed his face in his hands and groaned.

"Whatsmadda, Doc? You *moi moi*?"

"What?" he mumbled into his palms.

"You tired? Got da big sleeps dis noon? Dat what bodda you?"

"Yes. I'm very tired."

"Hey, no beefs, brah. I have you dere by yesta'day, cha? You g'wan n' catch some z's. I done take care a' ev'rytin'."

Kapono bounded onto the pier, tossed the mooring line into his boat, bounded back, and fired up the engine. Revving it, the entire craft shook and rattled and complained. It sounded like a legion of tortured souls cage-fighting inside a thin wooden box.

Jacob cringed. "Are you sure we can make it without sinking?"

"Whoa, chill dat kine' talk, dude," Kapono said, clearly upset. "Ain' nobody talk stink 'bout my tub."

Pretty sure he'd inadvertently offended his Hawaiian escort, Jacob held up his hands in a truce. "Sorry. I didn't mean anything by it."

The solid-bodied young man favored Jacob with a hard stare before an incredibly white, toothy smile split his face. "Oh, you jus' foolin', cha?" He laughed heartily. "Dat's sweet, brah. You done got me good. Me, I not use ta *haoles*. Didn' know dey could crack. Nex' time you crack, you smile so's I know id be a rib, cha?"

Jacob waved him off, not quite sure he even understood what the islander had said. "Fine, fine."

Kapono piloted out of the slip and headed toward the mouth of the harbor. Jacob kept a watchful eye for signs of additional water seepage.

"Man, you mus' be good blood wid da Robinsons, cha?"

"The family that owns the island?" Jacob asked. "No, not really. But I convinced them this would be good for the Ni'ihauans, so they said I could visit."

"Hey, it be total cool wid me, man. I mean, we get a few *haoles* on da beach time ta time, but ain' no one allow ta stay long time, right?"

"Yeah," Jacob concurred without enthusiasm.

Kapono's "tub" rattled and gurgled relentlessly. Once past the safety buoys, Kapono spread his legs a bit, leaned forward, and called back to his guest, "Hol' on ta yo' trunks, dude. We 'bout ta fly."

"Okay, sure." Jacob spun his chair to face the back so he wouldn't have to converse with Kapono the rest of the trip. The scientist in him didn't believe this mini-*Titanic* could go much faster than a sea slug on a dry beach.

The young Hawaiian shouted, "Cowabunga!" and slammed the throttle to the dash. The boat shuddered, coughed, then shot forward with surprising velocity. Jacob flew from his seat and slid to the back of the boat. He fought to right himself but could not even struggle to his knees. Kapono glanced back and laughed.

The boat must be used for smuggling, Jacob reasoned. No fishing boat or leisure craft could move like Kapono's tub did. The hull ricocheted off each wave crest like a stone skipping across a placid lake, spending more time out of the water than in it. By the time Jacob could regain his footing, Ni'ihau was no longer a blue smear on the horizon; it was a jagged, brown mass rising before them. He staggered to the chair and held on as if his life depended on it. It probably did.

Kapono was still whooping shrilly as he urged his "tub" to go even faster. Jacob wondered if his jovial young guide would be as happy to escort him to his island home if he knew everyone there would be dead within two weeks.

Chapter 16

THE CALL CAME VIA A personal satellite link, joining the United States with whomever the CFO wanted to talk to. The communications service had its own satellite, complete with an unbreakable, multilevel encryption algorithm—a key feature in its advertising pitch. The service was owned by Belize Securities, an unregulated Central American company that offered its clients a variety of discreet, untraceable finance, information, and communication services that were second to none. If you made a phone call where one or more parties needed to remain anonymous or needed to hide a multimillion-dollar profit from a questionable transaction, Belize Securities was your best friend. They didn't come cheap, but they were always worth their six-figure fees. It was a service the CFO used daily.

"Are you sure about this?" the man asked with a hint of an Arabic accent.

"I'm sure. I have the preliminary research notes, and everything looks very good. This will be the biggest medical breakthrough since aspirin."

"More 'preliminary' notes?"

The CFO on the United States end of the line swallowed hard. "Well, yes. But Dr. Cross has completed several tests, and they've all come out positive."

"Any field studies yet?"

"Well, no—but plenty of lab trials. If we do field studies, that will change its status from biochemical to bio*medical*. Then we'll have to file a new drug application with the FDA, which means we'll have to disclose all parties funding this research. Because your employer wishes to remain anonymous, we won't be able to proceed." The man allowed a fresh edge of annoyance to slice across the connection, indicating his impatience with the Saudi negotiator. "Is that the way your boss wants it?"

"Is that what *you* want, my friend?" the foreigner asked, equally impatient. "My employer has many investments in many countries, and all are profitable . . . except yours."

"But these things take time. Surely he understan—"

"Your venture is a sizeable sum of money," the liaison interjected. "That makes it a potentially traceable risk. How do we know your connection with us will remain a secret? How do we know it will bring us the investment return we seek?"

"Because it's a worldwide problem!" the CFO shouted. "Dr. Cross has developed a vaccine against the number one cause of death on the planet. Don't you realize what that could mean financially?"

"*If* it works."

The American was dancing a fine line between insisting and begging. "There are always inherent risks when developing a new medicine. Any fool knows that."

"Yes," the Middle Easterner said with measured patience. "Just as any fool would expect someone to blindly invest two billion dollars in a venture no one in history has been able to achieve. My employer is not a fool, my friend. He is shrewd and calculating, and, if need be, vengeful. We have had reports of . . . *issues* in Dr. Cross's lab trials. This concerns my employer greatly. I would hate to think of his recourse . . . if these issues are not resolved."

"Which issues?" The American already knew which issues. The very fact that Erin Cross was missing was what he hoped the investor didn't know.

"My employer has eyes and ears worldwide that penetrate very deep. But you know this, yes? We feel Dr. Cross is hiding information that could speed her tests to conclusion."

Having played all his cards except one, the American backed down. He didn't want to play his trump card just yet. "Now don't get all excited. I'm just saying it may take a little longer than we originally planned. Once we get the final research notes back, we'll be able to get production under way in less than a year."

"Get them back?"

"Um . . . yeah. Dr. Cross is doing some trial work on her own as we speak. Once she gets back, we'll be able to proceed at full speed."

There was an uncomfortable pause on the line. "Are you still in contact with her?"

"Yes, of course we are."

"I hope so—for your sake," he said with a hard tone of censure. "I will forward this information to my employer. I cannot say what his response will be, but it's not difficult to guess."

"Look, I promise you everything is under control. Just give me a little more time."

"What we require are results, my friend, not promises."

"I know, I know. Everything will work out fine, you'll see."

Another uncomfortable pause caused the American to break into a sweat. He stuck his finger under his collar and pulled it loose.

"One week," the Arabian said. "Contact me in one week's time with the complete documents. Understood?"

"Yes, but one week is not—"

The line went dead.

"Yeah. Good talking to you, too," the CFO grumbled.

The American CFO disconnected and moved to the wet bar in his office. He poured himself a shot of bourbon then made it a double. He hated balancing on a razor's edge between having ultimate power and money and total financial ruin . . . and possibly a horrific demise. But he'd played financial roulette many times before. The difference this time was the size of the gamble.

He took a long pull on his tumbler and closed his eyes as the hard liquor burned down his throat. What seemed like such an easy chain of events was turning into a length of barbed wire, where every surgically sharp notch had his name on it.

He regretted having to eliminate the night guard at TRI. He was a nice guy—a bit simpleminded, but he was good at his job. The CFO huffed out a short, sneering breath. How hard is it to sit at a desk all night doing nothing? In any event, the guard had questioned his presence at

TRI at such odd hours. Rather than risk a connection, he'd shot him then gone to the security center and erased the digital recordings of his snap decision. No—"snap" wasn't the word. His decisions were never knee-jerk responses. Everything he did was enlightened.

He returned to the wet bar and toasted his reflection in the mirror behind the assorted carafes and decanters. He smiled in self-adulation at his own duplicity. Dr. Cross's current research had little to do with what he was spending the investment capital on. The research he was funding would have a far greater impact than mere financial glory. He hoped his foreign investor didn't find out—at least not until he was ready to reveal everything. At that point the CFO could make whatever demands he wanted.

He raised his glass a second time. "Here's to you, Grand Prefect Magnus."

Still gazing into the eyes of the man reflected back at him, he paused and wondered if he should feel morally responsible for the people he was about to kill. He shrugged. History was replete with mass murder in the name of noble advancement. What was one more event?

Chapter 17

AFTER ERIN HAD DISCONNECTED, SEAN dressed quickly and sent her a text asking if she was still okay. A few minutes later his cell phone croaked like a frog, the sound assigned to text messages.

Can't talk. Might hear. Please text only. Trapped walmart cedar city. Tried kill me again.

Her simplified text proved what urgency she was experiencing.

He texted back.

Have you called the police?

Sean felt a strange connection with Erin Cross, even having just met her—and under less-than-agreeable circumstances to be sure. He felt an urge to be with her, to protect her. It wasn't any kind of love-at-first-sight nonsense. This connection was on a deeper level. And yet he wondered what *he* could do that the Cedar City police couldn't? He was no longer involved with the military or special ops of any kind. He was an author of children's books. Still, he knew he had to do *something*.

His phone croaked.

Dont know who trust. Police maybe involved?

Sean frowned. He had a deep respect for all law enforcement personnel. Yeah, there were always a few bad apples. Every profession had its share of system-abusers. But the good far outnumbered the bad.

His mind began to skip from one thought to the next. What if Dr. Cross had nefarious connections? Maybe she had upset the mob? No. Mob members don't go around quoting phrases in Latin. Maybe her employer, this TRI, was doing illegal things behind her back and she got stuck in the middle. Unlikely. Who's to say she wasn't making all this up? Sean hadn't seen the harassing texts she claimed to have been receiving. But she did show them to the police . . . or did she? Maybe, maybe, maybe.

Sean smacked his forehead with his palm. *Focus!*

Family? he texted.

No.

OK. How long will you be safe?

Don't know. They know I'm in WM.

Is there anyone in Cedar you trust?

Can't trust anyone. Don't know who involved.

Here was his chance for more information.

Involved in what?

There was a lengthy pause with no reply. Did that mean she was debating how much to tell him? Had he called her bluff? No. This woman was a known scientist working for an acclaimed research firm. There was no reason for her to be making any of this up.

She needed his help. And he was determined to give it.

Sean began gathering things he thought he might need. He could feel his former training kicking in again. It was a feeling he usually tried to fight. It was like an inner demon he was at constant odds with. Those feelings always led to the same end: the taking of a life—often, several lives. But this time was different, he reasoned. He was going to *save* a life, not take one.

With his anxiety on the rise, he stopped at his medicine cabinet and took the pill designated to calm his nerves. He then dumped all his pill bottles in a large ziplock baggie and tossed it in his duffel.

His phone croaked.

Cant tell now. Just come.

He texted back. *Be right there. Keep hidden. May be few hours.*

Sean filled a large pack, grabbing things by reflex, by intuition. He transferred a portion of his gun safe into a watertight duffel, turned off his computer, and headed out the door.

Sean drove an old Jeep Wrangler. He liked the sportiness of it as well as the security of four-wheel drive. He was an off-road enthusiast. He'd installed a Skyjacker off-road lift kit himself, along with an interior roll bar, an oversized gas tank, and a waterproofing kit for the engine that included a carburetor snorkel. He loved taking the road less traveled—loved spending time communing with nature. He respected the earth, but he was not an extremist. Environmentalism took things too far. He was a steward of the earth, not its savior nor its servant. The earth was created for him, not the other way around.

He remembered many times in Special Ops when he'd spend days outdoors running surveillance on a target. He knew terrain like he knew the back of his hand. Jungle, desert, forest, even urban—no two operations were the same, although they all seemed to have the same result. No, that wasn't true either. He wasn't *always* asked to kill. Many times his orders dealt more with capturing, interrogating, gathering target data. Those had been his favored missions. Sean had learned to case a situation in seconds and enact decisions even before he knew what he was doing. A split second could often mean the difference between life and death. That was why he reacted to the deli situation like he did.

His phone croaked.

They still here. Can hear them. Please hurry.

He replied to the text with, *On my way.*

Tossing his gear in his Jeep, Sean headed toward I-15. He had a high-tech radar detector that not only alerted him to a speed trap but also told him how far away and from what direction the radar beacon was broadcast. He couldn't remember where he'd gotten it, but he was sure it was a leftover from his military service.

Pushing the limits of safety, he drove south on I-15 at top speed. His alarm sounded several times along the way, but he was always able to quickly judge the potential of each encounter and the likelihood of his detection.

Thirty minutes later his phone croaked again. *Police here. Not good. They definitely with bad guys.*

Chapter 18

THE FRENZIED CLAMOR OF WEEKEND shoppers penetrated the small dressing room in which Erin sat. Every few minutes someone yanked on the door, trying to enter, sending Erin's heart into her toes. But Shaniqua or another associate always helped the customer to another booth. Occasionally, Erin would hear the static hiss of a two-way radio and the garbled crackle of code numbers and acronyms broadcast over the airwaves. *The police are still here.* She listened to Shaniqua give wonderfully sarcastic responses to endless questions as to Erin's whereabouts. They usually conversed right outside the dressing room door. Obviously, Shaniqua had intentionally led the officer or agent there so Erin could listen in.

A man's voice stated, "Security cameras show she came in earlier this morning. We have reason to believe she's still in the store. She's in her late twenties, medium blonde hair, kinda chunky."

Kinda chunky? Jerk face.

"Yeah, I seen two dozen girls like that in just the last hour," Shaniqua claimed. "This is a college town, honey. They wander through here in packs."

"Yes, ma'am, I'm sure they do. Here's a photo of the woman we're looking for. Does she look familiar to you?"

There was a pause before Shaniqua answered. "Not sure. Why? What'd she do?"

"I'm not at liberty to say."

"Oh, what-ev-er," the Wal-Mart associate groaned in a singsong voice. "It'll be on the six o'clock news, honey, so I'm gonna find out sooner or later. She a serial killer or she knock off a bank or somethin' like that?"

"Yeah. Something like that," the officer said.

"Well, all I can say is she's cute as a bug's ear, and from what I can see from this picture, not the least bit chunky . . ."

I love you, Shaniqua.

"But this short little gal a hardened criminal?" Shaniqua continued in a tone dripping with sarcasm. "Are you on crack?"

The click of a button and the snap of static sounded before the officer spoke. "Dispatch. She was definitely here, but there's no sign of her now. I suggest we widen our search."

Shaniqua huffed. "Honey, I told you I ain't seen her."

"And I never mentioned she was short," the officer said.

"Well, I . . . you . . . oh, whatever," Shaniqua fumbled. "Besides, you can kinda tell by the picture."

"Of course you can," the lawman said.

Erin listened to the officer's radio static fade as he moved away from the dressing rooms. The ensuing silence was suffocating. Shaniqua must have wandered off, too.

Erin scrunched tighter into the corner of the small cubicle and drew her knees to her chest. The already narrow space seemed to shrink even more. Even the air seemed to thicken and press down on her. Her mind spun, she felt nauseous. She'd been locked in the small space for nearly five hours. Her cramped muscles screamed for movement. She had to go to the bathroom. She needed to exit the claustrophobia-inducing space, but she didn't dare leave. She thought about texting Sean Flannery again but didn't want to scare him off with perpetual pleas. And Tom had probably turned off his cell phone for the weekend so nothing would disrupt his time with his grandkids.

It felt like a dispensation of time had passed before Erin heard Shaniqua's voice again. "The police are gone, but there's still some government types hanging around," the Wal-Mart associate said through the thin dressing room door. "Now's your chance."

Erin stood on burning, wobbly legs. She exited the dressing stall and stood there, not sure what to do next.

"Child, you look like a ghost," Shaniqua gasped, holding a few articles of clothing. "Here, change into these as fast as you can. I guessed you're just about a size fourteen."

Unfortunately, the calculating eye of the Wal-Mart associate was spot on. Erin had long dreamed of one day getting back into an eight. Well, okay, a ten.

With a weak smile, Erin grabbed the clothes and reentered the dressing stall. Shaniqua had chosen jeans that fit snugly but were still breathable, and a fitted, two-layered tee that was also a bit snug but not slutty. To finish off the disguise, she'd included a ball cap identifying the wearer as being on Team Edward. She pulled her hair into a ratty ponytail and fed it through the opening in the back of the cap. Because of her perpetually youthful face, the combo made Erin look like just another young college student on a shopping foray to the big-box store. The jeans might have been part of her wardrobe, but the other articles she'd never be caught dead in. *Ugh, bad choice of words,* she thought.

She exited the booth again and accepted a light jacket Shaniqua handed her. "You'll need this. It's getting right chilly outside. I've pulled all the tags and security tabs, honey. I have no idea what you did, but it can't be as all bad as these guys are making out. You just scoot, but don't be too obvious. There may be more of 'em outside."

Gratitude pooled in Erin's eyes. "I can't thank you enough, Shaniqua."

"Oh yes you can," the woman balked. "You can give me $108.89, so this doesn't come out of my pocket." The smile accompanying the statement was refreshing.

Erin pulled two Ben Franklins from her pocket and handed them to the associate. "Keep the change."

"Thanks, honey. I will. Oh, and don't forget these," she said, handing Erin a pair of sunglasses.

"Thanks again," Erin said, giving the associate a quick hug.

Using the racks of clothing and the chaotic mob of shoppers as a shield, Erin wound her way toward the front of the store. She headed straight for the bathroom. Afterward, as she tried to make the exit, a tide of McDonald's patrons seeking their afternoon installment of caffeine, carbohydrate, salt, sugar, and grease—America's five basic food groups—slowed her retreat. Part of the deluge included two dark-suited men holding cups of coffee. One of them was the bald man from this morning. They stopped and gave her a long stare. Erin's step faltered as her heart again dropped to her toes. *Turn and run or keep walking toward them? I don't know. Just act natural—*

"Hey, Melissa!" some guy shouted from off to one side.

Erin slowed her step but didn't turn.

"Hello? Melissa?" the guy called again as he drew closer.

Erin stopped and turned toward the shouter. It was Sean Flannery.

"Hey, Missy, I thought we were going to meet at the commons on campus," he said loudly, as if mildly perturbed.

Erin stood speechless. The two men in black watched the encounter with mild disinterest.

"What—oh, don't tell me," Sean continued. "Another late night with your boyfriend, right? Can't even make time for your study partner?"

It suddenly occurred to her what Sean was doing. She shrugged, "Well, he *is* captain of the football team. How can I resist that?"

Sean stepped directly in front of her and put his fists on his hips. He had on a ball cap worn backwards, jeans, and a frumpy sweatshirt. "So are we going to study or what?"

Erin huffed loudly. "Fine. Even though I don't like bio—"

"Business Admin is *always* important," Sean forcefully interrupted. "Now let's scram. I've got a report due Monday that I haven't even started."

They walked briskly past the two hit men, who were now looking off toward the center of the store.

Once they were outside, Sean said quietly, "My Jeep's over this way. They probably have your car bugged and under surveillance."

Erin numbly followed the man. She'd slept only an hour or two last night in her car, had not eaten since the incident in the café, and had been on anxiety overload for nearly twenty-four hours. It was all she could do to put one foot in front of the other. She was surprised she'd had the wherewithal to improvise their little performance in the store.

Sean opened the passenger door for her. Luckily, he had installed a foot bar that made it easier to climb into his raised Jeep. Once inside, she finally felt she could breathe.

Sean fired up the engine and headed toward the exit. A moment later, Erin's phone vibrated. She pulled it from her pocket and saw it was a call from Tom Jenkins. Apparently he *had* kept his cell phone on.

"Hi, Tom, thanks for calling," she said in a gush of gratitude.

"Erin! Are you okay? Where are you?" her boss nearly shouted.

"I just left the Wal-Mart in Cedar. I'm with S—" Sean reached over, yanked the phone from her, and closed it.

Her scowl said it all.

"Until we figure out what's going on, we trust no one," he growled as he accelerated past the tall lighthouse marking the Providence Center shopping complex.

Erin fumed in silence for several minutes before she thought to ask, "Where are you taking me?"

"Somewhere safe," was all he said.

Perturbed and frazzled, she huffed, "Can you be more specific?"

"No."

She bit back a retort and tried to remain focused and calm.

Sean drove through the main section of town and turned east at a sign marking the way to the Dixie National Forest. After a few minutes, Erin felt safe enough to close her eyes and relax—a little. Her emotions rocketed from one extreme to another, but she kept her thoughts to herself. She still wasn't sure of anything. Well, she was pretty certain Sean Flannery had just saved her life—again. Considering all that this stranger had done for her, she knew she should cut him some slack.

In a much calmer voice she said, "I guess I owe you thanks a second time now. I didn't know who else to call."

"You're welcome." It was a flat, monotone response. Sean then sighed heavily and shook his head. "Sorry for being terse. I'm just trying to underst—"

His words were cut short by Erin's phone ringing. Still holding it tightly in his grasp, Sean glanced at the readout. "Who's Tom Jenkins?"

"My boss and the company CEO," she said. "He's a very dear friend."

Sean slipped the phone into his pocket without answering it. "Wrong. Until I figure out what's going on, I'm your only friend."

Chapter 19

Kapono nimbly piloted his boat into a cove on the westward side of the island. The cove—no more than a dent in the rugged coastline—boasted a single, low, wood-plank dock, with what looked like a small tool shed where it met the shore. Twenty yards inland, the white sand gave way to red volcanic dirt, on which stood the tiny village of Pu'uwai.

Kapono helped move Jacob's luggage onto the dock. "Man, what'chu got in dese, Doc—rocks or sometin'?"

"Mostly research equipment, so be careful, okay?"

"Hey, no worries, brah." The young Hawaiian then bent backward with his hands on the small of his back in a groaning stretch. "Man, my legs feelin' like I been surfin' a *makani pahili*."

"A *makani*—what?"

Kapono made a sweeping gesture toward the ocean. "A hurricane, brah."

"Oh." Jacob looked inland at the primitive buildings and dirt roads. In spite of his exhaustion, he knew he couldn't rest until he got his larvae to the experiment site and tested the water. "Let me guess. No taxi service to Halali'i Lake, right?"

Kapono laughed. "You been smokin' *nahelehele*, Doc? Dere no taxi here. It don' take long time ta hoof it ta my hut."

Jacob's brow furrowed. He wondered if the young man actually lived in an open, thatched hut. Worse, he wondered if he'd have to sleep in it, thereby exposing himself to creatures of the night and hordes of mosquitoes. He thought it best not to ask. He reminded himself that this was a semi-covert operation—that no one was to know his true intentions and that the privately owned island was basically a former cattle and sheep ranch, not a Marriott resort. Besides, his foray to this antediluvian speck in the Pacific would last only a couple weeks. He could tough it out at least that long.

"Gotta warn ya, brah," Kapono continued. "Mos' people here can talk *haole,* but we mos'ly talk Hawaiian, ya know?"

"By *haole,* I assume you mean a Caucasian from the mainland who speaks English?" Jacob asked.

Kapono cocked his head to one side. "Ah, yah, sure. Okay."

"Yes, I was told the citizens here speak Hawaiian almost exclusively to preserve the language."

"Sweet. You know any o' da Kamehameha lingo?"

"*Aloha* and *mahalo* and a couple other words is all."

Kapono shrugged. "No madda, dude. Mr. Robinson, he say I was da only one you could talk wid anyhow, cha? Our privacy is sacred ting. You need anytin', you come ta me, cha?"

"Cha."

Walking up the dirt road instantly had Jacob's shoes coated with a fine red powder. He saw very few people, and those he did gave him only a furtive glance. They all bore classic Polynesian features: large-bodied, dark eyes, bronze skin, black curly hair, broad noses. Of the ones he saw, there was a distinct gap in their ages; they were either very old or very young. Only one or two islanders looked middle-aged. The old ones seemed annoyed by his presence but the young ones stared at him with open amazement. Jacob didn't know if it was because of his white skin or his white shirt and Utah Jazz tie.

Up ahead, nestled between two shade trees, stood a small bungalow with stucco walls and a corrugated tin roof. Tethered to a post next to the front stoop was a scraggly old goat.

"*Aloha,* Pegasus. You miss me, girl?"

The goat looked at her master and bleated nonstop for about sixty seconds.

"She want know who you are," Kapono translated for the animal.

Jacob smirked. "You speak English, Hawaiian, and goat." It was more of a statement than a question.

"Nah, man," he said with a chuckle. "I don' *speak* goat. But I unda'stan' wha' dey say, ya know? I unda'stan' goats an' fish an' birds an' . . . an' all Kahuna's creations."

Jacob was incredulous, but he couldn't fault in the young Hawaiian for feeling that way. He understood bacteria and viruses on almost the same level. To Jacob, the molecular choreography of endonucleases dancing along strands of RNA—copying, mutating, and splicing—was a breathtaking ballet. And the fact that he had created a similar dance himself placed him on the same level as God. Well, maybe not the same level, but at least on the same playing field.

Stepping inside Kapono's hut was like stepping back in time. While the exterior walls were painted stucco, the interior walls were lined with grass thatch; the ceiling was a weave of wooden poles and more thatch. A single cot stood along one wall, various piles of clothing and dive gear lining the opposite wall. There was no cooking area. No bathroom. Along the far wall hung a long, twin skeg surfboard dangling from two lengths of cord. A thin woven mat was all that covered most of the plank-wood floor.

"*Aloha e komo mai!* Welcome ta my home sweet home. Snap digs, eh, Doc?"

Jacob was speechless.

"I call id da 'love shack.'"

The goat bleated low and long.

Jacob was suddenly nauseous.

"We're *both* gong to stay here?" Jacob asked, dreading the answer.

"Right on, brah. Two bugs in a rug."

The cot looked barely wide enough to hold a bulimic supermodel. Pointing a hesitant finger at the makeshift bed, Jacob asked, "We're not going to . . . um . . ."

Kapono tipped his head back and brayed. "Nah nah nah, dude. Whoo, dat primo funny! I know fer sure you been tokin' da *nahelehele*. No way *we* be ridin' tandem on da night board, man. No offense, but I don' surf dat slope, cha? You take da board, I take da hammock outside."

Jacob chuckled. "Yeah. I was just cracking again."

Kapono wrapped a muscular arm around Jacob's narrow shoulders. "Ya know, when I firs' saw you in dem baggies an' dat nasty tie, I t'ought you was gonna be a mondo dweeb. A gnarly huge hodad, cha? But you all right, brah."

"Gee, thanks," Jacob said blandly. "Can we see the lake now?"

Kapono shrugged. "Sure, dude. Bu' firs' ya gotta lose dem uptight baggies, cha?"

"Excuse me?"

"Lose da preacha' threads, brah. They scream *haole*. Here," he said reaching into the pile of discarded clothing. "Use dese."

The young Hawaiian held out a pair of multicolored cargo shorts and a T-shirt emblazoned with the phrase *I'm a Local*.

"Not very accurate, is it?"

Kapono flashed another broad smile. His teeth seemed to glow in the shadowy hut. "Chill, dude. It not mine. A *haole* touris' lef' dem on my tub long time back. But dey be better'n' whad you wearin'. Be yours now, Doc. I waid outside while you change, cha?"

Jacob looked through the mosquito net window at the surrounding trees. A gentle breeze soughed through the dark leaves and pushed against the netting. He glanced through the doorless entry, wondering about privacy. Kapono was nowhere in sight. But the goat stared back at him with expressionless eyes while chewing a wad of cud.

"What are you looking at?" Jacob growled. He closed his eyes and held his fingertips against his temples. "Great. Now *I'm* talking to the goat," he said before loosening his tie.

Chapter 20

SUBORDINATES ADAMS AND JEFFERSON WAITED outside the Cedar City Wal-Mart. It wasn't long before a Prefect of the Order showed up. The Prefect gave the secret signs and identified himself as Franklin. Even though their dark suits were a bit formal for weekend shopping, the men received little more than occasional glances from passersby.

The initial excitement concerning Dr. Cross in and around the box store had dwindled. The Thanksgiving case lot sale was more important to the denizens of Cedar City than a reality show scenario. The police had impounded Dr. Cross's sports car and had left shortly thereafter. They would remain vigilant and asked that the store management do the same. The manager decided not to spread the word that a murder suspect was in the area. He didn't want to start a panic, after all, and lose his weekend sales.

"The police are stepping up their search to a state-wide sweep, Praeficere," Adams told the Prefect. "They said they'd contact us with any leads they encounter. We had no trouble convincing them we were with Homeland Security."

Franklin nodded, his eyes remaining steely. "And?"

"We were able to identify Dr. Cross from the store security cameras," Jefferson stated. "The DVR showed Dr. Cross entering the store and slipping into a dressing room. That was where she hid from us. I searched that area myself, but I was misled by a store employee, a Shaniqua Twillwater. We had asked to see the security recordings soon after we got here, but the assistant manager would not allow it until the manager showed up, and he didn't get here until about an hour ago. By then, Dr. Cross had already escaped."

"You were watching the front of the store?"

"Yes, sir. Store management was watching the back. We even had the local police combing the store."

"And yet she still got away," Franklin stated.

"Yes, sir, but she had help," Jefferson joined in, trying hard to sound emotionally detached while foisting the blame elsewhere. "She was in disguise. This Shaniqua woman waited until the store was very busy then brought Dr. Cross a change of clothing, a hat, and sunglasses. The employee claimed she was just doing her job. From the DVR it appears they had just met that morning, but we feel she knows more than she's revealing."

"So Dr. Cross changed clothing and just walked right past you?"

"Not exactly, sir. She met with a man. The two claimed to have had a prearranged meeting. They left together."

"Do we know who he is?"

"Possibly. We believe the man she encountered is Sean Flannery. We have a couple of images from the cameras, but they are not very clear. We identified him by his car. He drives a Jeep Wrangler that is modified for off-road driving. The parking lot cameras recorded his license plates. The images were fuzzy, but police were able to match the tags to the Jeep, and that's how we got his name. His address is listed in Orem, Utah. He's forty, dark brown hair, blue eyes, six feet even, about 190 pounds. That's all we know so far. We don't know what his connection is with Dr. Cross."

Franklin seemed more perturbed by the information than pleased. "So you, the store management, and the local police had Dr. Cross in a confined space for roughly . . . five hours? And she still got away?" It was more of a statement than a question.

"Yes, sir," Adams replied.

"With some help," Jefferson again added.

The Prefect was silent for a long time. His mouth was pursed in a tight line. His eyes were steady and hard. "You two are hereby commanded to enact order ninety-nine immediately."

"Yes, Praeficere," Adams said without hesitation.

"Yes, Praeficere," Jefferson softly echoed a moment later.

"Your keys, please."

Adams handed Franklin his car keys.

"Any idea where they were headed?"

"According to the police, Mr. Flannery and Dr. Cross were last seen heading east toward the mountains."

He nodded. "Your marks, please."

The two pulled out their billfolds and handed them over, money and all.

"Your rings."

They removed their rings, kissed the onyx stone, and surrendered them to the Prefect.

Franklin drew a long, steady breath. "*Meus vita pro novus ordo seclorum,*" he said with reverence. He then handed them each a folded slip of paper, which they each slid in their breast pocket without reading.

"*Meus vita pro novus ordo seclorum,*" the men repeated solemnly. "*Ego tribuo meus vita ut novus ordo seclorum.*"

The Prefect nodded and left. Adams and Jefferson walked past their sedan and continued on foot to the frontage road along I-15 until they came to an overpass. Walking beside the low guardrail, the two men stopped and faced the oncoming southbound traffic below. Despite the coolness of the late afternoon, both men had a fine sheen of perspiration on their foreheads. The traffic below zipped by at sixty-plus miles per hour. In the distance, a Peterbilt semi pulling a double trailer crested the rise and headed toward them, picking up speed as it did.

Both men climbed onto the cement abutment and stepped over the metal guardrail. They reverently kissed the gnostic tattoos on their knuckles. They patted the paper in their pocket. They knew it contained a false declaration of who they were and why they committed such a heinous act. Neither man made a sound as they waited for the precise moment they needed to fulfill order ninety-nine. It came within seconds. Leaning forward, the two jumped in tandem, falling directly into the path of the large tractor trailer. Their timing was perfect. They didn't even hit the asphalt before their lives were forfeited.

Chapter 21

As they wended their way east into the mountains along Highway 14, both Sean and Erin remained silent. He had a thousand questions, but he wasn't sure where to begin. He didn't want to reveal what he already knew about her—or rather, what he didn't know. She might misconstrue that as snooping or even stalking. And yet he didn't want to play mind games either. She was a major-league scientist—although you wouldn't know it to look at her. He stole a quick glance and had to smile at the *Twilight* cap she wore.

Sean was a voracious reader of pop fiction. He'd read Stephanie Meyer's popular vampire series and thought the author's syntax and first-person prose were quite good. It was the content that didn't thrill him. Oh, well. To each his own.

Coming out of a narrow canyon, the lowering sunlight pierced the overcast sky, briefly highlighting the area in an amber glow. The light also revealed the glistening remnants of tears on Erin's cheeks. She was currently sleeping. He could tell she was near total fatigue when he saw her in the store. He also saw the hit men and recognized them for what they were. He'd learned when dealing with their type it's often best to hide in plain sight. Plus, Sean and Erin had the advantage of being in a very public place. That's why he immediately started with the college student ruse, knowing Cedar City was home to Southern Utah University. Fortunately, she picked up on the charade. He was impressed. Apparently there was more to this woman than he'd first suspected. The big question was how much more?

Erin groaned and fidgeted. She must be fighting bad dreams. She definitely had the material for several nightmares. Sean again wondered who was after her. In normal circumstances, she'd be best served by going straight to the police. If it was a mercenary group or secret government agency, she'd still be safer with the local law enforcement. Only now the police were looking for her, too, suspecting her of murder. Perhaps it was some other group altogether—someone no one had ever heard of. Frankly, he was surprised she'd lasted this long.

They passed a road sign marking the boundary to the Dixie National Park. There was a rest area with bathrooms and tourist information. He didn't stop. He could use a stretch but he didn't want to disturb her sleep—even if it was fitful. Best to keep driving. The more distance he placed between the two of them and those chasing her, the better.

Those chasing us, he corrected himself. If they had the resources Sean suspected they did, they probably already knew who he was. He was certain the store cameras had glimpses of him. And the parking lot cameras undoubtedly had identified his Jeep and license plates. That made him an accomplice. But an accomplice to what? Certainly not murder.

He couldn't accept that Erin was a killer. Nor did he believe she was involved in any illegal experiments or business dealings. He didn't know why he felt that way. He just did. Sizing people up was an interrogation skill he'd honed working for the military.

Sean slowed to take a sharp turn. Rounding the corner, he saw a large whitetail buck standing just off the shoulder in a stand of aspen some distance ahead. He tapped his brakes to slow even more, just in case the animal bolted. Erin gasped and woke up suddenly.

"It's okay," he said softly. "Just slowing for a deer."

She looked ahead and squinted. "Where?"

He pointed. "Right side of the road, fifty yards, in the trees."

They covered half the distance before she saw the elusive creature. "How in the world did you spot him from back there in this low light? Are you a hunter or something?"

"No. I hate killing any living thing. I just have good eyes. Especially at night."

"Oh." She yawned and rubbed her eyes forcefully. She then yawned again, stretched, and groaned as if the motion caused considerable pain.

"How're you doing, kid?"

She raised an eyebrow. "Kid?"

He chuckled lightly. "Sorry. The outfit kinda takes the years off."

Erin took off her cap and tossed it in the backseat. She took a breath as if to say something but then exhaled slowly without a word. A few minutes passed before she spoke. "Thank you, Sean," she said softly.

"You already thanked me. Don't you remember?" he said, still trying to lighten the somber mood.

"Yeah, but it was my life you saved, and that deserves extra thanks."

He stared straight ahead. "I don't know about that."

A mountain rain shower had recently moistened the narrow road, darkening its surface. Sean listened to his tires hiss along the asphalt as he waited for her to speak again. Erin seemed lost in her thoughts. Her eyes had that vacant stare people get where they can't focus on issues clouding their mind.

"I think you do know about it, Sean. You saved my life twice already. I'm not sure I can ever repay a debt like that."

"Forget it," he offered. Then in a suddenly forceful tone, he said, "I think it's about time you tell me what's going on. Who's targeting you?"

"I don't know . . ." Her voice trailed off as she stared into her empty hands.

"You sure?"

Erin clenched her jaw and shook her head. She rolled down her window and took in some crisp mountain air.

Sean cleared his throat. "What—you don't want to talk about it?"

An angry frown furrowed her brow. "Talk about what? I just told you I have no clue what's going on. One day I'm eating lunch in a small deli, and the next thing I know I'm being threatened by men with guns! I'm just so confused. And I'm not used to being confused." Her voice raised in pitch as tears brimmed on her eyelashes. "And you. Who are you? And where did you learn all that GI Joe stuff?"

Sean's frown matched hers. "I already told you, in a past life—a life I don't like to talk about." He could actually taste the bitterness in his tone.

Erin shifted in her seat to face him. The frown slowly relaxed into a look of consternation. "Is there any reason why I shouldn't trust you?"

He shrugged but didn't answer.

Erin kept staring. "Well?" she prompted.

He briefly glanced her way. The look in her eyes was heart-wrenching. He shouldn't be so angry. This wasn't her fault. *Cut her some slack.* He smiled and winked. "Yes, there is. I usually take the biggest slice of cake and do so with little remorse."

She considered his answer for a moment before facing forward again. "I'll keep that in mind."

It was a few minutes before Sean spoke again. "Sorry. Just trying to lighten the mood. Look, we're both stressed out here. I get that way when I haven't taken my pills or haven't eaten in a while. It's been hours since my last meal. How about you?"

Erin huffed. "I can't remember. But I don't feel hungry."

"There's a mom-and-pop gas station up ahead. They have a small diner inside. We'll top off the tank and grab a quick bite. I think we have a big enough lead to give us a couple minutes of downtime."

Erin didn't respond. Even though Sean had a million questions for her, he respected her silence. He wondered what it would take to crack through her shell to find out what was at the core of this bizarre chain of events. He felt a curious empathy for her. It seemed her emotional shell was a lot like his—impenetrable.

Chapter 22

The diner was almost empty. Sean said he was surprised it wasn't closed, as late in the season as it was. Frankly, she didn't care one way or the other.

"You know there's an APB out on you?" Sean said between bites of cheeseburger. When Erin didn't respond, he added, "For murder."

Erin still said nothing. She felt too numb. Her mind would not stop swimming. Unrelenting fatigue from the angst of the past twenty-four hours had her body shutting down involuntarily. She'd caught a few winks while riding with Sean but nothing restorative. She was running on empty. The last thing she'd eaten was her croissant sandwich at Giamboli's, but she couldn't bring herself to eat any of the food in front of her. She simply had no appetite.

"A security guard at Timpanogos Research was shot and killed last night. They say you were there."

They think I murdered Harry Harriman?

"Care to tell me about what happened at TRI so I don't feel like I'm aiding and abetting a criminal?" Sean was a hundred percent serious. There was no jesting in his tone.

A tear of frustration escaped down Erin's cheek. She angrily brushed it off. "Harry is—*was*—a good friend. One of the few I have. Why would I want to kill him?" she snapped.

"I don't know," he snapped back then lowered his voice to a harsh whisper. "But a lot of people think you did, so you'd better start explaining things so I can figure out what to do."

"So *you* can figure—" she stopped abruptly. "What makes you think I need *you* to figure anything out?"

With a French fry poised at his mouth, he brandished a look of astonishment. "*You* called *me*, remember?"

She ducked her head and clenched her fists. He was right, of course. Why was she having so much trouble accepting that this man might truly want to help? *Why?* She knew the reason. She had no idea who he was. With all his talk of not trusting anyone, he had yet to include himself. Even so, she felt she *should* trust him. She knew so few people outside her work, and just as few inside. She wasn't antisocial. She simply got more enjoyment out of reading a book or working biochemical formulas at her computer than going to a singles dance or hitting a night club.

"Erin?"

"Yeah, sorry. It's just that . . . well, why would I kill Harry? We were close friends. I don't even own a gun. Here someone is threatening to kill *me,* and now they're saying *I* killed Harry? Honestly, I wish I had an answer to who they are and why they want me dead, but I don't."

"But you have your suspicions, right?"

She nodded—then shook her head. "A dozen names come to mind but none I could conceive is behind all this." She angrily dipped a French fry in a dollop of ketchup but didn't eat it. She *wanted* to confide in this man. She *needed* to confide in him. But she was serious about not trusting anyone until she could figure out what was going on. More than anything, she wanted to call Tom Jenkins at TRI. But like Sean said, what if he was involved?

"You feel alone right now, don't you," Sean said with surprising empathy.

Her gaze bonded with his. "Do you read minds, too?"

"No. But I'm pretty good at reading people and emotions. It's a skill I learned a while back."

Erin scrutinized the man across from her. He was serious yet approachable. He was good looking but not full of himself, as she'd initially suspected. What's more, he seemed like he was truly interested in her. Or at least in helping her. That was something she could trust, wasn't it? Hadn't he already proven that?

Allowing herself the slightest vulnerability, she asked, "I need to trust you, Sean Flannery, but first I need to know who you are."

He frowned. "I take it you want more than name, rank, and serial number."

"Yes, please. Once I tell you what I suspect is going on, you'll understand my hesitation for confiding in you."

Sean took another bite of burger and washed it down with Diet Coke. "Okay. One confidence for another." He nodded. "Fair enough. I don't usually open up to beautiful strangers. But this is a unique situation."

Erin's stomach fluttered at his "beautiful stranger" statement, and she felt her neck color. Wanting to sidestep the awkward comment, she said, "*Unique* is a mild way to put it."

"For want of a better word," he said with a shrug. "But I insist on one condition before I tell you anything."

"Yes?" Erin said with a raised eyebrow.

"You eat while I talk. You need the nourishment, and we need to keep moving. I figure we have maybe a fifteen-, maybe twenty-minute lead on these guys, but there's really no telling. We have the advantage in that Cedar City doesn't have any traffic cams—at least none that I could see. And there's dozens of side roads in this park. They have no idea which way we went."

Erin sighed and lifted the top bun of her burger to remove the pickle.

"So you don't like them either, huh?" Sean chuckled.

"Vile things, pickles. Did you know the chemistry used in making them is the same as the Egyptians used to make mummies?"

"Seriously?"

"Close enough. There's just something ostensibly wrong about eating an embalmed cucumber."

"No wonder I hate them." Sean chuckled through a huge grin. "'An embalmed cucumber.' That sounds like something my daughter would say."

Her eyebrow rose a bit higher. "So you do have a daughter. Is she more like you or your wife?"

Sean set the remainder of his burger on his plate and wiped his mouth. "Ex. That's where it gets complicated."

"Oh. Sorry."

"It's okay. Water under the bridge. Way under. Pretty much a dry gulch anymore. I never hear from her, which is fine with both of us."

Erin dropped her eyes to her plate. She didn't know what to say.

"I hear from Britt pretty regularly. She's attending Dartmouth College right now. Studying pre-pharmacy for some reason," he said with a jesting grin.

"She sounds pretty smart," Erin said.

"Oh, she is. I haven't seen her in a long while, but we communicate through e-mail and texts."

"Texts," Erin said as if revolted. "Speaking of which, I haven't received one in a while. I wonder why?"

Sean looked out the window at the darkening terrain. The afternoon sun was totally obscured by thick storm clouds. "Perhaps they're waiting for the right moment."

"The right moment for what?" she hesitated to ask.

He pointed at her plate. "You eat. I'll talk. Then we can take it from there." His voice had a strange finality to it—almost a sense of foreboding. Erin wasn't sure what to make of it.

Outside thunder rumbled in the distance. It matched her feelings to a tee.

Chapter 23

Jacob Krantz had done significant research about Ni'ihau before deciding to run his field tests there, but he was still taken by how un-Hawaiian the landscape looked. The Big Island of Hawaii was inundated in tropical splendor. Oahu and Maui were even more so. Kauai beat them all with its lush vegetation and scenic wonders, securing its title as the Garden Isle. But Ni'ihau seemed to be in a completely different weather zone. Although it was part of the Hawaiian archipelago, it was a surprisingly arid island. The textbooks claimed it lay in the "rain shadow" of Kauai. Plus it lacked mountains high enough to catch any trade-wind moisture. Pani'au, the highest peak on the small island—a mere 1,280 feet—was little more than a bump compared to the mountains of Kauai and the big island.

"Sure seems . . . dry here," Jacob commented between gasps for breath as they hiked toward Halali'i Lake

"Cha. We haven' had da konas yet. Dey usual set 'round end a Novemba' mos'ly. Mondo huge storms, fer sure. Tings really green big time den. Da rest a da year Kauai steal all da rain."

"I see," Jacob said, wishing he'd prepared better. He didn't think he was out of shape, but keeping up with the stout Hawaiian proved challenging.

After an hour of hiking, they crested a rise that overlooked Lakes Halali'i and Halulu, the two largest freshwater lakes in Hawaii. Jacob immediately noticed that Halulu, the smaller of the two, was not much more than a red-clay mud hole. Halali'i still had a large amount of water but even it looked murky. It was easy to see where the water line had been. The distance between the rim of the lake bed and the water was almost fifty yards. During wet years, the surface of Halali'i measured more than 800 acres. Presently, it was a fraction of that.

"I wasn't aware the lakes dried up this much," Jacob said after catching his breath.

"Cha, dude, 'special when id hot. Dis summa' ain' been too bad, but all da udda' lake be mud 'bout now. Hope id don' jack your study none. My people be very concern 'bout da Wes' Nile *gamboo*. Dat why Mr. Robinson let you come ta Ni'ihau. You 'bout da only *haole* dat visit in long time."

"Well, I'll try my best to put an end to it for you," Jacob said in a compassionate tone.

"Thanks, brah," Kapono said, slapping Jacob's back.

If you only knew.

The two went directly to the shoreline of Halali'i. "Are there any fish in this lake?" Jacob asked.

"Nah nah nah, man. Like I say, mos' da time da lake is jus' a gnarly mud hole. Notin' in dere but worms 'n' snail 'n' mosquita mos'ly. Notin' wert' fishin' for. Now, da sea bass off shore—dude! Dat some good chow, Doc."

"Actually, I'm more interested in what indigenous larval predators there might be."

Kapono gave Jacob a confused look.

Jacob held up his satchel containing the five plastic bottles. "Mosquito larvae are a primary food source for many species of fish and other insects. If these get eaten before they have a chance to grow into adults, my research will be ruined."

"No worries, man. Halali'i be mosquita luau. We usual stay 'way in da wet times. Serious, brah. Da lake have id own cloud—only id made of bugs, not rain."

"When was the last time anyone sprayed insecticide in here?"

"Oh not for long time. Since da ranch close, ain' nobody got no money. We a private islan', cha? We can no affor' dat kine' stuff."

"Perfect," Jacob said. His larvae were a hardy strain of *Plasmodium falciparum,* the species responsible for eighty percent of malaria cases and ninety percent of related deaths worldwide. They were also the most common species to carry West Nile virus and avian (bird) flu. It was the ideal vector for his designer blood-borne pathogen.

Armageddon. His creation. His meal ticket. His way to get back at all those who scoffed him and all those who continue to scoff—for all those who call him a madman. He could see it now: Dr. Jacob Krantz, President of . . . well . . . the World.

Jacob removed his shoes and socks.

"Whoa, chill a sec, Doc. You not tinkin' of going in dere, cha?"

Jacob gave his Hawaiian companion a condescending smile. Obviously this naive young man knew nothing about the life cycle of mosquitoes. His larvae would do nothing to him. Larvae didn't draw blood like leeches. While they may carry the sporozoites of a deadly virus, the only way the virus could enter his bloodstream was via an adult insect.

"It's okay, Kapono. I know what I'm doing," he assured the young man.

"But dat's—"

"Nothing to be worried about," he finished for the Hawaiian. "I'm the scientist, remember? I'll be just fine. It's important I do this to protect your people."

Kapono just stared slack-jawed.

Shaking his head at Kapono's naiveté, Jacob waded knee-deep to an area thick with vegetation. He removed a paper litmus strip from a small vial. Dipping the strip into the lake, he compared the resultant tint to a color-key on the vial. The pH was 5.9. A bit acidic, but not dangerously so. Probably due to a lack of calcium. That was common in the Hawaiian archipelago groundwater.

Jacob unscrewed the lid of the first bottle. He marveled at his foresight in filling the nipple with actual liquid soap then sealing the hole emptying into the bottle so none of it would enter. That's what the TSA agent had smelled. It was a good thing he hadn't actually opened the bottle.

He allowed a trickle of lake water to wash in. Luckily, the temperature of Lake Halali'i was almost as warm as the water in his bottle. He gently swirled the water then added a bit more. When the bottle was full, he poured a quarter of it back into the lake. He capped the small bottle with a fine mesh screen so no larvae would fall out. He repeated the slow addition of water until the bottle was full again. The whole process took nearly ten minutes. All that time Jacob stood in one place with his feet sunk a few inches in the muddy silt of the lake bottom. He repeated the procedure for each of the five bottles in his ziplock baggie.

Trudging back to Kapono, Jacob could not help but smile. The stout Hawaiian, however, was not smiling back. In fact, he was frowning. Well, that was to be expected. He didn't know any better. He would never know any better.

"Dat not a cool t'ing, brah," Kapono said angrily.

"Kapono, my friend. The mosquito larvae will not bite me, and I don't believe there are other parasites I need to worry about in there either."

"But da spirit of Halali'i not like it."

Jacob could not suppress a snigger. "The spirit of the lake?"

"Cha, man. Halali'i is a sacred lake. It holy water to da people of Ni'ihau. We not suppose ta drink from it unless it be a drought. An' we special not supposed ta swim in it." The look on Kapono's face was one of abject disdain.

More silly superstitions, Jacob mused. "I understand," he said in his best diplomatic voice. "But I believe the lake god will be kind because I am here to help your people."

The Polynesian's expression softened slightly. "I still t'ink it not a good idea, Docta Brown."

"I promise I won't swim or frolic in the water. And I will use only one small portion of the lake for my tests. How's that sound?" Jacob couldn't believe he needed to barter for permission to use the main location of mosquito breeding when they'd already okayed his visit. Where did they think the mosquitoes bred, anyway?

Kapono rubbed the back of his thick neck. "Well . . . if you t'ink it be da right t'ing. But I don'. You go in dere an' da spirit of Halali'i will be angry. He be one jealous dude. He always get even in the end."

Jacob nodded solemnly. But inside he was laughing.

Chapter 24

CFO Luther Mendenhall knew he was walking a tightrope that could easily be fashioned into a noose. He had made a decision. It wasn't a snap decision; it was one he'd spent many sleepless nights over. The investment capital necessary to fast-track the development of any drug was astronomical. His company was financially sound . . . mostly. True, they had funded a few projects that ended up being dead ends. In today's economy, such wrong guesses didn't simply bruise their accounts, it made them bleed.

This new project, however, was a guaranteed windfall. Well, "guaranteed" was a hopeful term. When researching anything of a biologic nature, there are no guarantees—and that went double for new medications. The current drug approval process mandated years of lab trials on hundreds of animals and eventually on thousands of people. But when a drug hits the market and is used by millions of people, unforeseen side effects invariably show up. Some are mere nuisance; others are devastating.

When the CFO first heard the idea for this latest venture, he scoffed. Was that even possible? And what was the profit potential? Dr. Cross said it would change the mortality rate of the world. The *world*! That was enough of a promise to channel significant amounts of money into the venture. Unfortunately, the company coffers were at an all-time low. Blame the economy.

Mendenhall had immediately looked for outside sources of financial support. Exhausting all his aboveboard resources, he followed a few leads to overseas investors that ostensibly had unlimited funding: oil barons, foreign officials, third-world royalty, and the like. One source led to another source, which led to a guy who knew another guy, and before long the American CFO was talking to someone with undisclosed connections in Saudi Arabia. Their ability to invest seemed endless. Having reached the end of his rope, the CFO signed his name with high hopes.

Then a national panic happened when the swine flu crept in from Mexico. TRI was asked to develop a treatment. Dr. Cross and her partner were asked to spearhead the project, which unavoidably put her project on hold. Things went well to begin with, but a serious snag stopped the project cold. Like a chain reaction, the snag shut everything down, including repayment of the loan.

A few months later, the Saudi investor's people began making calls. The first-installment deadline had come and gone. A few weeks after that, the CFO began receiving threats. He'd never experienced anything like that before, but he took them all very seriously.

Then a miracle happened. Well, maybe not a miracle, but certainly a fortuitous turn of events. The project partner made a secondary discovery—one that had further-reaching potentials than even Dr. Cross's original idea. It wasn't a shock, really. The scientist Mendenhall had brought on was there not only to help with TRI's discoveries, but also to make sure the CFO was fed all data and information—some of which could be used in other, less-than-humanitarian ways. This was one.

It was so simple, it came across as illumination.

Luther Mendenhall immediately removed Dr. Cross's partner from the project and assigned him to a lab in an ultra-secure facility. Within a few months, the scientist's project showed huge potential, mind-boggling potential. The CFO began channeling the Saudi funds into the second project. With any luck, he would never have to pay back the money. In fact, if the designer virus his scientist had created was everything it promised to be, the CFO could make any demand he wanted—for the rest of his life.

But that's where the potential for serious ramifications came into play. Dr. Erin Cross knew everything. And if she didn't initially put two and two together, she certainly had the brains to figure it out later on.

Mendenhall knew he'd have to remove her from the equation. But he couldn't simply have her eliminated. Where was the fun in that? She had cost his company a significant amount of money. And she had spurned his efforts to have her join in his vision for a new way of life.

Yes, he was going to make her suffer first—make her regret her former decisions, even make her question her sanity if possible. The fall of Dr. Erin Cross would be shrouded in mystery—just like his secret Order.

Utilizing his service with Belize Securities, he was able to send her untraceable text messages. Through the eyes of numerous field subordinates and a few high-tech tracking devices, he knew her whereabouts at all times. Those same subordinates had just informed him that Dr. Cross was no longer acting alone. A man by the name of Sean Flannery was helping her. The only things his minions had uncovered on the man were from the police reports on the incident at Giamboli's Deli. Flannery was a former Special Ops Marine. No wonder Dr. Cross had lasted so long. But knowing she had help added a new dimension to his game. It certainly upped the stakes, and not necessarily in a bad way. As his Luther Mendenhall persona, he'd be at a loss as to how to proceed. As Praefectus Magnus, he felt a surge of enlightenment in his quest to rise to this new challenge. Sean Flannery would have to die, too. Painfully.

Yes, this was going to be a very fun game.

Chapter 25

The determined look in Sean's eyes became distant, pensive. He remained quiet for some time, his glance drifting.

"I'm sorry, Sean. You don't have to say anything if it brings up bad memories."

He fixated on a random object out the window. "It's okay. But if I tell you some, I have to tell you all," he began softly. "Valerie and I got married when I got out of the service. Marines, Special Ops. I thought settling down would help me get past the . . . past the *issues* I dealt with overseas." He paused and glanced at her plate. "You're not eating."

Erin took a bite of her cheeseburger. She wanted to express as much sympathy as possible by being more interested in his story than her food. But as the taste of grilled meat, melted cheese, onion, and tomato hit her taste buds, her apparent lack of appetite instantly vanished. She was ravenous. Still, she ate slowly and with little emotion so she could concentrate on Sean's narrative.

"Anyway, I was fresh out of the service. We were both living in North Carolina at the time. I had a good GI pension, good insurance, a pretty decent nest egg. Valerie was beautiful and driven. She was one of those people who took the initiative in everything. But she also got bored easily. At first I was exciting to her. You know, in excellent physical shape, lots of money, had a past filled with intrigue and adventure. In spite of that, she starting becoming distant about a year after we said 'I do.' But that was probably my fault."

Sean took quick sip of soda, as if taking a shot of whiskey for courage. "I guess I talk a lot in my sleep. I had terrible dreams about what I did in Special Ops. I thought the nightmares would eventually go away. Some months were great. Some were terrible. I finally went to the docs at Beaufort Hospital—that's in South Carolina. They assigned me to a psychiatrist—a tall, black kid named Dr. Alex Wilder. Nice man. Had this really deep voice, like a bass in a fifties doo-wop band. Anyway, he had me start writing everything down—both as a release and a way to see things from another perspective. We got along great. Trouble was his tour was up a couple weeks after we started. He transferred out to some hospital in California, so they sent me to some other psych who loaded me up with pills that basically shut me down. I didn't like it. Valerie hated it. I was lethargic, moody, zero libido, zero . . . ability. Not much of a honeymoon husband."

"But those are side effects of the medication. It wasn't your fault," Erin offered.

He shrugged. "It went beyond that, I think. The new psych sessions I went to were weird. I'm not sure why they felt so strange. Each time I came out, I felt better but . . . different. None of the issues of my past seemed lifted like they did with Dr. Wilder."

He took another sip, this time long and drawn out, contemplative. Looking up, he asked, "You sure you want to hear all this?"

Erin nodded, intrigued more by his tone than the content. He sounded almost relieved to be sharing his past.

Sean looked out the window and continued. "Anyway, we thought maybe a change of scenery would help, so we moved to Littleton, Colorado. It's a city just south of Denver. That seemed to help at first. I've always loved the mountains, the clean air. That's where Britt was born."

A warm smile spread across his face, and his pensive stare softened. "She was a godsend. Valerie was able to focus on her instead of me and my issues." Sean's eyes closed. "I can still picture Britt's first steps, her first words and sentences. I loved the feel of her in my arms, the scent of her hair as she lay on my shoulder, rocking her to sleep after bedtime stories and prayers."

He paused a moment, not saying anything. Slowly, almost painfully, his smile sank into a look of regret. "But after only a few years of motherhood, Valerie lost interest. She'd become the housewife of a low-income yard man. She used to be 'cosmopolitan flash' but had somehow digressed into 'suburban drab.' Britt was just one more burden in her life, in her marriage." He swallowed hard. "I say *her* marriage because that's what she called it. Not *our* marriage. I tried to help by doing most of the housework and childrearing. I had a job in landscaping, see. I was busy during the summer, but the winters were long, so I had a lot of time at home. I went back to Beaufort for follow-up appointments, but I didn't feel they did anything. I always came back feeling so . . . empty. That's when I started writing—to fill my mind with good images and stories. That's what I do now. I write."

Sean started running his finger along the grout line on the tile tabletop. "Anyway, Valerie took a job with a dermatologist in Denver. Almost immediately I started to suspect something was going on between her and the doctor, but I didn't say anything. She seemed happy, and I wanted Britt to grow up in a house filled with happiness, not bitterness and anger." His gaze returned to the view out the window. "It took less than a year before Valerie left with the dermatologist. I say 'left' because the doc *had* to leave the state. He lost his license due to 'inappropriate patient contact.' At least that's the way the state medical board put it." Sean snorted in derision. "Apparently, Valerie didn't mind the injunction—or the inappropriate contact."

He went silent again. Lost.

Although her caution was still on high alert, Erin's heart went out to Sean. She felt she had learned more about this man than she'd ever known about any other man she'd met. It was not so much what he said as how he said it. These memories were from his soul. He wasn't the shallow individual she'd suspected he was. His past ran deep. He cared for his daughter. She'd obviously come first in his life—a feeling she never got from her father. And he had come to her rescue *twice*! She wanted him to stop his narrative, feeling she could deduce the rest of the story. But she also felt *he* needed to finish, to unload everything so there was no mystery, no unknowns between them as they battled *her* dilemma.

Softly, he continued: "She sent me divorce papers shortly afterward. She didn't want anything money-wise. She just wanted Britt. Can you believe that? Just a few weeks before, she could care less about her own daughter; now she wanted full custody. I consulted a lawyer about my chances of keeping Britt. He said—" Sean stopped abruptly. Erin saw his Adam's apple bob repeatedly in an effort to rein in his emotions. His eyes were distant, vacant. He forced a bitter chuckle. "He said because of my menial job and documented mental health issues, I wouldn't stand a chance. He suggested I request ample visitation rights and leave it at that. I—" He stopped again and swallowed several times. "I didn't know what to do. I guess all the things Valerie used to say to me about not being much of a father . . . or a man . . . well, I guess it must have had an element of truth to it. I had no backbone. I was a slave to my medications. I signed the papers, and my lawyer sent them off." He wiped his eyes quickly and forced a smile. "Sorry for being so depressing. Not all my life has been as bad as it seems."

"I'm sure it hasn't," was all Erin could think to say.

"Each time I went to Beaumont, I made a point of trying to see Britt. I made time to go more often, thinking that the extra visits to my psych couldn't hurt, and it would increase my chances to see my daughter. She was all I had. I'd do anything for her."

Unbidden thoughts of Erin's father flashed through her mind. Why couldn't he have felt that way about her? She shook it off. This was Sean's time, not hers.

"So . . . what do you write?" she asked.

"Children's books."

Erin barked out a sharp laugh then quickly covered her mouth. "Sorry. A former Special Ops Marine writing children's books? What—like, *How the Ayatollah Stole Ramadan*?"

Sean laughed. "No—but that's not bad. Can I use it?"

"Be my guest. It's just that you look more like a dashing CEO or a sportswear model than someone who makes up kids' stories." Erin stopped abruptly and shoved a French fry into her mouth. Did she just call him dashing? She felt the heat rise in her neck and cheeks from her Freudian slip.

Sean didn't seem to notice. "So that's it. I'm basically a single dad with a troubling past trying to be a nice guy. Britt's in college at Dartmouth studying stuff that's way over my head but apparently right up your alley. She likes it, anyway. I've thought about moving back East to be closer to her, but I feel comforted by the mountains. Strange, huh?"

Erin was silent for a time, mulling over everything he'd told her. "No, it's not strange at all. I feel the same way."

Someone as honest and forthright as this guy couldn't be all bad. She felt strongly that she was in safe hands. But as nice as he seemed, she still could not figure out exactly what he could do to help. She couldn't really ask him to be her bodyguard forever. Yet he seemed bent on helping.

"So what do we do now?" she asked, feeling the weight of his story on her shoulders.

Pling-buzz. Erin gasped and held her breath.

Sean calmly pulled her phone from his pocket. The call number was a string of zeros. He handed it to Erin. "They're back."

Taking the phone, she pressed VIEW.

Do not trust Sean Flannery.

Chapter 26

SEAN STARED AT ERIN, HOPING to see some compassion in her expression, maybe even a little sympathy. What he saw was confusion. "What's wrong?" he asked.

Erin closed her cell phone and slipped it in her pocket. "Nothing," she said before finishing off her chocolate milkshake with a slurpy finale.

She was hedging. "Come on, Erin. If we're going to figure this mess out, we need to be totally honest with each other, okay? What did the text say?"

She shook her head. "Just more stupid threats."

Sean tried to stare her down, but she kept her eyes glued outside. Was she regretting her decision to ask his help now that she knew the truth about his past? He felt strangely lighthearted after spilling his guts as he had. Expecting to be drowning in a tsunami of embarrassment, he instead felt buoyed up, as if recounting his history had confirmed his ability to carry on in spite of the sorrows he'd endured.

"Well, we've sat here long enough," he said, slipping back into his commando mode. "It'll be dark soon. And these clouds look like they've got some snow in them. We better be going."

Just then a large, silver Suburban with tinted windows pulled up next to Sean's Jeep. His pulse quickened, and his vision narrowed. He heard Erin draw a quick breath. Apparently, she had similar premonitions.

"Sean?" Erin said softly.

He could hear her, but his attention was elsewhere. He had a 9mm Glock 17 holstered at the small of his back. Seventeen-round magazine.

One round in the chamber. Depending on their firepower, he could probably take out three or four of them before they realized he'd taken the offense. Whoever *they* were.

Within a few seconds of the SUV parking, all four doors opened, and roughly a dozen Cub Scouts spilled out. Sean realized only then that his jaw was clenched tight, and he was holding his breath. He forced himself to relax, withdrawing his hand from behind his back. The sound of Erin's phone had thrown him into high alert. Every little thing was potential accelerant for his volatile nervous system. He got that way when he couldn't make things fit into black-and-white categories. Thus far with Erin Cross, everything was gray.

"Sean?" she said again.

He shook his head, clearing the sticky web of confusion within. "Sorry. My train of thought derailed."

She smiled.

"We need to get moving," Sean said with a touch of irritation "I've got a bad feeling about this. We shouldn't have stopped for so long. Come on," he said while sliding out of the booth.

Erin joined him as he paid for the meal in cash. They climbed in his Jeep and drove to a Maverik store at the end of the tiny town. Sean told Erin to wear her dark glasses just in case her photo was on the news again. They grabbed soup, canned pasta, cold cereal, and other storable foods. Erin selected a loaf of bread and a gallon of milk. Sean picked up lighter fluid, batteries, and a number of prepackaged food items. At the check stand, Erin noticed a bag of Double Stuff Oreos. Sean followed her line of sight and remarked, "Everyone has their addictions." He then added a bag of licorice to the pile.

"Are we planning on hiding out somewhere?" Erin asked, putting the cookies on the counter with the canned goods and other sundries.

"Maybe. I'm not sure yet."

"Well, as long as we have Oreos we'll be okay," Erin jested.

He smiled but kept his eyes locked on the young cashier ringing up their purchases.

Then Erin's cell phone rang.

The readout on the phone said Cedar City Police. She handed it to Sean and asked, "Shouldn't we answer that?"

Sean hit END and pulled her out of earshot of the cashier. "No. You said the police are involved," he whispered cautiously. "Once they make contact with you, if you don't go in, you'll be charged with resisting arrest."

"They *might* be. I really don't know. Besides, I always thought running was an *admission* of guilt."

"Only to the guilty." Sean then nodded toward the checkout. "Let's get moving."

The cashier hit the TOTAL button. "One hundred and twenty-two dollars and forty-seven cents, please."

Sean opened his wallet and paused. "Um."

"No cash?" Erin asked.

"Not that much. I don't want to use a credit card because they're traceable and—" Sean stopped abruptly and glanced at the cashier. To Erin he said, "You got any cash?"

Erin huffed and pulled a couple of hundreds from her purse.

"Wow," Sean said. "Pocket change, right?"

"Yeah," she said without humor.

Returning to the Jeep, they headed north, farther into the mountains. They traveled almost an hour before Erin's phone vibrated. The readout was all zeros. Sean pressed VIEW.

Enjoying the Dixie Forest?

"I was afraid of this." Sean turned the phone so Erin could see it.

"How do they know?" she asked.

"I'll show you in a minute," he said in a flat voice. Sean's focus was on the road, on the terrain and the weather. His training had gone back to firing on all cylinders.

Rounding a bend, he could see a scenic overlook. Sean pulled into the turnout and parked next to a Ford crew cab. The sun had disappeared but still lighted the underside of the looming storm front. Far below, heavy shadows filled the valley like a black sludge.

Sean removed the back from Erin's phone and popped out the battery. Underneath the battery was the SIM card. He removed the card and found a second, ultra-thin card about a quarter-inch square. Sean removed it and replaced the SIM card and battery. "Did you know this was in here?" he asked, holding up the tiny chip.

"I don't even know what that is," Erin admitted.

"It's a tracker chip. Sends out a signal every time you use your phone."

"But I haven't used my phone."

"The Cedar City police called your number. That's all it takes. Believe me, this card's not a standard feature. Your phone has been modified so someone can keep track of you."

Erin just gawked. Her eyes registered a mix of anger and fear.

"Does your cell have Internet?" Sean asked.

"Yeah."

"GPS?"

"Yes."

Sean turned the phone on. "Normally, I'd suggest we just pitch this in the trash, but I have a feeling it may help us figure out what's going on." He handed it to Erin. "Go into your apps and deactivate your GPS. Then delete the feature. They can track us through your GPS ID even if we're out of tower range. GPS works off satellite transmission, not cell tower. If you get rid of the GPS function, the signal just floats around in electronic limbo."

As Erin entered her password to edit her phone applications, Sean took the tracker chip and tossed it into the back of the truck next to them. "Now buckle up. From here on we go off-road."

"Off-road?" Erin asked with a gulp of anxiety. "Isn't it getting too dark?"

Sean smiled his lopsided smile. "So much the better."

Chapter 27

Jacob was very pleased with the results of his water analysis. Lake Halali'i was nearly ideal for breeding his mosquitoes. Not only did he need good aquatic conditions, but he also needed an unsuspecting, isolated population on which to test his virus. The Forbidden Isle was turning out better than he had dreamed . . . *except for the accommodations.*

After making sure his larvae were healthy, he had gone back to the hut for a much-needed nap. The anxiety of getting from Salt Lake to Ni'ihau had worn him thin.

As afternoon slowly faded toward evening, Jacob began his trek back to the lake. Like a faithful dog, Kapono tagged along. Although the constant companionship annoyed Jacob, he put up with it because of the mandate from the island elders. And it was free labor. Jacob burdened the strong young Hawaiian with a pack of research materials. Kapono took it in stride. He was excited about being part of a real scientific experiment. *If he only knew . . .*

Finding a location with the most likelihood of shade, a good concentration of plant growth, and at least twelve inches of water took about fifteen minutes. In its present state, the lake was small and fairly uniform. Jacob doffed his shoes and waded into the water. Kapono opted to stay on the shore. *Wimp.* The scientist carried an open box made of plastic window screen. Finding the location again, he pushed the box under water and lined the bottom with small stones to keep it stationary. The top two inches of box rose above the surface, creating an accessible aquarium that still allowed for water and nutrient flow. He then slowly introduced the larvae from his 100-mL bottles into the screened box. He returned to shore to collect a folding camp chair and went back out to the box to observe.

A full thirty minutes passed before Kapono called out, "Wha'chu lookin' ad, Doc?"

"I'm checking for water flow, potential predators, sedimentation rate of the silt I kicked up, sunlight refraction angles, that kind of thing."

"Wha'd you put der?"

"Mosquito larvae."

"Mosquita larvae? You mean da mosquita babies?" the young man gasped. "But you here ta kill mosquita, no'ta grow 'em."

Jacob smiled but did not shift his gaze from the partially submerged box. "These mosquitoes are a special kind," he said loudly. "I'm hoping these will make the mosquitoes that carry West Nile virus go away." He knew this was far from the truth, but that didn't matter. He figured the kid wouldn't know mosquitoes are not cannibalistic. "There are approximately 460 recognized mosquito species worldwide, Kapono. The ones in Hawaii are known carriers of malaria, bird pox, yellow fever, and West Nile virus."

"No crackin'?"

"No cracking. The funny thing is most mosquitoes are island-specific. That means they don't fly from one island to the next. So the mosquitoes on Ni'ihau will be easy pickings for my mosquitoes," he explained, pointing to the submerged box. "There's going to be a bloodsucker brawl when my mosquitoes hatch."

Kapono burst out laughing. "Now you crackin', Doc. You one funny *kané,* brah."

"Thanks," he said, grinning.

If his tests went according to plan, Jacob would be the only one laughing. He'd be laughing at all those who'd *ever* laughed at him. The vaccine that provided immunity to his deadly virus would be his gift to the world . . . at a price. Yeah, he'd be laughing at a lot of people then.

Jacob wished he could claim total creativity for the vaccine, but that didn't matter. Soon, no one would ever know. He glanced at his wristwatch. If it hadn't happened already, the true creator of the vaccine would be dead before he returned to the mainland. Then, total exclusivity would be his. *Stupid woman.*

Jacob sat in silent contemplation for close to three hours while Kapono wandered around the dry portions of the lakebed—the scientist watching the larvae, the islander looking at whatever caught his eye. An evening breeze brought the fragrance of dried grass and sweet brine. It was a nice change from the stagnant odors wafting from the lake.

A few minutes later Kapono called out, "Hey, you have da hungry yet, brah?"

"As a matter of fact, I do," Jacob said, remembering he hadn't eaten in a while.

"Well, we head back before da sun totally go gone, cha? I got coals back o' my hut. We can grill yellow fin. My cous'n say he leave id for us. Got plenny. 'Less you like 'em still swimmin'. We do dat, too."

Jacob stood and stretched. "I prefer my fish dead and cooked, thanks. Do you have any idea how many parasites one of those can carry?"

Kapono's toothy smile looked almost porcelain in the setting sunlight. "Nah nah nah, id be all *ono,* brah. Id come from da deep blue, id be good in you; id come from da shallow sea, id be good in me. You tread all God's creature wid respec', dey not go chunder down under, cha?"

He had no clue what the young man had just said, but he smiled anyway. "O—okay," he said, trying not to sound confused.

Jacob returned to the shore and handed his folding chair to the stout young man. "Whoa! Sweet tats, dude."

He looked at the three gnostic symbols on the knuckles of his right hand. "Thanks."

"Whad dey say?"

The scientist knew their meaning went much deeper than the young Hawaiian could understand. Jacob had received them after hiring on with New England Noetics at the request of Luther Mendenhall. The corporate hierarchy all belonged to an elite brotherhood that only a few were privy to. He was amazed at how closely many of the members shared his thoughts for the future of humanity. Jacob had joined the fraternity and quickly ascended the ranks of illuminates. Each symbol tattooed on his knuckles represented his level and authority in the Order. If his mosquito tests proved out, he'd earn another tattoo.

He knew of only one man who had all five gnostic symbols. He was determined to be the next.

"Oh, they are just different symbols representing my understanding of science. You have some nice tattoos yourself," he added nonchalantly.

The young Hawaiian glanced down at the classic Polynesian motif that adorned his entire shoulder and upper arm. "Thanks, man. Got dis da old fashion way usin' fish bone an' squid ink. It be a ting a beauty, cha? Dis be Tangaroa, God of da Sea. He protect me from all bad mojo. I never been sick a day since I got it."

"Very nice," Jacob said with mock admiration.

"Thanks, brah. Maybe you should get one too, cha? Dat way you be protected from walkin' through da Spirit of Halali'i's waters."

Jacob doubted the existence of any god, let alone a Polynesian one carved from wood or stone . . . or tattooed on the shoulder of a native islander. And even if they did exist, he doubted with equal certainty they could stop him. "I'll pass, but thanks anyway."

"No worries, brah. Let's chow."

Jacob glanced at his knuckles as they walked back to the village. While his tattoos didn't represent a particular deity, they did represent something very important to Jacob: his destiny.

Chapter 28

Sean drove a couple miles up the highway before stopping. To the right was a barely perceptible dirt road wedged between two huge spruce trees. In the remaining light of dusk, it was all but invisible. The road was overgrown with weeds and buffalo berry. He put his Jeep in four-wheel drive and pushed through the underbrush.

"Not much traffic through here," Erin commented.

"Which is a good thing," Sean confirmed.

The dirt road soon turned into a rocky path, and the two passengers were jostled relentlessly as they worked their way up the mountainside into thicker forest. Cresting a knoll, they headed along the ridgeline until another trail appeared. Turning, Sean followed the path down a slope into a swale choked with aspen and scrub oak. The fall leaves had long since blanketed the ground, leaving behind a skeletal forest. The clotting clouds churned black overhead. Erin couldn't see more than a few feet in front of her. In spite of that, Sean still had not turned on his headlamps.

"You sure you know where we're going?" she asked.

"Yep," Sean answered.

Branches scraped the sides of the Jeep while hungry potholes and small boulders caused the vehicle to lurch and bound like a mechanical bull.

"Shouldn't you turn on your lights?"

"Nope. I don't want anyone to know we're here."

"Okay. And where is *here*?"

"You'll see."

Erin looked at her cell phone and saw there was no signal. Good. At least she wouldn't be getting any more texts for a while.

A mile or so up ahead, Sean turned on his running lights, but not the headlamps. Following the trail for another hour, they both rode in silence. Erin's thoughts were not so much on where they were headed but on where she'd just come from. Her life was in turmoil. She hated feeling out of control. She hated feeling so flighty. She hated being needy. But her conundrum had left her few options.

Erin stared out the window, catching snippets of muted scenery through the trees. What she needed was a sign. *A sign?* she immediately scoffed. Who's to say her sign hadn't already passed by and she was too stubborn to see it? Was it fate that'd brought her to this point?

No. She didn't believe in fate. She accepted the concept of divine intervention but not predestination, like some board game she was forced to endure with paths set and a conclusion predetermined. She knew her life was a mix of personal choices with both gracious and hazardous options laid out by a loving Heavenly Father. That's how she was raised. And in spite of all the education she'd had that fostered a negative opinion on the existence of deity, she still felt it was the way things were. A Seminary teacher had once told her more atheists come out of college than go into college. A profound aphorism, to be sure. And she'd used it as a maxim of sorts, determining to study science as a pathway to truth, not as the absolute truth.

"Ah. Here we are," Sean said, disrupting her thoughts.

She looked out the windshield and saw nothing but dark scrub forest and a barely recognizable trail. Sean rolled down his window and bent his neck to peer up a rise to his immediate left. There was nothing there but a steep, thirty-foot embankment of barren rock and a few clumps of dried sagebrush.

Sean turned to her with a smile. "You ready?"

"For what?" she asked with trepidation.

"A bit of a thrill ride," he said with raised eyebrows.

Erin said nothing as he cranked the steering wheel over and gunned up the sandstone incline. Cresting the rim, she could not help let out a plaintive whine as the Jeep tipped forward and pointed down at an insane angle. The bottom of the grade was lost in shadow, making the slope appear endless.

"Wait! Sean! You're not going down—"

"Hold on!" Sean almost sang.

Shifting into a very low gear, Sean eased the Jeep down the seventy-degree sandstone slope to a river basin filled with sand, grass, and poplars. The length of the slope was only fifty yards or so, but to Erin it might as well have been five hundred. When Sean rolled onto the soft, level sand, Erin let out a breath that sounded like a horse whinnying.

"Why was *that* necessary!" she demanded.

"It's the fastest way to my cabin."

She swallowed and tried to steady her breathing. "You have—a cabin—out here?"

"Yep. And you can let go of the dash now. No more big drop-offs," he said just under a chuckle.

Erin had to concentrate to unclasp her hands from the padded safety bar on the dashboard. "H-h-h—how much longer until we get there?" Even she had to laugh at how shaky her voice was.

"About ten minutes." He glanced at his watch. "The rough part is over. Just a couple more turns and—" Sean suddenly veered under a large stand of blue spruce, killed the lights, and shut off the engine. He rolled down his window and stuck his head out. Moist, cold air flowed into the cab.

"What's wrong?" Erin asked, still trying to catch her breath.

"Shh."

Erin rolled down her window and leaned out. She couldn't hear anything except the keening of wind in the branches overhead. Then it came to her, faint but definite—the beating of propellers in the cold air. Growing louder. Heading in their direction.

Eyes wide, Erin looked at Sean. "Helicopter?"

He nodded. "They know we're out here."

Chapter 29

Soon, the thumping sound of the helicopter blades was unmistakable, but it wasn't until it was directly above them that they saw it. And even then, they could only see a dark shape slowly passing over them. The traditional safety lights on the aircraft were either malfunctioning or they were intentionally turned off. Sean figured it was the latter. Even the typical engine whine was greatly diminished through some kind of super muffler.

"They're flying covert," he whispered.

Although the rotor wash made it difficult to hear anything, Sean still thought it imperative to whisper. Modern audio detection tools could hear a gopher sneeze ten feet underground. He then noticed Erin's head was out the Jeep window trying to see the helicopter.

"Get your head in," he urged just before it passed directly overhead.

"What's going on?" Erin whispered back.

He held his index finger to his lips, indicating silence for a time. He kept his finger erect as a signal of when they could speak. The helicopter did not pause but kept a slow, steady trajectory along the canyon wall next to their hiding place. As it passed by, they got a better look at it: flat black paint, navigation lights extinguished, an array of surveillance equipment mounted to its belly, large sound dampeners on its engine. It was a covert reconnaissance machine designed for one purpose: intelligence gathering . . . a predator seeking prey. Them.

The canyon continued for a mile or so before it turned to the east. As soon as the black helicopter turned the corner, Sean lowered his finger. "I'm surprised they didn't see us."

"I could barely see them," Erin said. "No way they could see us."

Sean started up the Jeep and backed out from under the trees. "If they'd had infrared, they would have. We might be camouflaged under the tree branches and this roof," he said, tapping the fiberglass above his head, "but my engine is still hot. It'd light up like a signal fire. I have heat-diffusing padding under the hood, but if they have state-of-art equipment . . ."

"Do you think they do?" Erin asked in another whisper. "Have high-tech infrared, I mean."

"Yep. I recognized some of the gear hanging from it. But I didn't see any hardware like cannons or rocket launchers or mini-guns," he said as he drove without any lights along the negligible trail. "It's probably an older recon bird. The new ones don't have as much rotor noise. They're almost totally silent—perfect for stealth operations."

Erin alternated between staring at him and the path the helicopter took. "Exactly what did you do in the military?" she asked.

He shook his head. "It's classified. But even if it wasn't, I'd rather forget the whole thing. I did stuff I'm not proud of. Let's just leave it at that."

Erin continued to stare but honored his request. Sean was glad. He truly didn't like talking about it. Besides, his focus was on helping Erin Cross—trying to figure out who was behind the attacks on her and why they wanted her dead.

Driving more by memory than sight, Sean wended his way along the faint trail until they came to the bend in the canyon. From there the canyon continued another twenty yards before opening into a wide valley. At the mouth of the canyon, the faint trail headed down toward a verdant river bottom. Instead of following it, Sean veered left and paralleled a rock wall composed of irregular shapes and muted tones. Even in minimal light, you could tell the walls were not just pale sandstone but a myriad of earthy colors. No trail aided their trek, but the Jeep's suspension lift and massive tires handled the terrain without a hitch.

Working their way up a gentle rise, they leveled out onto a wide horseshoe carved into the rock wall by eons of elemental abuse. Abundant trees formed a natural barrier along the rim of a plateau, roughly a quarter-mile across.

Sean drove across a short field of tall grass and brush then eased under a stand of enormous, leafless cottonwoods. Adjacent to the copse of trees stood a cabin tucked inside a sandstone alcove. He shut off the engine and breathed slow and steady as he surveyed the small structure.

"Yours?" Erin asked softly.

"Yep," was all he said as he continued to check out the surroundings. Even though he felt confident his hideaway was safe, his training taught him to expect the unexpected. Opening his door very quietly, he whispered, "Stay here. I'll check it out and be right back." When Erin looked like she was about to protest, he added, "Look, I know you don't like being told what to do, but this will only take a minute. Lock the doors. If someone besides me comes out, take the Jeep and get out of here as fast as you can."

"But, Sean," she protested.

"No buts," he said, closing the door quickly.

Sean stood just outside the Jeep and listened. Crickets, a slight breeze, maybe the sound of a jet somewhere in the distance—everything sounded normal, natural. The horseshoe could play tricks with sounds. It'd been a long time since he'd been to the cabin, so he needed to acclimate to these environs again. He'd learned that you should never rush into any terrain—even if you were familiar with it—if there was a chance it was compromised. His last visit here was perhaps twenty months ago. Maybe longer. He couldn't remember.

When all seemed normal, Sean eased toward the cabin while staying in deep pockets of shadow. The ambient light revealed the things he expected: the cabin was butted tight against an alcove in the rock wall so that it had only a wide face and a bit of one side wall; its roof was made out of slabs of shale, which created an awning almost ten feet deep over a porch thirty feet wide; the face and side of the cabin were made of mortised river rock. The front wall boasted a good-sized picture window and a front door; the side wall had a small porthole. Both windows were boarded up with plywood. A flight of rough-hewn stone steps rose ten feet above where he stood. In all, the place could almost be mistaken for an Anasazi ruin—except for the solid wood door and the glass windows. From the air it was nearly invisible; from the valley below, the trees obscured its face. The only way you could see it clearly was to stand directly in front of it.

Sean mounted the stone steps and ascended quickly to the porch, where he paused again, listening, sensing. A patina of dust covered the porch, revealing only a few animal tracks: rats, skunk, coyote. In one corner a pile of guano indicated swallows had returned to nest in a nook over the porch. Cobwebs abounded. No human footprints were present. Excellent. This could work.

Sean unlocked the door and stepped inside. Although he was quite familiar with the interior of the cabin, he waited a moment for his eyes to adjust. Everything looked just as it should. Yeah, this could work out perfectly.

Chapter 30

Erin stood shivering on the porch as Sean backed his Jeep under a lean-to ensconced amongst the cottonwoods. He climbed the stone steps with three large packs across his back.

"You had time to pack all that?" Erin asked, surprised.

"Just two. The other is an emergency kit I keep in the Jeep at all times."

Erin was about to comment on the symptoms of clinical paranoia when she thought of her own 72-hour kit and secret stash of money and computer files.

"Good idea," she said instead.

The cabin was still extremely dark inside, but Erin could see enough to make her way to a counter that separated the kitchenette from the main room. She sat on one of the three bar stools. The place smelled of dust, old fires, and musty cloth. And it was cold. The cabin faced east, so it only caught a few hours of morning sun. Sean had probably designed it that way to keep the heat of the day to a minimum. Situated in Southern Utah, the cabin undoubtedly got very hot during the summer.

Sean set his parcels on a rustic couch in front of a river-rock fireplace and pulled out a flashlight. Keeping the beam pointed at the ground, he retrieved a lantern from a cabinet in the kitchen. From another cabinet he then pulled out a safety can marked LAMP FUEL. A box of matches was kept in a drawer next to the sink. Even in almost total darkness, he deftly filled the lantern, pumped the primer, and lit the filaments. As the lantern hissed to life, it filled the room with a rich, amber-yellow glow.

Erin looked around with unmasked admiration. The main room was about thirty feet wide, twenty feet deep. The small kitchen stood in the far back corner, and a narrow staircase climbed along the opposite wall to a loft over the kitchen and hearth. The river-rock chimney rose to a height of about ten feet, disappearing through the floor of the loft. The main window next to the door was about three by five feet, and the small one in the adjacent wall was about a foot square. Both had heavy-grade plywood panels bolted over them. The kitchenette had a sink with a faucet, a small refrigerator, and a stove. There were no electrical outlets she could see.

Erin's breath condensed in amber plumes in the golden lantern light. The place felt like a cold-storage unit.

"How about getting a fire going?" she asked with a shiver.

Sean nodded. "Only a little one for now." A small potbelly stove, about three feet tall, stood next to the fireplace. It looked like it could heat a narrow broom closet at best. Sean opened its grated door and began pitching strips of kindling and fuel into the stove.

"Cute," Erin scoffed. "How about throwing a tree in the real fireplace instead?"

"Oh, this little guy will put out the heat, don't you worry," he said while adjusting a flue on the vent pipe that disappeared through the ceiling. A single match got the fire going.

Erin sat on the floor next to the stove and held her hands to the grate. "Why can't we just get a bonfire going in there?" she complained, jerking her head toward the river-rock fireplace.

"These men are still after you. They probably know who I am, too, by now. A big fire would give off too much smoke, and the heat signature would show on any infrared equipment they have." Sean pulled a thick, woven quilt from the couch, shook it free of dust, and wrapped it around Erin's shoulders.

"Thanks," she said, shrugging into its weighty embrace.

"This little guy radiates heat like crazy," he said, tapping the cast-iron stove with a stick, "and the pipe vents into a crevice in the rocks behind the cabin. The smoke dissipates pretty evenly through the cracks, and the heat signature looks about the same as what a rock chuck would give off."

Sooner than she expected, the small stove began radiating a delicious warmth as it ticked and creaked with expansion. Erin immediately began to feel a deep drowsiness wash over her.

"How safe are we here?" she asked through a huge yawn.

"Pretty darn. That's why I brought you here."

"But they know who you are and that you're helping me."

Sean paused while emptying a duffel bag. "You sure about that?"

Erin ducked her head, ashamed that she hadn't told him about the previous text. "The message I didn't show you said your name. It said not to trust you."

He considered the information for a moment then said, "I'll take that challenge." He smiled and returned to emptying his pack. "They may know who I am, but they don't know about this place. Nobody does. I inherited it and the land from my dad when I was just ten. I own about thirty acres of forestland. The cabin wasn't here back then. My dad and I built it a bit at a time. He worked for the Bureau of Land Management before he died. He bought this parcel a long time ago, when the Department of Forestry was selling off bits and pieces for revenue. It's deeded to the Flannery Family Trust. But since I'm the only family member, no one but me knows it's here."

"Brother or sisters?"

"None. I am an only child."

"Your mom?"

"She died giving birth to me."

"Not even your daughter and ex-wife?" she asked as delicately as she could.

Sean shook his head. "I don't believe I ever mentioned it to either of them. This is my escape, my . . . my *retreat*. I come here to rejuvenate. I remember just sitting out on the porch with my dad watching the world wander by without it even knowing we were here." His voice caught, and he tried to pretend it was just a frog he was trying to clear. Erin detected a deep longing in his tone that she found extremely moving. Then, as suddenly as it came, it was gone. "But you can never be too confident, right?" he said authoritatively. "That's why you'll sleep upstairs in the loft, and I'll be down here by the door."

It took a few seconds before Erin realized what he was saying.

"You're not going to stay awake all night, are you?"

He stopped unpacking and came over to check the fire in the stove. "Nah. I'm sure I'll drop off soon enough."

Erin raised an eyebrow. "You're not a very good liar, you know."

He rubbed the back of his neck. "Well, I'm not sure I could drop right off, anyway. There's a lot on my mind I'm trying to figure out."

"You and me both," she said.

Sean stood and removed the 9mm handgun from the small of his back. Erin had no clue it had even been there. He checked the magazine and breech. "Do you know how to use one of these?"

Erin swallowed. "Um . . . point and shoot, right?"

"Basically," he said handing her the gun. "Just make sure you're pointing it at the right guy." He headed up the narrow staircase.

"Got it," she said to herself. "Is it loaded?"

"Of course," he called down from the loft. "What good is an empty gun?" There was a slight pause before he descended the stairs. "All clear. There're two twin beds up there and a small dresser. Take your pick. I'll be down here all night," he said, pulling an armchair to the front door.

"No, Sean, I don't wa—"

"No arguments," he snapped.

Although he tried to hide it, Erin could tell he was as fatigued as she was. They were both running on little fuel, little sleep, and frayed nerves.

"The next forty-eight hours are the most critical as far as your escape goes. We're not going to treat any of this lightly. Someone is trying to kill you, Erin. Someone with a lot of connections and money. You got me involved; *you* asked for my help. So here's the deal: you do exactly as I say—for the next forty-eight hours, at least. We should be able to figure things out by then. If not, we'll do things your way one hundred percent."

Erin bristled at first but knew this was definitely not her area of expertise. She was loath to let him make all the decisions but recognized she had little choice. If she didn't know him better, she'd swear he was showing off or playing the hero to the damsel in distress. But she did know him—or felt she was beginning to know him. The mysteries surrounding his insistent personality were easy to understand. They are what brought him through many crisis situations. She needed to trust him.

"Okay," she demurred, "but in the morning we trade. I stand guard while you get some sleep. Deal?"

Sean rubbed his eyes and mumbled, "Deal."

Chapter 31

On the trek home, Jacob and Kapono were assaulted by legions of mosquitoes. Normally, Jacob wasn't bothered by them much. He wasn't certain, but he felt it had to do with the excessive combination of nutritional supplements he took every morning. Walnut oil, two different kinds of fish oil, various herbs and minerals, and a cadre of antioxidants. He also ate tons of black licorice nibs, which he believed had significant antiviral properties. He concluded that his armada of supplements gave his sweat a certain odor that the insects abhorred. And although he was inoculated against every bug know to man—and one known only to him—he believed in hedging his bets. The only time he took chances was when the outcome was quantitatively in his favor. Like now. Yet these mosquitoes seemed even more aggressive than the ones he'd encountered before.

"Come on, Doc. We shoulda been home long time back," the young Hawaiian said as he walked a bit faster. "Mosquita are 'special bad dis time a day, cha?"

Trudging amongst the low-lying shrubbery and grasses, neither man required a flashlight. The moon and dense blanket of stars illuminated the rolling hills enough for them to avoid rocks and roots. Only an occasional cloud obscured a portion of sky as it eased by.

"You see, mosquitoes are lovers of afternoon to dusk temperatures in northern climes, but in the tropics they are out nearly twenty-four hours a day," the scientist lectured.

Kapono slapped the side of his face, leaving a fresh blood smear. "Bud at nigh' dey come ou' wid mondo appetites," he said while applying a fresh misting of insect repellant. "Dat why id crazy mad ta surf da moon beams, cha? Hey, you sure you don' wan some bug spray, brah?"

"No thanks, Kapono. They don't seem to like the taste of my blood."

"No offense, Doc, bud dat a total jacked way o' thinkin'."

As they headed down the slope to the windward side of the island, the mosquito numbers lessened considerably. Jacob pulled out a nib of black licorice and popped it into his mouth. Up ahead, the outline of a few huts and low bungalows hunkered against the scrub trees and red soil. Yellowish light spilled from their windows, giving the scene a "welcome home" feel.

"Da Robinsons, day be huge inta preservin' da nature of Ni'ihau; we be keepin' it real here," the islander continued. "Dat why nobody come here. Bud da Robinsons know da mosquita bring gnarly infections, and da only way ta no get *gamboo* is with *haole* medicine, cha? Dat why ever'body sleep wid mosquita net. Dey see you and me walkin' da moon beam an' dey think we be crazy or drunk. Me, I think you not 'fraid a nottin'."

If you only knew, Jacob thought.

"Well I'm certainly going to try my hardest to fix the problem," Jacob said magnanimously.

"*Mahalo, mahalo.* You good man, Doc."

They found Pegasus asleep on the stoop of Kapono's hut. Jacob stepped over the goat and pushed through a veil of mosquito netting. He set his gear on a small table someone had brought from town. Luckily, the ambient moonlight was enough to fumble around the small space with little hazard. He stepped outside to brush his teeth and use the outhouse. His apprehensions from the day before were rapidly dissolving as his plans fell into perfect sequence. With minimal contact on the island, he would not have to worry about making excuses or covering his tracks when the real outbreak occurred. Besides, most of those details were covered well before he took off from Salt Lake International.

His application for a visitor's permit under the auspices of an "entomologist with the World Health Organization coming to study indigenous mosquito-borne West Nile virus" had cleared all the usually insurmountable hurdles. The request was made via a research company specializing in blood-borne diseases. If anyone tried checking into it, they would find reams of documentation on research grants, income-tax returns, personnel profiles, and the like linked to a fledgling drug company in South Africa. It was proctored through Belize Securities in Central America. But the company existed only on paper. Not only was Belize Securities good at laundering money, but they also excelled at tweaking other forms of business information and communication. It always tickled Jacob that the company's initials were a well-known acronym for spreading false information. How ironic and yet apropos.

True, Jacob Krantz was a PhD, but of infectious disease, not entomology. True, a group of investors was funding his research, but not the one listed on all his papers. True, he was researching blood-borne diseases, just not the ones documented in the history of Ni'ihau—or anywhere else on the planet, for that matter.

Jacob returned to the hut and stepped over the goat again. This time he noticed a strange bulge under the blanket on his cot. For some reason he'd missed the lump just moments before. Drawing back the thin blanket, he saw a small child curled in a fetal position facing the wall. Jacob stepped back and frowned. His visitor's permit mandated he avoid contact with all islanders except Kapono. He stepped over the goat a third time and rounded the hut to Kapono's hammock. The young man was cocooned in a web of mosquito netting.

"Kapono," Jacob whispered.

The Hawaiian did not stir.

"Kapono, there's someone in my bunk," he said a little louder, nudging the hammock.

"Wha—huh?" the islander mumbled.

"There's someone in my bunk. A little kid."

Like a moth emerging from a chrysalis, Kapono shed the layers of netting and sat up in his hammock. "W'sup, brah?" Jacob couldn't believe the young man had fallen asleep that quickly.

"There's a child asleep on my bunk. Since I'm not supposed to interact with anyone but you, I thought you could chase him out."

Kapono rolled off the hammock and went inside the hut. From the window, Jacob listened to the conversations within.

"Kaile'e, whad you doin'? You know you ain' suppose ta be here, you lil' *kolohe*."

A groggy, very light voice answered. "I ain't no *kolohe*, brah. Da parents be beefin' again. Blah, blah, blah. I about to kotch, it make me so sick."

"Still, lil' sista', you nah suppose' ta be here, cha? I da only one dis *haole* healer suppose ta speak wid."

"Why? Is he a bad man?" the innocent, young voice asked.

"Nah nah nah. Don' talk no stink 'bout him. He here ta help us. He very *akamai*, you know? He 'bout da smartes' dude I ever meed. But he need ta get some *moi moi*, cha? He one tired mainlander."

"But where I sleep, Kapono?" came the plaintive wail.

"Shh, don' talk so loud, lil' sista'. You come sleep wid me in my hammock, cha? We let da doc sleep in here."

"Okay," the little voice said dejectedly.

Jacob stepped back and saw Kapono lead a little girl wrapped in a floral-print muumuu out of the hut. She looked about seven or eight years old. With a nearly full moon and a blanket of stars for illumination, Jacob could tell she was extremely pretty. Round face. Large, doe-like eyes. Dark, waist-length hair so lustrous the constellations above appeared to dance and cavort across it as she moved.

She looked up at Jacob from under dark, thick lashes. "*Aloha*, healer," she whispered.

"*Aloha*, sweetheart," he said, breaking his vow of no contact with the other islanders.

"Da shack be all yours, Doc," Kapono said. "Sorry 'bout dis."

"Hey, no apology is necessary. It was very good to meet you, Kaile'e."

The little girl beamed. "You know my name."

"Yes, I do. I heard it through the window. My name is Dr. Dan Brown," he said, remembering his pseudonym, "but you can just call me doc."

"*Mahalo*, Doc," she said just shy of a giggle.

Jacob was entranced. The little angel reminded him of his daughter, the one he had lost two years earlier. The viral infection had hit her so fast that even advanced treatments had no effect. She was gone in less than twenty-four hours. She had just celebrated her eighth birthday.

Little Kaile'e had just put an unexpected kink into Jacob's field tests.

SUNDAY
NOVEMBER 6, 2011

Chapter 32

THE MORNING BROUGHT A CRISPNESS that stiffened the joints. Erin was curled under a pile of thick quilts and blankets, dreading the foray into the light. The blankets had a musty, wood-smoke scent that was curiously comforting. The bed was old but not saggy. There was little headroom in the loft; it was made for sleeping not for recreating. And it was constructed in such a way that the stovepipe ran through the center of the loft floor with a protective screen attached to it. She felt heat radiating from it up until the moment she fell asleep.

Erin crawled out from under the blankets and peered between the balustrades over the edge of the loft. Bright sunlight seeped around the edges of the plywood covering the windows. Sean was sitting in a chair propped against the door. He wore a thick jacket and ball cap. A mean-looking rifle lay across his lap. With his head hung low and his breathing deep and steady, Erin could tell he was asleep. Her watch read 7:17 AM. Her stomach felt sour and very empty. She slipped on her shoes and headed downstairs. As she stepped on the bottom tread, it gave an almost imperceptible creak.

In a flash, Sean dropped to a knee with the assault rifle trained on her.

Erin's hands flew up. "Wait, Sean!" she screamed. "It's me!"

Sean was as motionless as a granite statue. No twitching, no blinking, no breathing. Erin held perfectly still, barely breathing herself.

"Sean, I'm Erin Cross," she said softy and steadily. "You are here to help me. Please put the gun down."

Sean frowned. His focus didn't diminish for another sixty seconds, but his shoulder did drop a titch. The tension between them arced like electricity. Erin slowly lowered her hands to her side.

"It's okay, Sean. Everything is okay."

Another electrostatic thirty seconds passed before Sean lowered the rifle. He exhaled slowly and shook his head as if to clear it. "Sorry. Instinct."

"Instinct or training?" Erin asked, still speaking softly.

He shrugged and stood. "Training, I guess."

"Did you get much sleep?"

"Not really. You?"

"More than I would have had you not shown up. I know I've already said thanks, but I'm not sure I said it right."

He looked off to one side and smiled. With sleep-tousled hair and a shyness in his eyes, his uncomfortable expression was adorable. "Well, it's accepted however it was delivered," he said. "Want some breakfast?"

"Heavens, yes. I'm starved."

Sean moved to the potbelly stove and stirred up the coals. He added some wood and made sure the fire was cheery before closing the grate. He then went to the kitchen, laid the rifle on the counter, and lit the lantern. "Sorry I can't offer you French toast or a Denver omelet. I can make you a mean cup of hot chocolate and a Pop-Tart."

"Perfect," Erin said.

She sat at the counter and pushed the rifle to the far end.

"Careful. The safety isn't on," Sean said as he pulled a box of Swiss Miss from a cupboard.

Erin stretched and asked, "How about some natural light? No offense, but I feel like I'm in a cave. You open the window, and I'll make the cocoa."

Sean nodded, slipped on some gloves, grabbed his rifle, and headed to the door. He unlocked it, slid three dead bolts from their seats, and opened the door a crack. He peered out at several angles before he stepped outside, closing the door behind him.

Erin felt suddenly defenseless. The shadow-choked cabin instantly closed in like a trap—as if it'd been biding its time, waiting for Sean to leave so it could spring shut. She tried to shake off the feeling but found herself heading toward the staircase with unwelcomed urgency. She'd remembered the handgun next to her bed in the loft. Taking the dark stairs two at a time, she probed around the bed until she found the weapon. Descending the stairs, she heard Sean working at the plywood covering the outside of the windows. She returned to the main room, slid the gun into her beltline, and held her frozen hands to the potbelly stove.

Soon Sean reentered the cabin with a bright halo of ice crystals dancing behind him like a heavenly shroud. He leaned his rifle beside the door and began untwisting the large wing nuts from the four corners of the plywood inside the cabin. As he lowered the panel, a flood of blinding sunlight filled the entire room.

"Wow," Erin gasped. "That's almost too intense."

"Yeah. The snow helps."

"Snow?"

"Yep. Four or five inches," he said, setting the plywood to one side.

"No wonder it's so cold."

Sean returned to the kitchen and pulled a jug of spring water from under the cabinet. "I'm afraid this'll have to do for a bit. You might have noticed I have a hundred-gallon tank in the loft, but it's empty. I fill it from a stream about a hundred yards down the hillside. There's a pipe buried a foot deep that runs from the cabin to the stream. It has a filter on each end so the water comes out pretty clean. But the pump requires electricity, which we don't have without running the generator—"

"Which is a bad idea because of the noise," Erin finished for him. "So my fantasies of soaking in a hot bubble bath while the snow falls outside . . . ?"

"Will have to wait."

"And the kitchen stove?"

"Oh, it's propane. Here," he said, moving to a cupboard beside the range. Inside were two five-gallon pressurized cylinders joined by a common regulator. Sean turned them on and used a match to light a burner. "Propane burns clean enough that you usually don't have to worry about an exhaust vent, but you can't run it all the time, like using it to heat the place."

Erin moved to the kitchen and set a pot of water to boil. She then found two enameled tin cups and poured a packet of hot cocoa mix into each. "So you don't have a water heater, then?"

"Oh, I do. It's under the sink. But it's a heat-per-need unit, which again runs on electricity."

"Dang it. I was hoping for a shower," she said, trying to sound playful even though it was the absolute truth.

"There's a swimming hole down at the creek," Sean offered.

"That's cold."

"Yes it is, but I doubt it's iced over yet."

She laughed then sobered quickly. "I'm sorry. Look, I don't mean to complain. This is truly a nice setup, and I know we're not here on vacation."

"Maybe another time under better circumstances," Sean said without looking at her.

Was that a come-on? Probably not. He'd been all business from the get-go. Still, the idea was not an unpleasant consideration. Erin shrugged. "So . . . how long will we stay here?"

Sean looked at her with tempered eyes. "That depends on how long it takes for you to tell me what's *really* going on."

Chapter 33

Praefectus Magnus listened, feeling the anger well within him. Blood pulsed past his eardrums with such force that it created a constant thump and swoosh in his head. He'd just been informed the two targets had disappeared. Again!

"I have no doubt they came this way," Prefect Franklin told him over the phone. "The cashier at the Maverik said she recognized Flannery's photo, although the picture we have is a few years old."

"And the woman?"

"She wore a ball cap and dark glasses. The cashier couldn't make a positive ID, but she said she was about the right size."

"Did she catch anything they said to each other?"

"Yes. She was certain they said something about hiding out, and they purchased a bunch of canned goods and sundries, as if stocking up for an extended stay somewhere. The woman wanted to pay with a credit card, but the man insisted on paying with cash because he said credit cards are traceable."

Magnus nodded on his end of the line. "That's a positive ID. Stocking up for an extended stay? Stay where? I thought the park was closed in the winter."

"They keep the main roads open for cross-country skiing, Praeficere. I haven't been able to go in deep yet. It was too dark by then, and I didn't have the right equipment."

Magnus's thoughts were rapid-firing. "Do you think he has access to a cabin in there?"

"We're looking into that, sir. Cedar Breaks has several campgrounds, and there are more throughout the Dixie forest."

"Ah. Has the forest service or Cedar City police sent out search and rescue yet?"

"No, sir. They won't without a valid missing persons request. And they won't file one of those until the person in question has been missing for more than twenty-four hours. I'm in the process of hiring a private helicopter to go searching, but it's Sunday, and no one seems willing to work today."

"I take it the roads are too numerous to follow?"

"Yes and no, sir. There are only two or three main roads through the park lands, but there are countless dirt roads and trails. They could have taken any one of those in his four-by-four."

"Any chance of following tire tracks?"

"No, sir. It snowed last night; almost half a foot in some places."

Magnus actually smiled at the news, his brilliant mind still working at top speed. "Ah. That also means if they try to exit the area, *their* tracks will be impossible to cover. They cannot make a move without us knowing it."

"My thoughts exactly, Praeficere. I have already sent subordinates to cover the main roads out of the park."

"And the unpaved roads?"

"Snowbound for now. Even his four-by-four would have trouble navigating them. If they do try to run, I feel confident they'll have to leave on one of the main highways. We pretty much have them boxed in."

"Excellent work, Prefect Franklin. Just remember, we had her boxed in that store in Cedar City and she managed to escape. We cannot be complacent with this one. The Grand Illuminate has taken an interest in this case."

"Yes, Praeficere. I'm compiling a list of all known motels, campsites, cabins, and building permits for cabins in there. I'll send an APB on Flannery through police and forestry service channels. Dr. Cross already has an APB on her thanks to the incident at TRI labs. As soon as I can, I'll get a helicopter in the air and check out possible routes from their last known location."

"Very good. This mess should have ended yesterday. See that you do not fail as the others have. I want Dr. Cross and Sean Flannery eliminated. They have vital information that could harm the Order."

"I understand, sir. I'll send you notice when I've received acknowledgment from all members in the area."

"Outstanding. I have every confidence in you, Prefect Franklin. *Novus ordo seclorum.*"

"*Meus vita pro novus ordo seclorum,*" Franklin said before disconnecting.

Magnus wrung his hands and sought immediate solace in a flute of vintage wine. But as he reached for the bottle, he checked himself. He was better than resorting to chemical tranquility. He closed his eyes and began a mantra he'd learned during his initiation in the chambers of Benjamin's Blood. He shouldn't get overly anxious. It wasn't in his nature. He would give his subordinates one more day. With Dr. Cross trapped in the mountains where there was no cell phone service, she wasn't an imminent threat.

Magnus reveled in the knowledge he was master of his universe. He could command legions of subordinates, prefects, and adepts to do his bidding. Those under him were mere pawns. Those not of the Order were puppets for his pawns. And his pawns were everywhere. Many lived ordinary lives. Most had joined his Order with the promise of fantastic rewards and greater illumination. Knowledge was easy to obtain. But Greater Understanding came from illumination. And only a select few made it to the level of true illumination. It had been that way since the beginning of time.

The quest for perfection.

As a reward for his own brilliance, he decided an indulgence was warranted after all. He poured himself a glass of Chateau Mouton Rothschild and held it under his nose. The combination of sweet and tart fragrances titillated his senses. At roughly $800 a bottle, it was perfection in a glass. An Andre-Charles Boulle pendulum clock moved in perfect synchrony on his Brazilian teak desk. The rare timepiece had once belonged to Louis XIV. Magnus toasted his reflection in the glass face of the clock.

To the next Grand Master. Me.

He sipped the expensive wine and held it on his tongue for a moment, savoring its sweet, dry flawlessness. Moving to the picture window of his top-floor office, he gazed out at the dawning sun illuminating the snow-covered tops of the Oquirrh Mountains.

Illumination. That's what it was all about. The only thing threatening *his* ultimate illumination was a couple of irritating scientists. Dr. Cross did everything by the book and even added her own chapters. That was only slightly less annoying than Dr. Krantz. He did everything by the book but *left out* several chapters. If Krantz didn't come through with his Armageddon virus, Magnus would be a dead man. If Cross couldn't be found and eliminated, he'd still be a dead man.

Regrettably, he concluded, there was only one way he could eliminate the uncertainty of both "ifs."

Chapter 34

The cabin had warmed considerably, but Erin still shivered—even wrapped in a thick quilt in front of the potbelly stove. Her feet were drawn up tight, her arms wrapped around her knees. She had rotated the couch to face the stove instead of the hearth. "You sure we can't get a bonfire going in there?"

Sean sat opposite her on the couch. "Not without attracting attention."

Erin frowned. "You know, it seems to me that your dad built this place with isolation and solitude in mind. If that's the case, then why build the hearth at all?"

"Back when he built it, this land was all wilderness," he said without meeting her eyes. "He wasn't real concerned about anyone ever finding it back then. I've kept the place just as he built it to remind me of him."

"Oh. Sorry. But . . ." She paused and shifted a bit. "Well, it still seems odd that you never brought your wife and daughter here."

Sean's shoulders lifted and dropped slowly. "I suppose." He pursed his lips and continued to stare at the stove. "I can't even say why. I have so few memories of ever doing much of anything with them . . ." His voice trailed off to silence. Then suddenly his focus seemed to sharpen. "Let's not get off topic here. I need you to tell me everything about what you do."

Erin's brow lowered into a troubled scowl. "Okay. But first, you should know that I have a very high government clearance. Like you, there's a lot I can't mention because it's classified. I'm not supposed to divulge anything that could jeopardize—"

"Look," he snapped, his eyes hard and narrow. "I've been shot at because of you. I've driven all night to help you. Now that they know who I am, my life is on the line, too. I haven't slept in almost forty-eight hours. I am a former Special Ops Marine and with a security clearance myself. And I don't believe we'll figure *anything* out with partial information."

At first, the offense in Erin's eyes matched the hardness in Sean's. As she considered what he'd said, her reticence mellowed. "You're right. I'm sorry." Her gaze shifted back to the stove. "I guess it all started when I began my research on swine flu."

"H1N1?"

"That's right. Remember a couple years back when it almost paralyzed the nation? The government contacted TRI to find a quick cure. What I found was that H1N1 wasn't all that unique. It's been around a long time; but because it hadn't shown up for a while, immunities had lessened, and people were more susceptible to it—especially children. Surprisingly, it really wasn't much worse than a typical seasonal flu. The thing that made the big difference was the severe diarrhea and vomiting. Most flus don't cause extreme intestinal symptoms, just respiratory ones and some body aches." Erin paused and glanced at Sean. He was again staring at the undulating glow through the grate of the stove, as if entranced by it. "Are you still with me?" she asked.

"Sure," he said without enthusiasm.

Erin couldn't blame his apparent lack of concentration. Most non-science people she knew zoned out when she started talking about her work. And it always annoyed her. She slid one foot from under the blanket and nudged him in not so playful a manner.

"Hey. Try to focus, okay?"

He nodded.

"Anyway, I was working on a vaccine to combat H1N1. See, what we do is take a live virus and kill it without destroying its outer membrane. That way your body can build antibodies that recognize that specific membrane. Some people refer to it as an 'outer shell,' but that's really a misnomer. Viruses don't have exoskeletons or chitinous tissues. Anyway, without getting into too much detail, something went wrong. Terribly wrong." Her voice softened considerably. "I . . . I made a mistake."

"What mistake?" Sean prompted.

"I found a way to 'attenuate' the virus—to leave a portion of it alive but not actively infective. A number of vaccines today are attenuated because they more closely represent a natural infection, which usually makes them last longer. Anyway, my attenuation caused antibodies to form not only to the H1N1 strain, but for several strains of *influenza A* virus. It looked to be the flu shot to beat *all* flu shots."

"Sounds ideal," Sean interjected.

"It would have been had I taken the time to develop it fully. But H1N1 had everybody scared to death. I had a number of friends sick with it. My employer was pushing for a vaccine. And I . . . I took some shortcuts that I shouldn't have taken. I knew my attenuated sample wasn't ready for field trials, but somehow an entire batch—that's more than a hundred doses—got out into public circulation before the final tests."

Erin was silent for a full minute. Her breath became shallow and she could not stop trembling, even under the heavy quilt. Her eyes burned—yet she was loath to shed any tears. It wouldn't help their current situation. Sean would probably think she was an emotional ninny. At the moment, that was uncomfortably close to reality. She hated dredging up these memories, but they somehow seemed necessary to give a baseline to where her research took her next.

"So people were given the vaccine before it was approved?" Sean asked softly.

She nodded. "Including some children. Ninety-six doses were administered. Sixty-six people died. Forty-two of those were children."

Sean drew a breath through clenched teeth. "I'm sorry," he whispered.

"Not nearly as sorry as I was," she spat. "We discovered too late that the attenuation didn't kill the infective properties of the virus, they supercharged them. Made them lethal."

"Antibiotics didn't work?" Sean asked.

She gave a derisive snort. "They wouldn't do anything. A virus is a totally different bug than a bacterium."

"Okay, anti*virals* then?"

She wiped at her eyes using the quilt. "They isolated the sick patients in clean rooms, loaded them up on HIV meds and antivirals, and fed them through IVs until their bodies found a way to fight off the virus. Of the thirty people who survived, more than half developed weakened immune systems and chronic irritable bowel syndrome. Eight of them ended up wearing ostomy bags. Knowing my part in their suffering, I was one step away from giving up on all research ever again."

Sean stood and walked to the front window. Erin closed her eyes and tried unsuccessfully to keep the images of the emaciated patients, the skeletal children, from her mind. But it did no good. She knew she would forever see their faces staring up at her for salvation she knew she couldn't give. "It got to where you could tell who would make it and who wouldn't by the look in their eyes."

"Did TRI blame you?" Sean asked while surveying the outdoors.

"No. They should have, but they didn't. It was deemed an error in quality control, not research and development. TRI was slapped with huge fines and some pretty substantial lawsuits. But they had a great team of lawyers and an ironclad insurance policy that kept the company from going under."

"Huh. I don't remember hearing anything about the accident."

"I think the insurance company acted pretty quickly to settle out of court and smooth things over."

Sean turned to look at her. "The thirty who survived: were any of them children?"

Erin tried to speak, but nothing came out. She shook her head.

Sean turned back to the window. "Is it common to give flu shots to children?"

She swallowed her emotions as best she could. "Yes, from six months to five years old for standard vaccines." She shook her head again. "But mine was anything but standard."

Sean walked up behind Erin and placed his hands on her shoulders. "But *you* didn't give it to them. It wasn't your fault."

"I don't know. If I hadn't developed the dumb thing, it wouldn't have killed anyone," she grumbled.

"That's not being fair to yourself, Erin. Come on."

"No, no, it's plenty fair. I was the one who said it was ready for initial testing."

"Yeah, but not random field testing, right?"

Erin didn't answer. She knew he was right. She'd thrown the same argument at herself for two years now. The batch was supposed to be tested in the lab first, on specific adult volunteers who could be monitored 24/7 while the effects of the vaccine were recorded. Someone else had moved the batch to the "cleared for distribution" phase without her knowledge.

Sean gave her shoulders a gentle squeeze. His hands felt strong and reassuring. "Right?" he repeated.

She nodded but was unable to stop the tears from tracing down her cheeks. "That brings me to what's happening right now. It's like the same thing all over again. Only this time, it could be worse. Much worse."

Chapter 35

Erin knew bringing up the H1N1 disaster would be painful but she didn't think it'd be this painful. She wanted to stop and simply forget the whole thing. But it wasn't that simple.

"Should I continue?" she heard herself ask.

Sean returned to the window. The sun no longer penetrated the room directly, but the reflective properties of the new snow continued to illuminate the cabin.

"Please do," he said in a tone that seemed a strange mix of concern, indifference, and anger.

Erin felt he was listening and that he was interested, even though he wasn't focusing solely on her. The guy could sure multitask. That was obvious. In fact, Erin sensed Sean was always mentally working through several things regardless of the current demands on his attention. He'd probably honed that skill while in Special Ops. She'd read where people in those lines of work learned to case a room in a single glance, identifying potential threats, pinpointing targets, and locating possible escape routes should the need arise.

Using a stick, Erin poked at the fire through the grate of the potbelly stove, soothed by its mesmerizing dance. "My focus has always been on helping underprivileged people overcome endemic illness—especially children. Swine flu is huge in Central America. AIDS is huge in Africa. Bird flu in Asia." She paused as if trying to organize the best way to present her thoughts. She turned to face Sean. "Do you know what disease is the number one killer worldwide?"

He shrugged. "Malnutrition?"

Erin bit back a condescending retort in favor of a gentler response. "While that's a very severe issue, it's not considered a disease."

"Oh yeah. I guess that rules out political corruption, too," he said with a bitter chuckle. "Okay then, um . . . is it HIV?"

"Nope, it's not AIDS. It's malaria."

Sean turned from the window. "Seriously?"

"Yes. Malaria is responsible for more than one million deaths every year. And even if the infected person doesn't die, they are often bedridden for months with debilitating fever and weakness."

"A *million*?"

Erin nodded. "There's a bunch of weird diseases out there, but malaria is the only one that has the potential of infecting half the world's population at any given moment. That's more than three *billion* people. Third-world countries have it the worst. In Africa, one in every five children dies from malaria, and a child dies from malaria every thirty seconds worldwide, every day."

"Children," Sean said softly, moving to a new angle to look out the window.

"Up till now, most eradication efforts have focused on killing mosquitoes, since they are the primary carriers of the disease. It makes sense. Mosquitoes are known vectors for several nasty bugs: malaria, Dengue fever, West Nile virus, bird flu, yellow fever, many types of fatal encephalitis. The list goes on and on, but without a doubt, malaria is the worst."

"So your research is about creating a better mosquito repellant?"

"Hardly," she said, trying to keep the offense out of her tone. "I wanted to get at the origin of the disease—not just the carrier. Eliminating the vector only slows the disease, it doesn't kill it. See, right off, it occurred to me that we're talking about an actual parasite, not just a bacteria or virus. It's a bug called *Plasmodium*. There are several species that infect humans, but the biology is pretty much the same in all of them. It's just a bug that uses human blood to propagate."

"Hang on," Sean said. "I took malaria pills a number of times on assignment in foreign countries. Can't you just distribute more of those?"

"While those meds are pretty good, they're not a cure-all. The trouble is supplying remote areas where outbreaks are the worst. Plus, they are pretty expensive, and you have to take them constantly while in the area; so they aren't very feasible for someone living there. Besides, malaria pills only work *after* the person is infected. By then it's too late for many of them because they were so weak to begin with, usually from a lack of food."

"Yeah, I know," Sean said flatly. "I did a tour in Somalia. The whole nation looked undernourished."

Erin gave him a long, hard look, trying to categorize the man under the hard, handsome shell. Was he simply agreeing with her or was he sincere in his expressions of concern? She took a breath and continued, unable to mask her excitement over the subject. "Anyway, I wondered why we could nearly eradicate epidemic infections like whooping cough and small pox, and yet can't control malaria."

Sean shrugged. "Aren't kids given vaccinations for that kind of stuff—DTP and MMR shots or something?"

"Exactly. So why don't we immunize for malaria?"

Sean turned abruptly. "Say that again."

"I developed a vaccine for malaria."

"You serious?"

Her previous excitement raised a notch. "Almost. I *think* it'll work. All my studies and projections say it will. All my lab tests have been positive. Even my preliminary tests on Rhesus monkeys proved successful. But there were some residual effects I was concerned with. Nothing serious, but enough of an anomaly that I wanted to study it further. Just to make sure so . . ." She turned back to the stove.

Sean rounded the sofa and sat on the arm. "So you didn't have a repeat of your swine flu experiment," he filled in for her.

Erin nodded and began to mindlessly pick at balls of nap on the quilt. "My research partner was really pushing me to go ahead with field tests. I refused. Tom Jenkins backed me up, although he was excited to see some results, too. The guy who was really pushing was Tom's partner, Luther Mendenhall. He's the company CFO, and he was still reeling over the losses from the H1N1 fiasco. But because I didn't want a repeat of that mess, I hid all my files on the malaria vaccine project. I've been working on it privately for about a year. Then, a couple months ago, I started noticing—"

"Shh," Sean said, standing. He moved quickly to the window and peered out from behind the wall.

"What?" Erin asked in a suddenly constricted voice. She was beginning to recognize Sean's erratic attention swings as the warning signs they were. Just then she heard the sound of rotor blades beating the air in the distance. *Another helicopter.* "Do you think they found us?"

Sean didn't answer. He probably didn't even hear her.

Chapter 36

The helicopter passed slowly overhead. Sean was confident they couldn't see his cabin or his Jeep. But then again, you never knew for certain. The aircraft's marking read IRON COUNTY SEARCH AND RESCUE. He watched the noisy machine pass to the far side of the canyon then follow the swale north, out of his line of sight. "Search and rescue this time," he commented. "Interesting."

"Do you think they'll send out bloodhounds?" Erin asked.

Sean snickered. "I seriously doubt it."

Erin did not look amused. "Listen, I don't know how this secret agent spy crap is supposed to go. I'm a research scientist, not some GI Jane. Like I said, I'm not even sure who *they* are."

Sean moved back to the couch and sat. It was not warm enough to sweat, and yet his forehead felt flushed and damp. "Hey, I didn't mean to laugh," he said, wiping his brow. "It's just that from what I've seen, the guys after you are high-tech all the way. Bloodhounds are too passé for them. But it's curious they got search and rescue involved."

"Why?"

"Before, if they succeeded in killing you, it would forever remain a mystery. Now that local government is involved, well, the bad guys can't simply bump you off anymore. You're too high profile. It makes me wonder if they've changed their minds and want to capture you instead of killing you now."

"Wow, I feel so much better," she said with acidic wryness as she moved to the kitchen. She scrounged through a cupboard and came back with a strawberry Pop-Tart. She offered one to Sean, but he declined. He felt empty but not from want of food.

"So I'm a target either way," she said after swallowing a dry lump of pastry. "I was about to tell you that I began noticing strangers looking at me more."

"Well, you *are* very pretty," Sean said before he could stop himself. When Erin favored him with a look blending confusion and delight, he cleared his throat. "So . . . um, when did that start? The strangers, I mean."

"It started a couple months ago. I don't know why. I just, well, they seemed to show up everywhere. They'd stare at me until I noticed them, then they'd look away, like they'd been caught. At first I thought I was simply being paranoid. But that's why I acted so aggressively to those texts messages." She snorted. "Obviously I wasn't delusional."

Sean sensed she wasn't being one-hundred-percent honest. There was still something she was hiding. It irked him that she could not reciprocate the efforts he'd made in her behalf. But if he pressured her, she might clam up. That wouldn't get them anywhere. He still couldn't explain why he wanted to help her so much. He didn't think it was a knight-in-shining-armor complex. Maybe she reminded him of someone. The mother he never had? The sister he never had? Probably not. You don't miss something you've never experienced. You may crave it, but you don't *miss* it. What then? Why did he feel so compelled, so driven to help her? He thought of the black helicopter last night. Definitely high-tech—perhaps even military-grade. Maybe that was a clue . . . ?

"Sean?" Erin said, bringing him back.

He shook his head to clear the mental cobwebs. "Oh, sorry. I don't have anything solid yet, but I think there may be a seam we could follow."

"A seam?"

"Yeah. You know, like a seam of gold in a mine that leads to the mother lode."

Erin nodded.

"Okay, look. We know that other people knew of your latest research and that this research could lead to something very lucrative."

"Okay."

"Can you list everyone who knew? I mean everyone, from CEOs and lab techs to the janitor who cleaned up every night?"

"Probably."

Sean went to the kitchen and searched for a scratch pad. The longer it took, the more frustrated he got. *It should be in that drawer!* He needed Erin to write down the names so they could examine each, one by one. *Where was that stupid pad?*

Erin joined him in the kitchen. "What are you looking for?"

"A scratch pad. I kept one in this drawer right here," he growled.

"I've got a spiral notepad in my purse—" she stopped abruptly. "Which is in my car," she added softly.

"I need you to write down those names." His voice was anxious.

"All right. Maybe there's a scrap of paper lying around somewhere—"

"Then find it!" Sean barked.

Erin stared at him with a frown. Sean knew he'd yelled. But he couldn't help it. This whole scenario was so . . . so frustrating!

"Look, this is *your* cabin. I don't know where everything is."

"Unacceptable," he snapped.

She stared at him with steely eyes. "Well, then let's just pack up and leave. You seem—"

"Negative! That's a stupid ide—" Sean clamped his jaw, feeling as shocked by his outburst as Erin seemed to be. He tried to focus but found it impossible. Why had he snapped like that? He certainly didn't mean to. He plopped onto the couch and put his head between his fists.

A full minute passed before Erin spoke. "Are you okay?" There was true concern in her voice.

Sean took a deep breath and released it in a tremulous sigh. "Sorry. Listen, it's past noon already. Let's make some sandwiches, and then we'll work on that list, okay?"

"In a minute," she answered. "Why did you bite my head off just now? What's wrong with you, Sean?"

He knew the reason but was too embarrassed to reveal it. Still, she had a right to know. It wasn't fair otherwise. He returned to the kitchen, opened one of his duffels, and pulled out several amber prescription pill vials. "When I got out of Special Ops, I had a pretty hard time adjusting to civilian life. Like I said, they sent me to Beaumont for stress evals and mental health assessments. They said I had a severe form of PTSD."

"Posttraumatic stress disorder," Erin said.

Sean sniggered bitterly. "I guess they were right. I didn't feel stressed, just angry, like I'd been used. It's . . . it's hard to explain." He opened a vial and dumped a small blue tablet into his hand. "This one's for anxiety." He opened a second and shuffled out two capsules. "These are for mood control." A third vial dispensed a two-toned capsule. "This is an antidepressant." He pointed to several more vials, saying, "I'm supposed to take this one, this one, this one, and this one every morning; this one, this one, this one, two of these, and this one at night; and these during the day if I feel I need them. I take so many freaking pills I'm surprised I don't rattle when I walk."

Erin smiled tenderly. Sean appreciated that.

"I don't even know what most of them are for," he said bitterly. He shook his head as if adjusting something inside. "No—I mean I know what they tell me they're for, but I don't know why I take them."

"Isn't that saying the same thing?" Erin asked without malice.

"Yes . . . and no. I don't feel I need them. But when I try to go without, I get these weird feelings. I hear voices, only they're not voices. They're in my head, not in my ears. Sometimes I go to my computer to write and just sit and stare at the screen. Sometimes I find myself surfing the web, and I don't even know what I'm looking for. I'm trying to find something that is just beyond my reach. And when I can't find it, I get angry even before I feel any frustration building. When I take one of these," he said, holding up the blue tablet, "I calm down to the point where I can focus again."

Sean left the kitchen with a bottle of water and again plopped on the couch. He swallowed his pill and stared hard at the lingering glow in the potbelly stove. "Let me guess—now you're wondering what kind of a drug-addled psychopath has locked you in his cabin in the middle of nowhere, right? What can a pill-popping loser do to help you figure out your problems, right?"

Erin didn't move. Sean hated that he had exploded like he had. But it wasn't fair to her not to know what he was like. What he was *really* like.

Erin cleared her throat and absently clicked her teeth together—as if deciding how best to tell him she was leaving. He'd seen that look before when he tried going out a couple of times after Valerie had left. When women found out about his mood swings and his need for medication, they always found some excuse to terminate the relationship without mentioning his hang-ups. How thoughtful.

Instead of answering his self-effacing questions, she casually said, "So. You were just about to explain why you thought leaving was a stupid idea . . . ?"

Sean answered softly. "Um . . . yeah. Sorry about that."

"Don't be." Erin dumped a can of stew into a pot and fired up the stovetop with a match. "If it's a stupid idea, then it's a stupid idea. I just want to know why."

"There's a number of reasons—why it's not a good idea, not why you're stupid." Sean again clamped his head between his fists as if willing it not to explode. "No—not that *you're* stupid. I meant the idea—um, okay, listen. We're in a hot zone right now. Our last known location was only a few miles from here, and because of the rugged terrain, they know there's only a few places we could have gone. That's where they will focus their search. With the fresh snowfall, leaving tracks will be impossible to avoid. And any heat signature we put off will be easier to spot because of the cold environment."

"See?" she stated offhandedly. "It *was* a stupid idea. Now we're getting somewhere."

Sean just stared at the woman in his kitchen. If he was curious about her before, now his wonderment was off the charts. Who was Erin Cross really?

"So since we're gong to be here a while, and you believe we're hidden well enough for the time being, why don't we use a scientific approach to get to the bottom of this. Instead of hit-and-miss guesses, let's write everything down we know for certain, then we can analyze it for similarities and connections."

Now Sean was gawking at her. He was about to say something when she started placing his prescription vials back in his bag as if the embarrassing quantity was no big deal. "Let's clear this area and work on a flow chart. I'll begin as you suggested with everyone who knows about my research; you come stir the stew. Then—oh, here's your scratch pad," she said, pulling out the spiral-bound ledger from the bottom of the duffel bag.

Erin bent to the task and began scribbling. Reluctantly, Sean made his way to the stovetop. His body ached from head to toe. Just as he started, he heard Erin gasp loudly.

"What is it?" he said, turning to her.

"I just remembered you got a bag of licorice and Double Stuff Oreos," she said with eyes wide.

Sean frowned. "What?"

"Where'd you hide them, Sean? Come on. If we begin holding out on each other now, we'll never get anywhere."

Grinning in disbelief, he opened a cupboard and removed the treats then returned to the stew. "Glad I'm not the only one who thinks black licorice is one of the four basic food groups."

Erin's mouth opened, but no sound escaped. A moment later she whispered, "What did you say?"

"Um, 'Glad I'm not the only one who thinks licorice is one of the four basic food groups'?" he hesitantly quoted himself.

Her eyes were wide with both anger and enlightenment. "Not just licorice—*black* licorice." She reached over and grabbed his forearm. "I think I know who is behind all this."

Chapter 37

A COOL BREEZE BROUGHT THE smell of fresh rain—none of which fell on the village of Pu'uwai. Even so, the kiawe trees and low-growing scrub were spangled with dew drops refracting the first rays of the morning sun. But even the ubiquitous morning dew was not enough moisture to keep the small island lush and green.

Jacob dropped his legs over the edge of the cot and put his head in his hands, waiting for the morning dizziness to pass. He stood then jumped back onto the cot. It felt as if he'd stepped on needles. He carefully ran his hand over the mat on the floor. It was dry and rigid, but there were no sharp edges he could feel. Checking his feet, he found a smattering of tiny red dots. Putting pressure on his feet again, the same prickly pain shot up his legs. The dots itched, too. Mosquito bites? The bumps didn't look like typical mosquito bites, but he wasn't an expert on that kind of pathology. Well, it didn't matter. He was inoculated against just about everything a mosquito can carry—unlike everyone else on the island.

He pulled some cortisone ointment from his personal pack. Daubing the ointment on the red dots diminished the pain and itch. He slid on his borrowed baggies and tee, socks and sandals, and stepped outside. Pegasus was tethered to a tree off to one side. She rocked to her feet and bleated.

"Yeah, good morning," Jacob mumbled. In spite of how favorably things were going, he did not sleep well last night. The primitive surroundings and noises woke him often, the air travel still haunted him, the rough boat ride, the cot, the smelly goat—it all added up to a undeniably miserable experience. And now he had stupid bug bites on his feet. He closed his eyes and inhaled deeply the sweet, briny air. At least he still had his larvae. And then there was the little girl too . . .

Someone hollered his name. He looked toward the village and saw Kapono coming at him carrying a bowl that vented wisps of steam.

"*Aloha kakahiaka,* Docta Brown. I make you poi for breakfas'."

Ugh, poi. Jacob was hoping to avoid the bland, sticky, starchy vegetable mush. His sponsor had paid for two weeks' worth of meals while he was on-site, but he wasn't given the luxury of a menu from which to order. Whatever the islanders provided was what he would eat. *Oh, well,* he thought, looking down at the way his shirt hung from his belly instead of his chest. *A couple weeks of dieting might not be such a bad idea.*

"I know mos' *haoles* don' do da cold poi. So I heat it up. An' I add some coconut and honey for flava', cha?"

"Oh, thanks," Jacob said flatly as he accepted the steaming bowl.

"Hey, no worries, brah. You need anyting else?"

"How about some freshly drawn crepes with Maine blueberries and sweet cream?"

Kapono just stared at him. "Ah, sorry, Doc. Ain' nottin' like dat on da island." The young man seemed truly saddened that he couldn't give Jacob what he'd asked for.

Jacob waved him off. "I'm just crackin' again."

Kapono slapped his hands together as if giving himself a high five. "Brah, you one mondo funny dude. Good ting I ain' on my board righ' now, 'cause I wipe out laughin' big time."

Jacob smiled as he stabbed at the pasty porridge with a spoon. It looked like purple wallpaper paste. He took a small bite and had to suppress a gag reflex. The taro from which this poi was made was dry and fibrous, and the coconut was old and tough to chew. If honey had been added, it wasn't in copious amounts. He could not taste any sweetness.

"You like?"

"Delicious," Jacob said after a hard, lumpy swallow.

"Dat cool. My lil' sis make id for you."

"Kaile'e?"

"Dude, you remember her name! Man, you mus' be smard as dey come. I know you take down da mosquita in no time."

"Yeah, speaking of which," Jacob said, "let's go check out my larvae before it gets too hot."

"Righ' on, brah," Kapono said, leading off with a brisk pace.

As soon as the Hawaiian had rounded a corner, Jacob set the bowl of poi in front of Pegasus. He grabbed his field satchel and followed the young guide.

The hike to Lake Halali'i went faster than the day before, mostly because Jacob wasn't as nervous about his larvae. He felt confident they were safe in their new aquatic nursery. He took the time to memorize aspects of the trail Kapono took as they meandered toward the site. By the time they crested the rise overlooking the lake, Jacob had worked up a sweat. He pulled a water bottle from his fanny pack and took several long gulps.

At the lake's edge, Jacob removed his sandals and socks and ventured into the water.

"Doc, I'm still thinkin' thad nod a good plan, ya know?"

The scientist turned. "I told you not to worry about the larvae," Jacob said as he resumed his trek. "And I believe your god is on my side. You'll see."

At the screened box, Jacob pulled a magnifying glass from his satchel and bent over to examine his brood. To his delight, he saw a hundred or more pupae clinging parallel to the surface of the water. They formed a nearly solid mat from one edge of the box to the other. There were just as many discarded larval shells floating at various levels in the box. The sight was expected and encouraging. Each larva molts four times before becoming a mature pupa. In roughly two more days the pupal skin would split, and an adult mosquito would emerge.

"Whacha see, Doc?" Kapono called from twenty yards away.

"A thing of beauty, my friend. My mosquitoes look healthy and will probably hatch in a couple days."

"What?" the Hawaiian shouted. "Whad yu mean—you *want* dem to hatch? I though' fey was der ta eat da udda mosquita babies, man."

Jacob trudged back to the lake's edge, where his companion waited. "Using your strange vernacular: no worries, brah."

Kapono's look of astonishment morphed into one of confusion. "Why dat?"

"You see, my mosquitoes are all male. *And* they are all sterile. That way, when they mate with the females mosquitoes on Ni'ihau, nothing will happen. No fertile mosquitoes means no West Nile virus."

The mental battle raging behind Kapono's eyes looked fierce. He wrestled with the information a moment before his eyebrows rose triumphantly. "So you sayin' we don' have ta spray no more?"

"Nope."

"No more mosquita net?"

"Very little."

"What abou' da ones dat blow over from Kauai?"

"Well, you may see some strays occasionally," Jacob said, drying his feet and putting his socks and sandals back on. "But when they get here and find no *kanés* to mate with, they'll turn around and go home."

Kapono burst out laughing. "You righteously funny, brah. You crack like no one else. No *kanés* for da *wahinés*. Dat be a mondo bad scene, dude. I almos' cry for dem bugs now." He continued to giggle as he spoke, play-acting between male and female voices. "All da girls sittin' 'round wailin', 'Ohhh, ohhh, da gods mus' be angry. Where all de cute *kanés*? How we make da baby now?' and da *kanés* say, 'Sorry, sista' mosquita, you be surfin' 'lone for long time, brah.' Dem mosquitoes will be eitha' very broken heart or very mad. Gonna blow der top, like Mauna Loa."

The Hawaiian walked off holding his ribs, intermittently laughing and coughing—almost to the point of vomiting, Jacob suspected.

The scientist smiled. He should have been an actor; his guise was water-tight, his material was unquestionable, his delivery perfectly executed. He stopped short and smiled again at his clever choice of words. Perfectly *executed*.

Kapono turned to face him from some distance off. "No *kané* mosquita for da *wahinés*. Man, you *serious* funny, Doc. Dem *wahinés* mosquita will be very, very mad."

"Oh, I'm sure they will find a way to get even," Jacob said with just the hint of laughter.

Chapter 38

Erin opened the Oreos and twisted one in two. She had no interest in the licorice. "About two years ago, Tom okayed Luther Mendenhall to hire a researcher from a company back east called New England Noetics. Noetic science studies the effects our conscious has on the physical world. Most scientists believe it's pure malarkey, but I think there may be something to it. You know how the scriptures say faith can move mountains? You got to wonder *how,* right? The idea is that our spirit and even our thoughts are photon-based. They act on Bose-Einstein principles of quantum mechanics. Even Joseph Smith—the founding prophet in my church—said that all spirit is matter, but that it can only be discerned by spiritually pure eyes." She paused and arched her brow. "Are you still with me, Sean?"

"Nope. You lost me just after Luther Mendenhall," Sean said, still engaged with the simmering pot of beef stew.

"Doesn't matter. The researcher was Dr. Jacob Krantz. He's a virologist—he studies viruses. He said New England Noetics had him trying to discover a connection between various bacteria, viruses, and prions, to host cells to see if they operated on more than a physical level—like a noetic connection." She snorted. "When I first heard that, I thought, 'oh please!' But the more we worked together and swapped ideas and suspicions, the more it began to seem possible on an as-yet-undiscovered level."

"Prions?"

"They're basically highly infectious proteins particles that cause abnormal folding of brain proteins. Like what causes mad cow disease."

"Oh." Sean brought the pot from the stove and set it on a hot pad. "You actually study this stuff on purpose? I think I'd fall asleep just entering your lab."

Missing the jest, Erin bristled. "Look, I'm trying to simplify this as best I can. You need to know some background to understand why I think Dr. Krantz is behind this."

Sean had just put an Oreo in his mouth. He chewed and swallowed quickly. "I was teasing, Erin. Honestly, I'm glad you're dumbing this down for me. So . . . you worked with this Krantz guy? In what capacity did Tom hire him?"

Her mood had turned pensive, troubled. "It was for his expertise on viruses. It was a temporary position. He was bringing his knowledge of noetics to our work on antivirals and vaccines. He was to be my assistant in my swine flu studies. In all fairness, Krantz was able to take my ideas and extrapolate them to amazing levels. I was able to develop a vaccine from his work on my theories."

"But I thought that didn't work out."

Erin poured equal amounts of stew into two bowls. She slid one to Sean and began randomly stirring hers without meeting his eyes. "Krantz was the main person who wanted to push it through before all tests were done. The man was highly intelligent . . . but he was also . . . oh, I don't know. He was more than driven—he was obsessed. But he was careless, too. When I refused to proceed with early testing, he went over my head."

"To Tom?" Sean asked, scooping up a spoonful of stew.

She shook her head. "I think he went *above* Tom. I'm not sure to whom, but it must have been a sponsor or investor, because the next day I was pulled from all other projects to focus on the H1N1 cure. Krantz assumed the lead role, and I was left with the choice of cleaning up his sloppy technique or bowing out altogether. Since I already had tons of time invested in the project, I stayed."

Sean cocked his head to one side. "If he was such a bad scientist, why did your bosses hire him?"

"Oh, he's not a bad scientist. The man's just shy of brilliant. But he's misguided and often lets his enthusiasm override his caution—and his morals. He was arrogant and rude to everyone in the lab, including me. At least until he saw his experiment go awry. Then he was all charm and schmooze." Erin scoffed, still poking at her stew. "He even asked me out several times . . . in the interest of bringing the project back in line. I agreed—once. We went to dinner then back to his apartment."

"Whoa, really?"

Erin took a sip of stew then slid her bowl to one side. "He said all his research notes were there—which actually wasn't a lie. He had whiteboards everywhere with chemical formulae and notes scribbled all over them. None of it was concise or orderly. It looked like he was doing some kind of free-association while smoking crack. Seriously. There were phrases in Latin and Greek, I think, and scripture references from the Koran and the Talmud as well as the Bible. I know because he even scribbled down the references. It was creepy stuff, Sean. Words like *doomsday* and *apocalypse* and *Armageddon*. I asked him what it had to do with our vaccine. He said it was another project he had started as a side interest. The guy was seriously strange."

"A real nerd, huh?" Sean said, scraping the sauce from his nearly empty bowl.

"No, not so's you could tell at a glance. He actually looked quite normal. Put him in a white shirt and tie and you'd think he was just coming home from church. But when you got him talking about the future and where our research could go—what it could do for mankind—he'd go all schizoid. His eyes got this glossy emptiness, and he'd babble things about his destiny in mankind's future. He said he found my mind worthy of such a future, 'because only the enlightened would survive.' Seriously, Sean, it freaked me out. Well, that night in his apartment, he lapsed into one of those moods. He started hitting on me big time, calling me his Eve. He turned into a disgusting octopus, hands and arms everywhere. I kept saying no, but he wasn't listening. I finally had to punch him in the nose. I broke it, too."

Sean gave a low whistle. "Remind me never to piss you off."

A fleeting smile passed across her face. "He left just after the H1N1 disaster took his only child—a daughter, I believe. She was one of the first tested on his new drug—by his own hand. I have no idea where he went after that. Tom didn't either. He just vanished. Like I said, that was over two years ago, so I haven't given it much thought since then."

"Until I mentioned licorice," Sean prompted.

"Yeah, *black* licorice—the real stuff, not just the flavored kind. He ate it all the time. He said it had antiviral properties. That's partially true, but I don't believe anyone's done any real studies on how effective it is in treating viral disease." She took a sip of water and added, "It swore me off black licorice ever since."

Sean looked over at Erin's nearly full bowl. "Not hungry anymore?"

She sighed and picked up her spoon. "No, but I know I've got to eat."

"So, you think Dr. Krantz is trying to have you killed," Sean said without a hint of flippancy.

Erin shrugged. "Kind of a stretch, huh?"

Sean's focus had narrowed. The hardness in his eyes suggested he was giving this serious thought. Erin appreciated that tremendously. "Not at all. You have a photographic memory, right?"

The blush she'd never been able to control when asked that question colored her cheeks. "Not really. I have *eidetic* recollection, meaning I can recall precise facts and figures and such."

"Did Dr. Krantz know about it?"

"I guess."

"Then he's worried you might be able to recall everything he talked about or had in his apartment that evening. If he's working on something only you could link him to, then the easiest thing to do is eliminate you."

Erin dropped to a bar stool, her brow furrowed. "But that was *two years* ago. You think he really remembers me? His memory was good but not eidetic."

Sean's focus remained sharp as he though for a moment. "In Special Ops we learned that people tend to remember things associated with life-altering events. You said you spurned him."

"My rejection of his sexual advances was life-altering?" Erin scoffed with a chuckle. "That's flattering, Sean, but not very realistic."

"Hey, a guy like that probably has an ego to match. That means he weighs praise and rejection equally. Plus, you said his daughter died as a result of your tests."

"*His* tests. He was the one who gave it to her, counter to our timeline," Erin corrected him.

He shook his head. "Doesn't matter. It was *your* idea to begin with. To his way of thinking, you rejected him *and* killed his daughter. Yeah—he remembers you, all right."

Erin placed her face in her palms, trying to mentally avert the headache coming at her like a tsunami. Even though it was still afternoon, she could tell it was going to be a very long night.

Chapter 39

"Kapono, I really need to contact my company. Where is the best place on the island to get a cell signal?"

"That be anywhere on da east side. But da best be on top of Pani'au. But that a long hike, brah. It take a long, long time, cha? You sho' you up ta it?"

The young Hawaiian had a point. A gathering of cumulus clouds gave intermittent shade but not enough to keep the temperature from pushing close to eighty degrees. Add to that Pacific island humidity and you got an altogether miserable hike. But it had to be done.

Jacob donned his tennis shoes and a wide-brim hat made of palm thatch. Before making the trek, he and Kapono had a quick meal of some kind of sautéed meat and rice. Kapono didn't offer to tell what kind of meat it was, and Jacob didn't ask. It was just better that way.

They followed a trail that paralleled the shore. A perpetual breeze from the ocean helped to keep the temperature tolerable. Five hours later, as they neared the southern end of Ni'ihau, the terrain began to rise. It was gradual at first then climbed sharply near the coast. Jacob was panting hard by the time they crested the top of the thousand-foot range. Solid cliffs of volcanic rock dropped precipitously to the ocean, some four hundred feet.

Jacob stood at the highest point he could find and turned his back to the wind.

"Da wind always blow here, cha? We call it *pu'ukani pali*: da singing cliffs."

Sure enough, the cliff howled and whistled with the constant battering of trade winds. Jacob slipped on his Bluetooth phone, stood the computer pen on a rock, and angled the red beam to a piece of card stock. It took an uncomfortably long time for the QWERTY keyboard to show. Perhaps the signal wasn't very strong. He shrugged and typed:

This place is more primitive than we thought. They live in the Stone Age here. I'm standing on a mountain peak. Only place I can get a signal. Only one bar. I hope this gets through. Islanders don't like visitors. My escort can barely speak Pidgin English. The weather's hot and dry, but the lake has enough water in it to breed my mosquitoes. The test should go well.

He paused and looked out over the blue-and-white expanse of windswept ocean.

One more thing, he typed. *I am still concerned about Dr. Cross's elimination. Please confirm it was taken care of.*

He paused again and wondered if he should mention the little Hawaiian girl. It might be good science to inoculate one more person just to be sure the vaccine worked as well as the virus. He looked up and saw Kapono watching him from several yards away. As friendly as the young man was, Jacob sensed a large measure of distrust from him. There was no way he could know Jacob's true intentions, of course; he'd have to smile as often as possible to maintain his ruse. In the end, his smile would be for a completely different reason.

He hit ALT-S and waited for the beep from his ear piece signaling the completion of the transmission. He saw Kapono looking toward the lowering sun, obviously concerned about getting back before dark. Probably not a bad idea.

Jacob shrugged again, closed the file, and pocketed his earpiece and pen.

MONDAY
NOVEMBER 7, 2011

Chapter 40

Jacob waited until after nine for Kapono to show, but he never did. The time was getting close to the final molting, when the pupa would emerge as full-fledged adults. Knowing he couldn't miss it, Jacob ventured off to the lake on his own. The sky was overcast with the threat of rain, although he doubted they'd get any. Perhaps it was the preamble to one of Kapono's *konas,* his winter storms. That'd be fine in a day or two. Just not now.

Arriving at the lake, Jacob felt a couple of raindrops on his face. The wind hadn't picked up to more than a breeze, but the clouds loomed dark and heavy. A sultry gloom permeated the area around Halali'i Lake, giving the air a heavy, oppressive feel. He removed his sandals and trudged out to the box, carrying his folding beach chair. He didn't wear any socks this time, because the rash on his feet and ankles was almost gone. The cortisone cream had done its job. He grinned. *Science: 1. Polynesian god: 0.*

The pupae were squirming, trying to shed their adolescent cocoons. A few adult mosquitoes sat on the water's surface with wings extended.

"Yes!" he cheered the insects. "Come on, Team *Anopheles.*"

He sat mesmerized by the activity in the box. Maybe he should have been an entomologist instead of a virologist—

"What they doin'?" a young voice asked, startling Jacob out of his chair. He jumped to one side, but because the mud at the lake bottom was like tar, he ended up floundering into the knee-deep water.

Kaile'e covered her mouth as she giggled at his clumsiness.

Jacob blustered and fumed. "What's the big idea creeping up on me in that slimy way?"

Kaile'e's giggling switched to full-out laughter.

Jacob struggled to his feet and wiped algae from his sodden baggies. "I'm glad *you* find this humorous."

"Kapono is right—you one funny mainlander," she said as she continued to snicker.

Jacob righted his chair and sat with a harrumph. He glanced quickly at the little girl. "You're not supposed to be talking to me, remember?"

The young girl shrugged.

"Well . . . aren't you supposed to be in school or something?"

"The satellite goes down with too many clouds," she said, pointing overhead.

"Satellite? I thought everyone here was opposed to modernization," Jacob said.

"Nah nah nah, doctor man. Not at da school. Our 'lectricity come from da sun. Dat why school is out today."

"Solar power? That's cool."

She shrugged again.

Jacob returned to examining his insects but continued the conversation. At least Kaile'e's English was easier to understand than her brother's. "So where is Kapono today?"

"My brodda be fishing. He don' let anyone drive his tub, an' da elders say we need fish. So he fish." She moved closer and peered into the screened box. It was only then that Jacob saw she was wearing rubber hip waders.

"Um, aren't you afraid of being in the water?"

She cocked her head to one side and pointed at her waders. "I not in da water. See? I not wet, so I not touch da water, cha?"

Jacob laughed, convinced this little girl was destined to be Ni'ihau's first lawyer.

"So what they doin'?" she repeated.

"Molting."

"What stage? Larva or pupa?"

Jacob looked up, still grinning. He had not expected such astute queries from the pretty little Hawaiian. It was a question his daughter would have asked had she been there . . . and alive. "Pupa, actually, molting into adults. How do you know such things?"

"Duh. I go da school, remember? We get Discovery an' Nat-Geo an' Animal Planet. I like da science shows most. You a scientist, right?"

"Why yes, I am. I'm a virologist." Just as Jacob said "virologist" he realized he'd blown his cover story. He was supposed to be an epidemiologist . . . or was it an entomologist? Or—oh, who cares? The little girl probably didn't know the difference anyway.

"Oh, dat right. You study West Nile *gamboo*. Dat what Kapono say."

Jacob continued to smile. He couldn't help it. "That's right."

"Hey, der's some adult mosquitoes already," Kaile'e said, pointing in the box. "Dat da final stage, right?"

"Correct again. They sit on the surface of the water waiting for their exoskeleton and wings to dry and harden. Then they fly off in search of their first blood meal."

"Dat so totally cool," she said as if awestruck.

"I agree, Miss Kaile'e."

"But when dey suck da blood, dat when da sickness spreads, right? I know cuz dat what I learn in school. Da female mosquito is de only one dat bite, and dey has forty-seven teeth she use to poke through da skin."

"Well, they're not really 'teeth' like you and I have," Jacob explained. "They have four sets of serrated cutting tools on their proboscis—that's their nose—which penetrate the skin and inject an anticoagulant into the puncture site so the blood won't clot while they feed."

Kaile'e frowned at him as if perturbed. "I think it easier to call 'em 'teeth.'"

He chuckled. "Perhaps you're right."

Jacob's daughter had been as inquisitive as this little girl. Kimberly had dark brown hair and light brown eyes, but she was about the same size as Kaile'e, and her mind was equally as sharp.

"Boy, you sure are smart, you know?" he said cheerfully.

"*Mahalo,* doctor man."

"Oh, you can call me dad—I mean Jacob. That's my name, Jacob Kra—I mean Jacob Brown. Dr. Jacob Daniel Brown. But I usually just go by Dan. Or Dr. Brown." He couldn't believe how much trouble he was having maintaining his cover. Something about Kaile'e stirred memories he'd buried deep because of the pain they brought. And yet, as those memories resurfaced in the presence of this delightful little girl, the pain was not there. It felt strange but very, very welcome.

Jacob went back to concentrating on the hatching adult mosquitoes, hoping the girl had missed his identity slip. He asked her to call him dad. It shocked him that he had said it, to the point that he felt his cheeks flush. Yet the little girl hadn't seemed to notice.

While pretending to watch the pupae molt to adults, Jacob watched the gathering breeze caress Kaile'e's hair into a fluid dance. Her flawless brown skin and large eyes were the stuff of postcards and travel brochures. She even had a beautiful yellow hibiscus flower tucked behind one ear. Kimberly's hair had been almost as long, but her skin was not nearly as brown. Jacob's mind involuntarily transposed one child with the other: same age, same size, same personality. It was difficult not seeing his daughter standing next to him.

Kimberly's innocence was what made her death so reprehensible, so brutal. She did not deserve to die such a horrible death. If Erin Cross hadn't developed that vaccine . . .

"Kapono say dese mosquito can't have children," Kaile'e said, as if saddened by the fact. "That's too bad. Children are a gift from God."

Jacob could see the threatening clouds reflected in her anthracite-colored irises. Such turmoil seen inside such purity seemed the ultimate contradiction. It wasn't right. It shouldn't be allowed. It *couldn't* be allowed.

The quick decision was absolute—it came unbidden but with finality. Jacob would inoculate Kaile'e against the Armageddon virus—not for her sake, but for Kimberly's.

Chapter 41

SEAN AWOKE WITH A START, unsure of what had roused him. He rolled to a sitting position on the couch and placed his hands on both sides to steady himself. The initial vertigo of waking so abruptly passed quickly. He cased the cabin in a quick 360-degree scan. His mind processed everything as fast as his eyes and ears took it in.

Thankfully, he felt much more in control; his medications had finally kicked in. Good. He hated the chaotic, rollercoaster pattern of his thoughts and emotions and dreams. More than that, he hated not having any influence over them. Well, dreams were beyond most people's ability to restrain, but the other things weren't. The only time he *did* feel in control was when he was actively doing something. Like right now. Gathering and analyzing intel was what he did best—as far as he could remember. He usually did it alone, but this time he was glad he had some help.

He glanced back to the kitchen and saw Erin poring over numerous papers on the table.

"Good morning, sleepy head," she offered with a smile. "I'm glad to see you moved from your chair to the couch."

He gave her a limp wave and smiled back.

"You were dead to the world when I came down this morning. That's why I let you sleep in. It's almost noon." She jerked her head toward the table. "Now that you're up, come look at this, tell me what you think."

Sean moved slowly to the table, recalling what he could about last night. He had stationed himself in front of the door, rifle in hand, just like the previous night. He didn't remember moving to the couch. Apparently, Erin had spent most of the evening mapping out the chain of events leading up to the shooting at Giamboli's.

He looked over her latest work. She'd listed all possibilities she could think of for what was happening and why it was happening. Her logic algorithm was meticulous.

Everything Erin Cross did impressed him. *Doctor* Erin Cross, he reminded himself. Considering she knew she was the target of a major player, Erin was handling the situation amazingly well. He had been trained to dissect and project possible outcomes of situations such as hers. He had learned to dodge, to blend in, to disappear at any given time. But where did *she* get such training? Certainly not in college. Certainly not studying science.

He shook his head. Of course that's where she learned it. Not the clandestine maneuvers, of course, but the extrapolation of information. Science was all about examining facts from numerous angles and distilling the most likely, most logical conclusion. Her career was built on deductive reasoning and systematic elimination of unplausible possibilities.

"Sean?" Erin's voice broke into his thoughts.

"Oh, sorry. Yes?"

"You zoned out just now." Her voice was filled with concern, not anger. "You sure you don't need more sleep?"

"No, I'm good. Sorry about that. I was just thinking how impressed I am at your ability to evaluate things."

Erin flinched. "Impressed that I *can* evaluate or impressed with the outcome?" Her tone sounded a bit defensive.

"Oh, definitely with the outcome. This is tight," he said, pointing at her work.

"Thanks," she said, returning her focus to the papers in front of them.

"So you're pretty sure Krantz is the guy, huh?"

Sitting at the kitchen table, Erin ran her finger along one of the columns, as if reconfirming her algorithm was correct. "Yeah, but he must be working *for* someone. He is a pretty smart guy but not much for organization or seeing the big picture. I have no idea what he's up to, but if I had to guess, it'd be an offshoot of our H1N1 studies."

"Did he have any input on your malaria vaccine?"

"I don't think so. I had some preliminary theories stemming from the swine flu study, but I didn't really start the research until after he left."

"What kind of an offshoot would Krantz have followed?"

"I don't know. That was years ago," she said with a tinge of frustration.

"Did you ever suspect he was doing something other than what TRI was interested in? You know—any signs that seemed out of the ordinary?"

She tapped a pen against her lips as she studied the scribbling in front of her. "The man himself was way out of the ordinary. But as far as what he was testing . . . no, not . . . really . . ."

As Sean leaned closer, his stomach gurgled loudly.

"Now there's a sign I *do* recognize," she said, laughing. "In scientific terms it's called 'borborygmi.'" She stood and moved to the kitchen cupboards. "You must be starving. What would you like? We've got eggs and sandwich fixings, Pop-Tarts. You can have Cocoa Puffs if the milk's still good."

Instead of answering, Sean walked to the door and took a quick look outside. He then unscrewed the plywood covers he'd put back in place last night. His mind was clear but anxious. He was definitely in need of food, but something else was gnawing at him besides hunger.

After removing the window covers, he said, "Be right back," and quickly stepped outside, shutting the door behind him. The mountain chill was biting. Most of the clouds had moved north, and the sky was a hard, pale blue. A steady breeze hissed through the pine boughs and made the bare cottonwood branches click and tap together. He inhaled deeply several times. The air was clean—no smoke from a fire or exhaust from an engine.

He took out his cell phone and pulled up his call log. No new messages or calls. Not surprising. Although his phone didn't indicate he was out of a serviceable area, there were no bars on its signal strength. Of course, he didn't expect any. The only way to get a signal was to hike to the top of the canyon wall above his cabin—and that was something he loathed to do with Erin in tow. However, he may not have much choice.

He moved to the edge of the porch just before Erin stepped outside. "I'm heating the pan for scrambled eggs whenever you're ready."

"Thanks," he said. Taking one last look around, satisfied they were still alone, he went back inside.

As they ate, Erin said, "Can I ask a couple questions? They're about your past—if that's not too personal."

Sean shrugged. He didn't mind. The past was past. Water way under the bridge, as he'd said earlier. "Go ahead."

"Do you remember much about the birth of your daughter?"

Sean smiled—then slowly it faded. "No. I guess I don't. I think I was back at Beaumont Hospital when it happened. I remember getting a phone call from the Littleton hospital saying Valerie was in labor. I had that new psychiatrist back then, and he was loading me up on heavy meds. But I remember everything after that: holding Britt for the first time, helping change her, feeding her, walking her at night." The smile returned. "I did quite a lot of that because Val returned to work during the day after her maternity leave was up."

"And your time in the service? How was that?"

"Pretty average, I guess. The Special Ops stuff was thrilling . . . and painful . . . sometimes."

"Can you tell me about that?"

Sean knew he couldn't because of clearance issues. He shook his head.

"I don't mean the missions you went on or what you did on them. I'm more interested in your training; it might help us take a new angle on this Krantz problem."

Really? Well . . . why not? He nodded. "Okay. What do you want to know?"

"Were there many other guys in your training squad?"

He thought for a moment. "Yeah, there were about a dozen, but . . ."

"But what?"

He closed his eyes and shook his head. Why couldn't he remember? Fighting against a huge blank spot, Sean lightly pounded a fist against his forehead. "I don't know."

"Don't know what, Sean?" She was speaking softly now but with greater intensity.

"I can't remember any of their names."

"Really?"

He shook his head again, almost convulsively. "Just nicknames: Shark, Acer, Jax, Buddy, names like that."

"That's okay, Sean. The names aren't important. But they were good friends, I'm sure."

Yes. He was pretty certain they'd all been friendly enough. "Yeah, I think so. I know they were with me on most of my ops. You had to rely on each man to do his duty so you could focus on yours."

"Did you guys do a lot together off the clock? You know, go to parties or the movies or anything?"

With his eyes still closed, he placed his palms flat on the table and commanded his mind to open and reveal. It was kind of like sitting at his computer willing his mind to create fantasy for his books. Except this time, the memories came more easily. "Sure. They dragged me to a bunch of ball games and such. That was okay, but I didn't care for the bar-hopping. I'm not much of a drinker. They pretty much had to drag me there, and then I'd end up dragging them home."

Erin laughed. "I bet. Did they also have to drag you to the tattoo parlor?"

He shook his head. "No. I don't remember that."

"Really? Then when did you get those funky symbols on your knuckles?"

Chapter 42

Ritualistically turning a small crystal pyramid with the precision and reverence of a Japanese tea ceremony, Praefectus Magnus pondered on the events of the past two days. He struggled to remain calm. Reading the latest printout had made his anger boil anew. His adepts were not adept at anything. His prefects were prima donnas. His subordinates were mere sycophants. How hard was it to find one woman and one man and kill them? This wasn't simply some flippant wish or childish vendetta. Magnus *needed* Erin Cross dead.

Pacing in his office, he looked at the reports from his feckless minions. That's what he thought of them. They didn't deserve the title of servant. *Servant* denoted some kind of skill set. These men were mindless, obsequious devotees. On the one hand it was good to have people you could command to do anything without question or pause. Occasionally that kind of blind obedience was optimal. On the other hand they sometimes needed to act for themselves—to interpret and adapt and respond to unexpected situations. In spite of intense training, so few of them actually caught this vision. They followed orders simply to say they had followed orders. The outcome meant nothing to them.

Now the one man he hoped would rise above the mediocrity of his subordinates was also failing. Magnus had had confidence Prefect Franklin would be able to ferret out Cross and Flannery. At one point Franklin had honed in on her tracker, only to have the signal stop when he was within a half mile of it. Pity.

When Magnus contacted Belize Securities about it, they said Cross's phone had suddenly stopped transmitting. Not only was the tracker chip gone, but she had disabled her GPS function so their satellite couldn't locate her, and she had moved out of range of any cell phone tower in the area. They were no longer receiving information of any kind from her phone. Was she really that smart? Or was this Flannery's doing?

Prefect Franklin's report guessed they were hiding in the wilderness of Dixie National Forest. After patches of snow had melted, he'd found where their tire tracks led into the back country, but he'd lost them a few miles in. The search-and-rescue helicopter hadn't found a thing either. Franklin said he was going to hire a tracker he knew of who did everything old school. If there was a haystack with a needle to be found, this old-timer would know right where to look. *Hire an old tracker? Was he serious?* They had access to the best surveillance equipment on the planet, and his prefect wanted to rent a pack of coonhounds and some old coot on a donkey.

Magnus paced his office, trying to recall the techniques he'd learned under his master to calm his mind so he could find enlightenment. But it was no good. He couldn't stop focusing on why everything seemed to be going wrong at the same time.

Even Dr. Krantz was proving unreliable. He was more devoted to his little science experiments than to the Order. That wasn't right. It was shaky ground on which to operate. The man was supposed to check in every evening, and yet Magnus had received only one report—and that was to say he'd cleared security in Salt Lake. That was inexcusable. If Krantz's tests proved successful, then Magnus would begin full-swing infestations. He'd begin in Saudi Arabia, Spain, France, and Italy. Saudi Arabia because he needed to kill those to whom he owed money; the other countries because that's where the Old Order resided. They called themselves the Grand Order, but Magnus felt that title was self-inflated. Grand? No way. Old maybe, but no longer grand. Their heyday had come and gone centuries ago. Just a bunch of old men reveling in past dreams . . . *as long as their Alzheimer meds keep working,* he snickered.

Magnus saw the true future of the Order. He saw world control with himself at the top. Strange how the one person he felt could stop him was this stubborn female researcher.

Erin Cross. If his minions could just find her.

He swore under his breath. He couldn't trust anyone!

Like many other operations within Benjamin's Blood, Magnus found himself needing to become personally involved. *He* sent the threatening texts to Dr. Cross (though he did have fun doing so). *He* shot Harry Harriman when the man got in the way of eliminating Dr. Cross himself. *He* had risked everything by borrowing money from Saudi militants. The only thing he hadn't done was personally monitor the mosquito tests in Hawaii.

Yet.

Why couldn't his men be more like himself? Everyone was so untrustworthy, so beneath him.

He blew out an exasperated sigh. How hard were these tasks, anyway? When he was rising in the ranks of Benjamin's Blood, no job was too difficult or morally objectionable for him to carry out. That was what the Order required: total, unequivocal obedience.

Was he going to have to eliminate Cross and Flannery himself? Was he going to have to fly out to that speck in the Pacific and make sure Krantz went through with the tests to ensure complete population annihilation?

Hopefully, Franklin would come through for him. He must be patient. Hopefully, Krantz would see his project to fruition. He must have faith. And hopefully it would all be done before his Saudi lenders decided to make *him* a target.

Chapter 43

Sean rubbed a finger over the markings on his knuckles. "To be honest, I don't know where I got these."

Erin favored him with a skeptical smirk. "Oh, come on. You sure it wasn't some drunken binge or secret initiation ceremony?" She found she loved the way he blushed so easily.

Sean squinted and flinched as if he'd just bitten into something extremely sour. He pressed his hand on either side of his head and grimaced. It wasn't the reaction she expected.

"Sean? What's wrong?" she asked, very much confused. The lighthearted tenor of the moment had vanished.

"These tattoos. They *are* symbols. I don't know of what." His voice was dry, almost painfully. "But I know the mean *something*."

"Come on. Let me see," she said, reaching. She took Sean's right hand and examined the greenish black markings. They looked ancient in design, not like some modern knockoff of oriental characters or arcane calligraphy. Erin had covered quite a bit of anthropology while obtaining her PhD in epidemiology. The study of civilization and the ebb and flow of populations was paramount to understanding modern cultures. And cultural changes were often predicated by religious influences. The symbols on the first and second knuckles of Sean's right hand looked gnostic.

"I'm not a symbologist or an iconographer, but this first one looks kind of like the Star of Ishtar. It's Mesopotamian, I believe. The eight points of the star represent the movements of the planet Venus. The inner circle is the eye of deity, and the outer circle represents eternity."

She looked up at Sean, who was staring at the symbol with glassy eyes. "Does that sound familiar?"

"I . . . I'm not sure."

"This other one looks like a druidic Triskellion. It represents threeness, which is a common theme in nearly all cultures throughout history. The godhead: Father, Son, and Holy Ghost; man, woman, and child; prelife, life, afterlife; good, evil, man . . . There's hundreds of examples. They are all religious in nature." She smiled playfully. "You didn't go join some cult after the service, did you?"

It was a few moments before he could speak. "I—I don't know." He again pressed his hands to either side of his head and issued a low moan.

"What's wrong, Sean?"

"It hurts to think about it, to talk about initiation and symbols and cults. I don't know. It's like my mind just short-circuits into a headache rather than allowing me to open the topic."

"It *hurts*? You mean actual pain, not just emotional?"

"Yeah. Weird, huh? It's like I blank out with pain, and yet I'm still fully awake."

"Huh. Do you get migraines?" she asked.

"Yeah, I do. All the time, in fact," he said while gingerly rubbing his temples. "But this isn't like that."

"What is it, then?"

He didn't answer. He stared at the tattoos again and poked at them hesitantly, as if he expected them to skitter from his touch. His breathing grew shallow and his brow furrowed.

"Sean?"

"I'm fine," he said flatly. He then stood and began feeding wood into the potbelly stove.

"Sean, I'm just concern—"

"I'm fine," he hissed, moving to the door and exiting the cabin.

Erin sat in a stupor. Her heart went out to the man. There was something about Sean that was intriguing and strong and yet so innocent. He obviously had some inner demons he was fighting. He'd had a rough past and had lost a lot, but he was resilient and seemed to be on top of his challenges. Mostly. His bipolar tendencies concerned her but only superficially. His past was *his* problem, not hers. *No*—she shook her head. *That sounded mean.* Erin was pragmatic enough to understand there was ugly history behind his idiosyncrasies. Yet it was those same idiosyncrasies that had brought him to her rescue.

She rolled her eyes. *Her rescue. Sheesh, that sounded so corny.* But it was a fact. And now he was risking his life to protect hers. Yeah, he had his quirks, but overall she trusted him completely. And the dark hair, pale blue eyes, and crooked smile didn't hurt either. *Sheesh!* She rolled her eyes again but could not stop smiling.

Erin went to the kitchen to make some hot cocoa to calm her worries. By the time it was done, Sean still had not returned. She removed the cocoa from the burner and went to the main room. She remembered seeing a paperback on the hearth. Finding the book, she curled onto the couch and began to read. It was a Dean Koontz thriller. Great! As if this situation wasn't already scary enough.

After two hours, Erin's worries had morphed into cold fear. She decided to go find him. The front porch was empty; the hazy sun was already dropping to the western horizon. Long shadows stretched like black fingers across the canyon. No breeze stirred the skeletal trees or made the pine boughs whisper. The multicolored rock formations stood as rigid sentinels against a densely blue sky. The stillness of the scene was unnerving—almost eerie.

"Sean?" she whispered forcefully.

Looking down the slope of the hill, she saw the Jeep still tucked between the rocks and trees. She leaned against a support pole on the porch, which caused a sprinkling of ice crystals to dust her face and arms. She shivered against the cold but didn't go back inside. Something wasn't right. Sean had acted so strangely just before leaving. She figured he just wanted some fresh air to clear his head—but he had left without his jacket, and he'd been gone so long.

Night was fast approaching.

"Sean?" she whispered again.

Still no answer.

Erin moved down the stone steps while concentrating on any noise that might sound out of place. Perhaps he was sitting in the Jeep, away from the cold. A cup of hot chocolate might be just the thing he—

What was that? A man's voice? Sean's? She wasn't sure. The furtive sound came and went like a breeze. But she knew she'd heard *something*.

The Jeep was empty. She turned and looked up at the cabin. It stood firm and silent in its rocky nook. The face of the wall rose some fifty feet above the cabin. Silhouetted against the hard sky was the form of a man. He stood with his legs spread to shoulder width; one arm was cocked with his hand to his ear, as if talking on a phone. Erin started to wave then caught herself. How did she know it was Sean? From the sharp angle and the backlighting, Erin could not tell if the man was facing her or looking away. If it wasn't Sean, then who was he?

In a panic, Erin sprang up the stone steps and flattened her back against the door, dislodging more ice crystals. Her breathing was raspy; the icy air made it feel like she was inhaling needles. A snap decision had her bolting into the cabin and up to the loft. She scrabbled around the dark space seeking the handgun Sean had given her. She turned the small nook upside-down. Finding nothing, she returned to the main room and searched around the couch and hearth. Still nothing. She had to find that gun! She dashed to the kitchen and checked every cupboard, every drawer. She heard herself whimpering. She was panicking—becoming the flighty woman she swore she'd never be. But this situation was unlike any she'd ever been through before. *Think, Erin! Where was the last place you saw the gun?* The loft. *Check it again.*

She bounded up the stairs and began searching the small area inch by inch.

Just then she heard the cabin door open and shut. She eased to the edge of the loft and looked down.

Sean was staring at her with a look of arrogance, of danger and sadistic humor. In his hand was the Glock 17, pointing at her. "You looking for this?"

Chapter 44

Erin tried to swallow her shock. It was one thing for Sean to hold the gun, but it was totally another to point it at her.

"Yes, as a matter of fact, I *was* looking for that," she said with as much bravado as she could muster. "You went off to who-knows-where, and I wanted the extra protection. Thank you for finding it."

Sean held the gun in a casual stance. His elbow was cocked but loose, his shoulders relaxed. But the 9mm Glock was still pointed at Erin, and his expression was anything but teasing. His look was terrifying.

When he didn't answer, Erin stepped lightly to the stairs and began to descend them slowly. She had no idea who he'd been talking to up on the cliff—or even if that *was* him—nor did she know what had brought on this change in his demeanor. She knew talking about his tattoos had triggered something in him that seemed beyond his control, causing him to act confused and . . . lost. But his current expression was almost predatory; his were eyes focused, dangerous, and yet somehow . . . empty. Plus, the way he'd said, "You looking for this?" had had a dark undertone to it. Staring down the barrel of the handgun convinced Erin that Sean was not in control of his faculties. He was not himself.

Rather than questioning anything that might trigger his anger—or his military reflexes—Erin decided to keep things nonthreatening. "I made some hot cocoa if you'd like something to warm you up." She reached the bottom of the stairs and passed right by him, using all her willpower not to look at the gun. "I sure wish we'd thought to get some grahams and marshmallows and chocolate bars so we could make s'mores."

Sean stayed by the door, his gun still trained on her. As she reheated the cocoa, her eidetic memory brought to mind some of her previous texts:

You can run but you can't hide. —sender unknown
Have you called the police? —Sean. Her answer: *No.*
Family? —Sean. Her answer: *No.*
Is there anyone in Cedar you trust? —Sean. Her answer: *No.*
Do not trust Sean Flannery. —sender unknown

It occurred to her just then that he was making sure no one in Cedar City could come to her aid. His former comments echoed the conclusion. *Don't talk to the police. Don't talk to Tom Jenkins. Don't use a traceable credit card. Disable your GPS so no one can find you.*

Now she was trapped in a cabin no one knew existed—and he was pointing a gun at her.

She stirred the cocoa, refusing to look at him. Her hands trembled uncontrollably. She found herself breathing through her mouth in rapid, staccato puffs. His footfalls steadily headed toward her. Was he pointing the gun at her back? At the base of her neck? Was he planning an execution-style shot? Was he going to knock her out? What did he want from her? Why were they here? She knew there was little she could do to defend herself against him. Her self-defense class had taught her only the basics. Even if he didn't have the gun, she knew he could physically subdue her without a second thought.

"Smells good," he said, only inches behind her.

Erin flinched at the sound of his voice then covered it by claiming some hot chocolate had spilt onto her hand.

"Have a seat, and I'll pour you a cup," she said in forced cheeriness. Her tone sounded so contrived, so obviously fake. He *had* to know she was scared to death. She turned off the burner and stirred the cocoa some more, trying to buy time in which to steady her nerves. When she did turn around, he was sitting at the counter.

She couldn't see the gun.

She grabbed a cup from the sink and slid it in front of him. The thought crossed her mind to toss the hot liquid in his face and make a run for it. *No, that's just silly,* she scolded herself, mentally rolling her eyes. *He'd be on you before you made the door.* She moved slowly as she turned to the sink to retrieve a second cup. Her nerves snapped and sparked like the arcing of a blown electrical circuit. Her thoughts whirled from questions to answers to more questions. Was he really here to hurt her? No. That couldn't be it. He'd opened up his past to her—a painful past at that. *He's risked his life for you. He brought you to his cabin—not to hold your hostage but to help hide you while everything settles down. Stop second-guessing him.*

Is there anyone in Cedar you trust?

"Erin?"

She turned with her cup in hand and offered a halfhearted smile. "Sorry. Wandering thoughts again."

He met her gaze and held it a minute before forcefully rubbing his eyes. He raked his fingers through his hair as if he was trying to pull it out by the roots. In a voice filled with more humanity than it had in the last ten minutes, he said, "I know just what you mean. I think it's time for my meds. I can't seem to focus on anything lately."

Erin nodded and filled his cup. Sean stretched then moved the gun from his lap and to the countertop. She had to force her eyes away from it.

"Thanks," he said, picking up the steaming cup.

"Sure," she answered. After they sipped at their cocoa, she brought the small bag containing his medications from a cupboard. "Which one of these do you need?" she asked, staring at the half dozen or so amber vials in the tote.

"The ones labeled 'Take at bedtime,' I guess, seeing as how I missed my morning meds."

"You guess?" she asked somewhere between disbelief and confusion. "You mean you don't know?"

He shrugged. "I'm not much of a chemist. Maybe you can help me with that."

"O . . . K," she said warily.

Erin dumped the vials onto the counter, wondering what was so difficult about following directions on a label. There were eight vials of varying size. Erin had plenty of dealings with modern pharmacology in her research but not enough to recognize all of the drug names that were on the market, especially the generic names. She immediately noticed they were not all prescription medications. One vial said OMEGA 3 FISH OIL, another BILBERRY EXTRACT, still another DAILY JOINT COMPLEX, which contained glucosamine sulfate and hyaluronic acid. One said CYMBALTA, another ABILIFY, both of which Erin knew were antidepressants. The remaining three were chemical names she didn't recognize. But the drug names were secondary to what really caught her eye: the labels themselves. Instead of being from a mainstream pharmacy like Wal-Mart, CVS, or Walgreen's, these meds were from a place called ProChem Labs, Harrowsmith, Ontario, Canada. There was no address or phone number. Erin knew both criteria were required by law. The labels merely listed Sean's name, the name of the medicine, and how to take the drug. Nothing else.

"These two say take at bedtime," Erin said, gently agitating the Abilify and one of the unknown medication vials.

"Okay," Sean said, pouring himself another cup of chocolate.

Erin opened the vials and shook out the suggested dosing. "So how do you get refills on these? There's no phone number or anything on these labels."

"Oh, they just send them to me. I don't have to ask for a thing. They said it's part of my military retirement package. I think it's pretty slick—one less thing I have to worry about."

Erin simply nodded, but her heart had almost stopped. Sean's erratic moods instantly became crystal clear to her. Sean was being duped. No hospital or pharmacy would simply send out meds without proper identification, contact info, doctor's name, etc. That was illegal. Something was going on that Sean had no clue about.

A curious mix of emotions swept through Erin. She knew Sean was not a threat to her—at least not when he really was Sean. Conversely, when he was under whatever was adversely influencing his mind, he was as dangerous as those chasing her. Yes, she was running for her life. But she was convinced Sean was, too—only he didn't know it.

Chapter 45

Jacob sat alone at the test site gnawing on his black licorice while trying to focus on his mosquitoes. They were hatching like crazy; almost all of the nymphs had molted into adults. By tomorrow morning all his brood would be flying off in search of a blood meal. He'd have to be sure to remember to wear some DEET. He wasn't afraid of contracting the Armageddon virus. He simply didn't want to risk being infected with any number of other bugs the bloodsuckers might be carrying.

He looked to the west. Tall columns of billowing cumulus hovered just above the horizon, obscuring portions of the sun while creating a fresco of rainbow-colored auroras. A thin ribbon of silver outlined each cloud, highlighting the multitextured mass within. It was as if Kapono's Polynesian god Tangaroa was gifting the Ni'ihauans this breathtaking sunset at the same time he was refusing to grant any moisture to their dry island.

Along with the distant beauty, a cooling breeze teased the surrounding vegetation and fluttered Jacob's short hair. If Kaile'e was beside him, he knew he'd be transfixed by how her long tresses would dance with the fluidity of a reed in a meandering brook.

Kaile'e. She was the cause of his trouble focusing on his mosquitoes. So much like Kimberly. Even their initials were the same: KK. Sure, many of their physical traits were different, but overall Jacob could not shake the characteristics that were identical. They would be the same age—had Kimberly lived. They both had dark hair and brown eyes. They both possessed entrancing, dimpled smiles. They were both inquisitive and confident in their ability to learn about things they didn't understand. They were extroverted and unafraid. They were smart and hungered for knowledge. They were adorable, friendly, loving—oh, how he missed Kimberly. Over the past two years he'd been able to build a mental wall around the memory of his daughter. He allowed a few vignettes to filter through but only on rare occasions and only when dealing with basic information about her. If he allowed even a tiny crack in his mental wall, it would burst into a flood of remembrances that would inundate him with sorrow and encase him in a coffin of depression and remorse.

He had been so sure the H1N1 vaccine was safe. Even Erin Cross's data backed up his predictions. If only he'd been allowed to read *all* her notes. He always knew she was keeping something from him. He had tried everything. He showered Erin with attention and praise and gifts. He took her to a classy restaurant. She seemed so willing when he suggested they go back to his apartment. Everyone knows what that usually means. It's the twenty-first century, after all.

Yeah, okay, so he claimed it was to go over a new aspect of their research. But he never said what kind of aspect. Then she punched him in the face. Broke his nose! He'd decided then and there he would do whatever he could to ruin her career—beginning with the H1N1 treatment. He would fast-track it on his own so that he would garner all the accolades. That's why he tested it on his daughter. And she died from it. Clearly, that was the work of Dr. Erin Cross. Kimberly's death was attributed to swine flu complications, but Jacob knew better. Kimberly's blood was on Cross's hands, not his. It was a cloud that darkened his life to this very day.

And yet, just as the waning sunset demonstrated, every dark cloud has a silver lining. Erin Cross's theories were the epiphany Jacob needed to develop Armageddon.

Finally, the time came to test his virus on a large population. It didn't matter who. At least, it didn't matter initially. That was before Kimberly resurrected in the form of Kaile'e Kahuleula. Well, this would be a true test of the vaccine as well as the virus. If she survived, he would adopt her. It was that simple. She would become the reincarnation of the daughter he lost to a similar virus. And this time, there was nothing

Dr. Erin Cross could do about it. *I mean, what can she do if she's dead?* he mused.

He wondered how Kaile'e would feel about changing her last name.

Chapter 46

"I THOUGHT YOU WERE COOL, Docta Brown. I thought we was tight," Kapono grumbled as they sat by the cook fire outside his hut.

"Look, I still don't see what the big deal is. I was watching my mosquitoes hatch, and Kaile'e just showed up. I couldn't leave my research project to run away so there'd be no contact. I'm sorry I talked to her. I'm sorry I broke my promise of no contact. But she came up to me, not the other way around."

The constant badgering Jacob had received ever since he spoke with the little Hawaiian girl was annoying. The whole "no contact" thing was overkill in the first place. He hated being treated like a leper whose lips might fall from his face should he speak to anyone. He thought his presence as the scientist sent to save the islanders from the ravages of West Nile virus would endear him to the people. But that was not the case. They wanted nothing to do with him. Aside from Kapono and Kaile'e, no one on the Forbidden Isle would even make eye contact for very long.

"That not matter, Doc," Kapono continued. "She in big trouble, and da elders are meetin' about whad ta do wid you."

"Well, if they're thinking about tossing me in a volcano, they should know I'm not a virgin," Jacob said with a grin.

Kapono didn't smile. He looked genuinely mad. He paced back and forth around the fire while Jacob sat in his folding camp chair. The Hawaiian was stripped to the waist and wore only a short sarong of tie-dyed cloth. He was sweating profusely—from exertion or the warm night, Jacob couldn't tell. But he was an intimidating sight. His young frame sported muscles Jacob didn't know existed. And the Polynesian tattoos on his shoulders and across his chest and back looked downright menacing in the frenzied pulse of firelight.

"Look, Kapono. I've already said I'm sorry. What else can I do to make it up to you and the village elders?" He had to check his tongue to make sure he didn't slip and say "village idiots."

The stout Hawaiian folded and unfolded his thick arms several times. "I don' know, man. Dey say you should leave. I tol' dem it not a good ting. You have ta finish your work or we will all get sick wid West Nile *gamboo* again."

Actually, just the opposite, Jacob didn't voice.

"I tell 'em I stay by you all da time now. Dey want fish, dey have to fine anudder fisherman, cha? In da meanwhile, dey lock lil' sista in da school."

"What?" Jacob yelled, jumping to his feet, causing his chair to topple back. "You can't lock her up like some criminal. That's illegal and immoral. All we did was talk. She is a very bright girl. She could probably teach your elders a thing or two about science and discovery and—and . . . well, just about anything. You can't punish her for simply talking. There's no law against that."

"Nah nah nah, Doc. It no a punishment. Kaile'e love da school. Dey have cots in der for sleeping an dey feed her good. She jus' there for tonight."

Jacob thought about the dose of vaccine he'd prepared for her back in the hut. How was he going to inoculate her if she wasn't allowed to talk with him anymore? The final molting would be complete by tomorrow. The adult anopheles would be scouring the island of Ni'ihau in search of blood, carrying with them the deadly Armageddon virus. Within seven to ten days, everyone would be infected. Within ten to fourteen days they'd all be dead. If they called for help, there was a chance the virus could spread to the other islands. But that was unlikely. This was the Forbidden Island. No one was allowed here without express permission. After the last of the islanders was dead, he'd take Kapono's tub and travel back to Kauai with Kaile'e. He even entertained the idea of taking the fishing trawler all the way back to California. Anything to get out of flying again. Only, this time he'd have Kaile'e to distract him. She'd probably love flying. They could plan for their future. Jacob would send her to the finest schools, he'd shower her with gifts, he'd give her everything he wanted to give Kimberly but was robbed of the opportunity to do so.

Kaile'e . . . that even sounded a bit like Kimberly.

Chapter 47

Sean handed Erin the Glock. "Take this upstairs with you. I'll stay by the door again tonight."

Even with gun in hand, Erin felt insecure around Sean. He was a ticking bomb with an unreliable timer. Perhaps now that he'd had his meds, he'd stabilize.

"Thanks," she tried to say casually. "Are you sure you don't want to sleep in the loft, and I can take the couch? This place is so isolated I seriously doubt anyone will come barging in during the night. And you do need more rest."

"I'll be fine. Honest."

They sat on the couch, talking softly and watching the pulsing glow of embers in the potbelly stove. They'd had a dinner of tuna sandwiches and tomato soup. They also finished off the Oreos. Erin made a pretense of brushing her teeth with her finger. Why she hadn't thought to grab a toothbrush and toothpaste at the Maverik store she didn't know. Perhaps it was the anxiety of the moment. She also desperately longed for a shower, but, obviously, that would have to wait.

What she really needed was to find out two things: was that Sean she saw up on the ridge, and if so, who was he talking to? She hoped she could field both questions in one. She swallowed back her fear and asked, "So did you get any cell reception up there?"

He nodded happily. "Yes, I did. I was just checking in with Britt."

"Your daughter? How's she doing?" *Keep the mood light.*

He yawned and stretched his legs out in front of him. He looked exhausted. "I asked her that myself. She's got an anthropology exam tomorrow."

"Hey, that's right up my alley," Erin said.

"Yeah, that's what I said. She asked all sorts of questions about you. She said she was impressed."

Erin sat up straight. "You told her about me? I thought we were to remain covert."

"My daughter is in New Hampshire. She's safe as far as this mess is concerned."

Erin considered his words in silence. What he said made sense. His relationship with Britt was endearing—even if it was a bit odd. She forced a smile. "What else did she say?"

"Well, after we discussed you, I asked her to look into Dr. Jacob Krantz and New England Noetics, since they're both from back East, close to where she is. Not to do any real snooping or anything dangerous, of course, just some local inquiries."

"What?" Erin almost shouted. She was astounded he would put his daughter in such jeopardy. What was he thinking? How could he claim Erin's nemesis was a "major player" and then throw his daughter into the fray? From the way he spoke about her, Erin assumed there was a tremendous bond between them—the kind of bond she'd always wanted with her father. She was at once disappointed and angry at Sean. "Tell her not to do it. Please."

"It'll be fine, Erin," he assured her.

"I can't believe you'd get her in the middle of this! What kind of a father are you?"

Sean's eyes hardened. "She's an adult and very headstrong. I've given up trying to tell her *anything*."

Erin met his glacier-cold stare with an icy one of her own. She wanted to retort but she could not form her frustrations into words. Finally she blurted out, "You haven't seen her in years. The next time you do it may be in a casket."

Sean got up and began pacing in front of the door. "What—don't you think I'd love to see her again? Don't you think I still picture her as a little girl I can carry on my shoulders instead of a grown-up twenty-year-old who lives clear across the country?" His voice went from angry to remorseful, etched with pain. "I have asked her countless times to come visit—begged her even. But she never does. Not even at Christmas. She's always too busy, 'but maybe next year,' she says. Do you know how many 'maybe next years' I've agreed to? More than I can count. She says it's nothing to do with me, but I know it is. How would you like to know your father is a hopeless schizophrenic with delusional tendencies? How would you like it if he was a freaking Dr. Jekyll and Mr. Hyde—depending on which pills he'd just swallowed? How—" He suddenly went silent; the pain in his eyes washed out any anger that was there moments before.

Erin's heart went out to Sean, because she could relate so well to what he was saying. How many times had she longed for union with her father only to be shoved aside by a football game? How many times did she hear "maybe next time" when she asked her parents to go to her science fair or some other academic achievement?

"I'm sorry, Sean," she said softly. "That was unfair of me to say."

He stopped pacing but said nothing.

"When was the last time you *were* together?"

The remorse in Sean's eyes was excruciating. "I can't remember," he barely whispered.

"Seriously?"

He nodded.

"That's not right. It seems . . . well, it's just not right."

Erin went to the table and stared at the diagrams once more. Something was churning and tumbling in the back of her mind—an idea spinning around a central focus that would not sharpen into a clear picture. There was a connection in all this, a fundamental hub that radiated spokes to several portions of the story. Why couldn't she see it? Her inability to resolve the conflicts ate at her.

Perhaps it was a good idea to let his daughter turn up some dirt. Maybe it could help. But Erin wanted to make sure she would be extra cautious in her digging. "Sean, may I see your phone?"

He pulled the small unit from his pocket but didn't immediately hand it over. "Why?"

"I want to try to text Britt to tell her to be extra careful."

"I already did that."

"Please, Sean. This'll be from one woman to another."

Slowly, he handed her his phone. Erin flipped it open and cued up the message center. Her eyebrows pulled together. "You said Britt is attending Dartmouth, right?"

"Yes."

"You know I have the ability to memorize facts at a glance, right?"

"Okay?"

"Well, Britt's phone number begins with a 011 39 calling code."

"So?"

"So the area code for Dartmouth College—in fact all of New Hampshire—is 603. This number, 011, is the code used to dial out of the United States. And 39 is the country code for Italy."

Sean's eyes narrowed. His head cocked to one side. "Are you sure?"

"Yes, Sean, I'm sure. I've dealt with enough foreign countries working at TRI and in my own research that I have quite a number of those codes memorized. Do you use a phone service to make international calls?"

"No, never."

"Not even in the military?"

"No. I was under orders to remain anonymous. Besides, I was strictly recon. Communications was left to another guy. I never had to learn those codes."

Erin folded her arms. "Then someone is listening in every time you talk to Britt."

"But I don't ever *talk* to her."

Erin blinked. "But you said—"

"We text. She asked me to text only."

"For four years?" Erin was shocked.

"Even longer." The look of humiliation on Sean's face was devastating. With misty eyes he stared at the floor and shrugged. "Ever since she left with Valerie. That's the way Britt wanted it. I get the feeling she's still mad at me."

She took a few steps toward him. "Mad about what?"

"About the divorce. About my condition, my meds. About everything."

"Is that Britt talking or Valerie?"

"Does it matter?"

Erin felt her temper rising. "When was the last time you actually heard your daughter's voice?"

He moved to the couch and sat on the arm. "I can't remember," he said softly.

"And that doesn't bother you?" Erin was almost yelling now. "As close as you claim to be to her, you can't even tell me when was the last time you told her—not texted, not e-mailed—*told* her you love her?"

"I, um. I'm afraid of pushing her away. Like I did with Valerie."

"That was completely different. Valerie was selfish and uncaring. I'm sorry, but that's the way I see it. She left you to be with her rich sugar daddy doctor because she couldn't handle the fact that her marriage had a few bumps in the road."

"More like deep potholes," Sean said with a half-smile.

"Call it what you like, but I believe it's those potholes that make a marriage strong. The more you put into it, the more you get out of it. Nobody has a perfect life, Sean. You're not perfect; I'm far from perfect. Anyone who claims to be living the dream is talking about a pipe dream. It's not real. What is real is the love of family—of husband and wife, of children, of making things work regardless of the situation. I can't believe you're—" Erin stopped herself and took a deep breath. She had no right to lecture him on family life. Hers had been far from ideal. And here she was almost thirty and still not married or even dating. Who was she to be lecturing anyone?

"You can't believe I'm what?" Sean asked without malice.

Erin grabbed her coat from the wall hook. "I can't believe you're so afraid of your only daughter that you haven't had any *real* communication since she left."

Erin hated herself for saying it so bluntly, but she felt it had to be said. Sean Flannery was a good man—there was no question there.

But he was a man whose past burdened him with more challenges than most people could handle. She knew he had slipped into a comfort zone where the possibility of emotional pain was minimal. But the avoidance of pain did not guarantee happiness. Her own life was proof of that.

"That's not altogether true," Sean said. "If I was afraid, I wouldn't contact her at all."

"I said *real communication*." Erin shook her head and sighed. "Sean, listen. It's easy to write something down but it's not so easy to actually say it. My dad always sends me birthday cards, Christmas cards, and such, and he always writes 'I love you,' but he has never *said* it to me. I—"

She paused again to collect her thoughts. She was rambling and she knew it. She was releasing her own pent-up emotions and she didn't like it. *Dr. Erin Cross is not like that,* she chastised herself. *She is a confident, successful, strong woman. Right. And she is more lonely than she will ever admit.* She suddenly realized with painful clarity she was trying to justify her own wounds by pointing out his.

Sean moved to the kitchen and brought her a paper towel. She didn't even realize she had started to cry.

"Thanks," she said, drying her face and eyes. "I'm sorry, Sean. I didn't mean to . . ."

Sean took her into his arms and held her tightly. He didn't say anything. There probably wasn't anything *to* say. Erin appreciated that. They stood and silently embraced, not in a romantic way but as two people with identical scars who needed the balm of true friendship.

After a time, Sean whispered, "You're right. I need to *talk* to my daughter. Let's go. Right now. Before I change my mind."

Erin looked up at Sean with pain-filled eyes. "Sean, that's what I was trying to get to before I unloaded on you."

He tilted his head. "What?"

"I'm wondering if it's really Britt you've been texting to all these years."

"Oh, come on." He chuckled.

"I'm serious, Sean. Your phone calls are being routed from Italy, not New Hampshire. It could be anyone sending you those texts."

"That's ridiculous. Then whom have I been communicating with?"

She looked at her watch and was shocked to see it was almost midnight. "That's what we're going to find out first thing tomorrow morning."

TUESDAY
NOVEMBER 8, 2011

Chapter 48

THE DAWN SKY WAS PERFECTLY clear as a million stars twinkled their good-byes to the unlikely hikers. Having no cloud cover made the high mountains of Dixie National Forest bitterly cold. Even the dirt was so frozen it crunched under their shoes as they walked.

Plumes of frost billowed from Erin's mouth with each exhalation. She said her skin felt rigid—that it was difficult to form words.

"I—am—so—cold," she whispered.

"Keep walking. Flex your muscles every other step. It'll help," Sean replied quietly. Even though they were in the middle of nowhere, they both felt the need to speak softly.

Sean carried the assault rifle in one hand, the other holding Erin's hand tightly. He chose a path that followed a couple of switchbacks so the climb wouldn't be so grueling. It took nearly an hour, but by the time they crested the ridge, they were both plenty warm. The eastern sky was just turning from deep purple to slate. Everything was ghostly still.

"My sweat is freezing to my face," Erin said. At least she was able to articulate now.

A stiff wind had picked up from the east bringing with it shrapnel-like spicules of ice. Sean led Erin to a stand of Ponderosa pines that sheltered them from the worst of the buffeting. He leaned the rifle against a boulder and pulled out his cell phone. "I got a signal."

"Me, too," Erin said, holding out her phone. "And I have a bunch of text messages. Should I go through them now?"

Sean punched a key. "Yeah, I've got a couple myself. From Britt."

"Well, that takes precedence. Most of these are from my jerk face stalker. They're all zeros."

Sean wanted to use the retrieve function on his phone but he was hesitant. If Erin was correct, and he wasn't really talking to his daughter, then whom was he talking to? He frowned at a headache suddenly building behind his eyes. It didn't seem plausible. He knew how Britt used words, her wry sense of humor; he knew everything about her and she about him. How could the person sending the texts *not* be his daughter? It was crazy. It was ridiculous.

"You think I'm wrong, don't you," Erin said, hugging herself tightly.

He shrugged. It hurt too much to even consider. "I don't know what to think. If you're right, then whom am I communicating with, and what have they done with my daughter?"

Erin slid her hand through the crook in his arm and hugged it. "Can I see?" she asked softly.

Sean opened the phone to her. The incoming number started with the international prefix and the country code for Italy. "That's not from New Hampshire, then, is it?" It wasn't so much a question as a conviction.

Erin shook her head. "I'm so sorry."

"Should I open it?"

"Yes."

He placed his thumb over the key but couldn't depress it. The conflicts tearing his mind apart reached icy claws down to latch hold of his heart. His hand froze, his entire being felt iced over—and it had nothing to do with the weather. His daughter was everything to him. She was the one thing that kept him going day in and day out. It was ridiculous to think it wasn't really her. It had to be Britt. It had to be. The phone number was simply a mistake by the cellular service. *Yeah, that's it.* And yet he could not bring himself to push the key.

He shivered deeply and handed the phone to Erin. "You do it. I . . . I can't."

Erin took the phone and looked up at him. "Remember, Sean, we're in this together."

He nodded and mouthed *thanks*.
She pressed the RETRIEVE MESSAGE key.

Chapter 49

The wind buffeted Erin as she fought to keep from shivering. The sun had just breached the horizon and was trying its best to warm the frozen environs, but with seemingly little success. Erin read the screen on Sean's phone a few times to be sure she understood its meaning. Her college Latin was a bit rusty. "It says, '*Meus cruor pro specialis. Meus corpus pro obsequium. Meus vita pro novus ordo seclorum.*' What do you make of that?"

Sean leaned in closer. "What was that?" The wind whistling through the pines must have made hearing difficult for him.

"It's Latin. It says 'My blood for secrets. My flesh for obedience. My life for the new world order.' Here, take a look." Erin handed him the cell phone.

Sean looked at the screen and frowned. His head gave an odd jerk and he blinked very hard. Erin assumed it was the cold—until he did it again and again and again.

"Sean?"

He didn't answer. He just kept staring at the screen on his phone and doing his odd head snap and forceful blink. In a hollow tone that sounded as if spoken from within a catacomb, Sean said, "*Meus cruor pro specialis. Meus corpus pro obsequium. Meus vita pro novus ordo seclorum.*"

"Yeah. What does it mean?" Erin asked.

Sean's eyes remained fixed on the small screen. It was as if he'd forgotten she was there. His lips moved, mouthing the words with only the slightest plume of breath indicating he was speaking. After reverently repeating the phrase three times, he pressed the REPLY key and began entering text.

Erin leaned her head on his shoulder so she could read what he entered.

Meus vita pro novus ordo seclorum. SEND

"You know Latin?" she asked with unmasked surprise.

He didn't answer. He didn't acknowledge that her head was against his shoulder. Erin realized he must have slipped into an altered state of consciousness.

A moment later, he received a new text.

Hi, Daddy. Your mandate has changed. You are to take Dr. Erin Cross to Kanab Municipal Airport. A jet will be waiting to take you to Las Vegas. The way will be cleared for you. From there you will escort her to Kauai, Hawaii. A helicopter will be waiting to take you to Ni'ihau. Do you understand?

What? Erin was in shock. She looked from the small screen to Sean's face and back. The questions assaulted her. Sean was being ordered to take her to Hawaii? Ordered by whom? What was all the Latin for? And *Daddy*? Why would the sender call him Daddy? Was Britt telling him what to do? Or was it someone *pretending* to be his daughter? Was it the same guy who'd been texting her?

Sean typed, *I understand.*

Erin couldn't breathe. Her mind fought to escape the sticky mire between disbelief and anger—her stomach roiled with feelings of betrayal and duplicity. Someone wasn't simply pretending to be his daughter; they were using the façade of a daughter to forward commands to him. Giamboli's deli, Cedar City Wal-Mart: her *hero* hadn't simply acted out of chivalry; he was fulfilling an order! How long had this been planned? How long had he been watching her, waiting for his chance to *kidnap* her? It was almost inconceivable he'd been lying all this time. Were the stories he told, the tears he shed, just playacting?

The proof was there on his cell phone. She felt belittled, used. She seethed with rage. Her hands trembled uncontrollably. Her vision narrowed on him—the object of her hatred. *We'll give the man an Oscar for Best Actor,* she snarled in her mind. *As soon as he gets out of the hospital!*

Erin lashed out to punch his face, but her movement was stopped by Sean's forearm. His cat-quick reflexes and dominant strength were no match for her attempts to physically vent her anger. She grabbed at his phone, but he held it out of her reach.

"Don't," he said in a flat, hard voice.

"Don't what—use your phone to call the police? To find out who's been texting you all this time behind my back?" She was screaming. "Jerk face! You're working *for* them, aren't you? Aren't you!"

If whoever was looking for her was close at hand, they'd surely hear her. But she didn't care. It didn't matter anymore. She was already caught, ensnared by the man she had believed was her hero. The only man she'd ever let past her bulletproof exterior. She'd opened up to him—and the first thing he did was betray her trust!

She ceased to feel the bite of the cold wind. She felt her knees giving out, and she staggered against a tree. She called Sean names she didn't even know she knew: vile, crude, shocking names. She wanted to run, wanted to hit him again and again, wanted to hurt him with the same intensity that she hurt. But she suddenly had no energy. Every bit of strength was sapped by her emotions. She slumped to the ground and felt tears freeze on her skin.

Sean was fixated on his phone, waiting for a message he somehow knew was coming. When his phone croaked, Erin believed the mysterious entity had changed his mind and had just ordered her execution. Sean studied the screen then calmly typed a reply. She watched him push SEND. He turned to her with an eerily blank expression. And yet there seemed to be . . . what—happiness in his eyes?

His phone croaked again. He pressed a key, nodded to the phone, and entered another set of words. As he pressed the SEND key, he whispered, "Good-bye, sweetheart. Daddy loves you, too."

Chapter 50

Magnus looked down between his feet from the copilot seat in his private helicopter. He loved watching the ground pass by from this angle. It felt like he was walking on air. The terrain under his feet was arid desert with sporadic splotches of green where some industrious farmer tried his hand at turning barren desert into a land of milk and honey. Occasionally, a tiny pocket of civilization would clot around a vein of highway like an ischemia. Other times, a snowcapped mountain peak would pass uncomfortably close beneath the helicopter's skids.

He smiled, thinking how that idiot scientist Krantz would probably have soiled himself by now. Dr. Jacob Krantz had an encyclopedic knowledge of viruses, but what he lacked was a backbone. That's what worried Praefectus Magnus. Even though Krantz had gone through the initiation into Benjamin's Blood and had received the programming given him, Magnus wasn't confident the man would follow through.

Over the years Magnus had noticed one irregularity with implanting command codes into the human brain. It seemed the weaker the mind, the stronger the control. When dealing with someone as smart as Dr. Krantz, it was lucky he'd absorbed any programming at all.

The Praefectus Magnus shifted his gaze from the ground below to his right hand. His tattoos were so meaningful. They represented decades of tradition and secrecy, centuries of knowledge and enlightenment. He wondered if Krantz truly understood their meaning. More to the point, he wondered if the man appreciated what they signified: A new type of leadership. A new way of life. A new world order.

Just thinking of Jacob Krantz gnawed at his spine. Magnus worked hard to control his temper. Frustrations always led to anger, anger to poor judgment. But the scientist had failed to check in again. In fact, he'd only made one contact the entire time he'd been on this assignment. That was unacceptable. What was so hard about sending an update? Just type and send. Imbecile.

Was it a mistake to assign him a task so important? Magnus opened a file on his laptop and scanned the contents. By now he had the prospectus of Krantz's Armageddon virus memorized, but Magnus liked letting his eyes roam the pages of text absorbing the patterns created by words, sentences, and paragraphs. Sometimes the patterns resembled blocks of knowledge randomly metered while elegantly conjoined, like the multicolored tiles in an old-world mosaic. Other times the patterns were serpentine, sinuous, like blood vessels pumping plasmatic information through a body of living text. The patterns in this report were the latter, which seemed enormously apropos. Krantz was testing his designer virus in blood. Or he was *supposed* to be. Magnus didn't know, because the man never checked in.

After about three hours of flight time, Magnus heard his pilot radio for clearance to land at LAX. His private jet, a Global 5000, was waiting to take him to Hawaii. He hated having to micromanage his people. Normally he let decisions and actions run their course. If fate had it in mind to curtail his plans, then it was meant to be. But this assignment was too important to leave in the unpredictable hands of fate—or in the hands of a self-centered scientist. This project had to produce results in his favor. Even a mild success would be welcomed. Then he could begin to pay some of the astronomical debts he'd accrued. Even better, if the field tests proved a complete success, his debts would no longer be a concern. World domination would be within his grasp. He could demand and receive without question.

Magus had it all planned out. A day on the tiny island of Ni'ihau, then, if his subordinate Franklin hadn't done so already, he'd fly back to clean up the mess with Dr. Cross. He closed his eyes and began reciting a mantra of Latin poems to calm his mind. Everything was going to be fine. Soon, he wouldn't have a care in the world. *Because the world will be mine.*

Chapter 51

NEARLY ALL OF THE MOSQUITO pupae had molted into adults and had flown away. A few stragglers hung around the plastic screen box like children afraid to go to their first day of school. That sometimes happens, Jacob reasoned. Although he couldn't fathom why.

The scientist bent over the box with a gleeful smile. "It's okay, little ones. Spread your wings and go infect the world. Make your daddy proud. And rich. And powerful." He started laughing and almost lost his footing in the muck of the lake—which made him laugh even more. He never did like his own laugh. It was low and pulsating, coming out in harsh, bellicose bursts. He sounded like a sinister villain in a cheesy melodrama: squinty-eyed, black top hat, stringy handlebar mustache—someone who cackles maniacally at the thought of kittens drowning, or one who dreams up a way to rid the world of too many warmhearted people.

Oh—wait. He *had* already done that one. He tipped his head back and laughed even more.

"Whad'chu crackin' 'bout, brah?" Kapono asked from the shore line.

When he could speak, Jacob said, "Just having some funny thoughts. Don't you ever just start laughing because you feel like it?"

Kapono gave him a concerned look. "Had an auntie do dat all da time long time back. Dey put her on medication and now she better. Dat what you need, Doc?"

Jacob started laughing again. "Nah nah nah, bro," he said in his best Hawaiian accent. "I got me all da medicine I need for what coming."

Kapono chuckled nervously. "What do ya mean? What be comin'?"

Jacob began sloshing his way back to the shore. "The end of the world, my friend."

The Hawaiian folded his muscular arms then unfolded them. He scratched absently at his cheek, all the while regarding the scientist with a questioning scowl. "You crackin' again, Doc?"

"Oh come on, Kapono. You can't tell me there's no story for the end of the world from Hawaiian folklore."

"Dude, we have plenty dat story. But dey don' scare me like yours do. You soundin' plum crazy, brah. Whad you talkin' 'bout, da end o' da world? You got ta lighten up, cha?"

"Oh, I'm feeling plenty light right now. All my mosquitoes have flow away. That means they survived and will start to feed and spread their dis—" He stopped and feigned a coughing fit. "Ach-*ahem*. Sorry about that. Swallowed wrong. *Ahem*. I mean the *wahiné* mosquitoes won't be making any babies, remember?"

Kapono's face relaxed a little. "Right, right. Now dat was crackin', man." He paused and looked around as if guessing which way the doctor's mosquitoes had flown. "So what you do now, brah?"

Jacob was still bursting at the seams with elation. "Let's get back to Pu'uwai and grab some chow. I'm starving."

Kapono scratched his chin. "It still morning, brah. Didn' you get enough poi for breakfas'?"

Jacob put his hand on the young man's solid shoulder. "Kapono, my friend, poi may be able to carry you through the day, but it passes right through me—if you know what I mean. And even garnished with honey and coconut, I can't quite seem to get over the pasty texture. No offense taken, I hope."

Kapono looked stricken, then slowly his wide, toothy grin broke across his face. He tipped his head back and laughed. "Now dat is righteously funny, dude. You tink *I* eat dat stuff? No way, brah. It be a traditional Hawaiian food but not many Hawaiian go eat it. I give it ta you because I though' you wan' ta taste real Hawaii."

Jacob chuckled sourly. "If I hadn't actually eaten that revolting stuff, I'd think that was funny, too."

Kapono clapped Jacob on the back. "Come wid me, brah. We go

fishin' and catch some mahi-mahi or swordfish for lunch, cha? Den we eat like kings."

The scientist looked back at the mostly submerged box and decided there wasn't much more he could do now except wait. He was supposed to send information on the progress of the molting, but what did it really matter? Even his superior could do nothing until the virus took hold and islanders started dying.

Walking four hours to the south end of the island just to send a one-line message seemed like such a waste. What could Mendenhall do with the information, anyway? He was almost three thousand miles away.

"That sounds great," Jacob said, popping a licorice nib in his mouth. "We can consider it a last meal of sorts, cha?"

Kapono gave him a quick, confused glance then echoed, "Cha."

Chapter 52

BACK IN THE CABIN, SEAN moved with measured efficiency. He created small groups of all his belongings, grabbed his three duffel bags, and began stuffing the materials inside.

"Get your things packed," he said flatly.

Erin moved as if in a dream—languid, unhurried, yet with a sense of desperation. She had resigned herself to her destiny—whatever that may be—but was not going to give up just yet. An unresolved quandary kept her mind in a vortex. The gunman in Giamboli's had quoted a Latin phrase. She could swear it had something to do with a new world order: *novus ordo seclorum*. It was the same phrase Sean had used. And yet Sean had stopped the gunman from killing her. She initially thought they were on the same team, but now she wasn't so sure. Why would one man kill the other if they were striving for the same goal?—*her* death.

Entangled in a vast web of confusion, she saw no way to break free. All she could do was obey and perhaps prolong the inevitable. If Sean was going to kill her, there was nothing she could do about it. She climbed to the loft and looked around before she realized she was wearing every bit of clothing she owned. Peering over the ledge, she saw Sean checking the magazines of each of his guns. He was in his Special Ops mode. She'd seen him like this before: focused, unerring, lethal.

Her eyes narrowed as a new thought came to her. She *had* seen him like this before, a number of times. And each time she had, she assumed he was simply haunted by his past. More importantly, she had unwittingly talked him out of each episode. She wondered if the Latin primer would work in reverse.

She took several calming breaths and descended the stairs. Reaching the bottom tread, she cleared her throat and said, "*Meus cruor pro specialis. Meus corpus pro obsequium. Meus vita pro novus ordo seclorum.*"

He spun around—one hand out in front of him for balance, the other notched behind his back, undoubtedly gripping the gun tucked back there. His stare was cold and calculating.

Erin continued as if nothing was wrong. It was the most difficult thing she'd ever done. "You are no longer required to take me to Kanab as previously ordered."

The gun came out, was steadied by the other hand, and was pointing at her faster than she could blink. "Don't," Sean said in a hard, explosive bark.

Erin froze. *Okay, maybe not.* "It's okay, Sean. It didn't mean anything." She spoke softly and easily. *Keep it positive.* "You know, I'm actually kind of excited about getting out of here. And I've never been to Hawaii before. I wonder what it's like this time of year." She walked slowly past him and began emptying the cupboards. There wasn't much left. "We should take this stuff with us so it doesn't spoil and stink up the cabin, don't you think?"

Sean still followed her every move with granite eyes and the pointed gun, but his shoulders seemed a little more relaxed.

"You want me to douse the coals in the stove?" she asked lightly.

He blinked a few times, lowered the gun, then nodded. "Okay."

"Okay. Should I dump the ashes or just leave them inside?"

It took a few seconds for him to answer. His eyes flickered to various points around the cabin. "Dump them."

"Sure, Sean. Where?"

He shook his head and let his arms slowly fall to his sides. "Um, hang on a sec." He stuffed the gun behind his back and moved to the kitchen. In a cupboard next to the stove he removed a large red metal can marked FLAMMABLE. "Scrape it all in here. We'll dump it down by the stream."

His voice sounded almost normal again. Erin didn't allow herself to relax. This was a little like running a psychology experiment—except that instead of pass or fail for a grade, it was pass or die.

They packed their belongings, secured the cabin, and were in the Jeep within thirty minutes. The sun was painting the canyon bright yellow, highlighting the red and orange stone. The temperature was approaching forty. Wisps of steam rose from sandstone formations like genies released from magic lamps. Yet in spite of the beautiful surroundings, Erin saw little of it. She kept her eyes peeled for any sign of someone watching them—and on Sean.

After a few minutes of driving, Sean asked, "What's wrong?" His tone was surprisingly lighthearted.

"Whoever was after me is probably still out there, right?" She knew she had to tread carefully with her questions. Anything could trigger another episode where his mind block would take over. That's what it had to be—a mind block: a subconscious programming that turned him into an automaton. She knew such things were possible, although they were considered highly unethical. She'd never experienced anything like it firsthand, but she was convinced that a mind block was exactly what Sean was dealing with. The obvious trigger was that phrase in Latin. She'd look into that one later when she had a chance. *If* she had a chance.

Sean leaned forward to look at the sky through the windshield. "Yeah, probably. It's the helicopters I'm worried about. Once we're back on the highway we'll be okay."

Erin was about to ask about the police APB on her, and most likely on Sean's Jeep, but she didn't want to slip into dangerous conversational territory. Then again, why not? Before she knew Sean was involved, she'd asked whatever she wanted. The worst thing that happened was he slipped into a funk for a while then would bounce right back. Well, she'd read the message he received from his "daughter." She said the way would be cleared. If Sean trusted in that assurance, she would too.

They covered the trail faster than they had last time. Then again, the last time was in the middle of the night. When they came to the sheer embankment, it didn't look as bad in the day as it did at night—until they drove up it. Sean dropped the Jeep into low gear and assaulted the slope, and Erin found herself staring into a partly cloudy sky. As they crested the ridge and dropped down the other side, Sean let out a gleeful *wheeeee!* The sound Erin made was anything but gleeful.

They made the highway in roughly thirty minutes. It was perfectly devoid of traffic. Sean drove past the Maverik and the diner, and came to the intersection of Highway 14. Instead of heading toward Cedar, Sean turned left heading toward Duck Creek Village then onto Highway 89. Then south toward Kanab near the state line. They traveled unmolested the entire route, passing only an occasional RV or minivan. The way *had* been cleared. *How much power do these people have?* Erin wondered.

Just as they entered Kanab, Sean's phone croaked.

"Here, check this, please," he said, handing his phone to Erin.

Wait. He knew she knew about him. He *had* to know. She'd read the last transmission. He saw her do it. So why was he trusting her with whatever message was coming across? Perhaps . . . perhaps he *didn't* know. At least not while he wasn't in his alter ego. Did that mean his trance had worn off? Was there a time frame associated with each primer?

She pushed VIEW.

Meus cruor pro specialis. Meus corpus pro obsequium. Meus vita pro novus ordo seclorum.

"What's it say?"

Erin cleared her throat. "Um, it's from your daughter."

"Oh, really?" The joyous surprise in his voice saddened her. "What's she say?"

She typed, *Meus vita pro novus ordo seclorum.*

The reply came. *Hi, Daddy. Your plane is waiting at hangar five. It is imperative you keep Dr. Cross safe. Her life is in danger. Do you understand?*

Erin took a steadying breath. "She says they've already had a foot of snow at Dartmouth."

Sean chuckled. "She's always loved the snow. I bet she's happy. Tell her we haven't had much snow yet."

"Okay."

She typed, *I understand.*

Erin wanted to ask the sender some questions that might reveal who they were. But the line went dead. Erin considered giving Sean false directions, saying that Britt told him to drive to the police and turn himself in. Then she remembered they were being tracked. How else would they know they'd arrived in Kanab? If Sean didn't do exactly as they commanded, they'd know he'd been compromised. Then they would both be killed. Curiously, Sean didn't even blink at the mention of his daughter. He honestly believed she had mentioned the snow. Erin didn't think he was acting either. If she played along, she might have a better chance of escaping later on. After all, they commanded him to protect her because her life was in danger. Maybe they weren't the same ones who wanted her dead. Maybe they—

Sean glanced over at her. "Did you send it?"

"Yeah. She, um, she must have hung up."

Sean chuckled again. "Yeah, she sometimes does that. She says she gets busy or her battery goes dead a lot. It's okay."

Erin smiled and slipped his phone in her pocket. "So what do we do now?"

"We go to the airport," he said as if it were the most obvious answer in the world. "We have a plane to catch."

Even in his normal state, his subconscious still remembered the previous command.

Chapter 53

Magnus boarded his Global 5000 from a terminal reserved for private jets at LAX. His pilot welcomed him aboard, and a buxom flight attendant offered him a brandy as soon as he was seated. A copilot was the only other person in the aircraft.

"What's our ETA, Justin?" Magnus asked the pilot.

The young man turned to answer. He had a lean, chiseled look and a perpetual two days' growth of beard. "We should arrive in Kauai around 1500 hours, Pacific Time, sir."

"Ah. Excellent," the Praefectus Magnus said as he swirled his snifter.

The flight attendant brought him a tray of pecans baked in caramelized sugar and dusted with cinnamon. Magnus knew he should not indulge his sweet tooth so much. But the combination of dry brandy and the sweet nuttiness of the cinnamon-sugar pecans was a temptation beyond compare. He reclined in his seat and watched a sixty-inch plasma screen broadcast four different satellite channels at once: CNN, Bloomberg, MSN, and Fox Reality. The first three kept him abreast of news and financial doings around the globe. He viewed the last as a reminder of how superior he was to the rest of humanity. Well, the rest of the United States, anyway.

"Oh, Natalie," he said to the attendant.

She turned from talking with the pilot and sauntered up to him. "Yes, sir?"

"What do we have for our lunch this afternoon?"

She presented a choice of three dishes, each of which would cost close to two hundred dollars at a five-star restaurant. Magnus wouldn't have it any other way. If he was to represent the embodiment of perfection, then what he put into his body should be no less perfect.

As they taxied to their runway, he created a mental list of ways he could eliminate Dr. Krantz once the test results proved positive. The man was an annoyance. A necessary one for now, but an annoyance nonetheless.

Magnus booted up a notebook and reviewed all the data he had on Krantz. Bachelor's degree from Brown University, PhD in infectious diseases from Duke, employed with Dow Chemical for five years, and the Centers for Disease Control for three. Recruited to Timpanogos Research Industries by himself, worked there a year before working on Armageddon. An impressive education, but the man had his foibles. Before his recruitment, he had lost more than $90,000 in Atlantic City, $120,000 in Las Vegas, and close to $200,000 with online gambling sites. It was easy for Magnus—then Luther Mendenhall—to impress the misguided scientist with showings of opulence and decadence. The young Krantz had an alcoholic wife who disdained him and vice versa. He kept saying when he made his big break then he'd retire, divorce his lush of a wife, and spend the rest of his life traveling.

Then Luther told him about the marvelous plans of the Benjamin's Blood Order: bold plans, daring projects, all with phenomenal potential for wealth and power. Krantz had joined immediately and participated in the initiation rites and secret combinations. He loved the idea of the tattoos but never caught on that they meant anything other than signifying his place in the Order. After his initiation, Luther Mendenhall became Magus to the scientist. A new relationship began, one of obedience and submission. As long as he was provided with funding and state-of-the-art facilities, he didn't seem to care where his research would lead. In fact, the more insidious it became, the more he enjoyed it.

Magnus transferred Krantz to TRI to combine forces with another brilliant researcher. He was to learn from her and, if possible, convince her of the potential of their Order. But Dr. Cross had spurned him. She wanted nothing to do with his secret life and twisted plans for the future. But it wasn't a total loss. Krantz was able to glean enough from Dr. Cross to develop his Armageddon virus. Of course, he also lost his beloved daughter through oversight. Magnus deemed it an acceptable loss.

Now Krantz was on some tiny island in the middle of the Pacific testing the virus on an unsuspecting population. Only, he was not following protocol as he'd been instructed. Again!

Magus drained his brandy. Stewardess Natalie was at his side with a decanter before he finished his last gulp. At least some of his staff was efficient. Some didn't need constant reminders and micromanaging. He swirled his snifter, watching the liqueur change colors as it thinned out along the upper edge of the vortex. *Now, how to eliminate one parasite after he's perfected a new one?*

He smiled and allowed himself a brief chuckle. *Oh, the cleverness of me.*

Chapter 54

"I wonder where we're supposed to go," Sean said as they drove down Kanab Road.

"From what I can see, we don't have many options," Erin said, looking out the window at the single runway facility.

Even though the municipal airfield was quite small, Sean still approached it as if he was lost. His eyes darted back and forth, his foot repeatedly tapped the brake, and he nervously tapped a rhythm on the steering wheel as if he were a boy approaching a first date. Erin knew he'd received a command to take her to the Kanab airport, but only she knew exactly where.

As they entered the airport parking lot, Sean came to a stop. His head repeatedly turned right and left, searching for something that would give him a clue. Erin figured she would just remain silent and see what happened. But as he continued to seek for a sign, his anxiety grew exponentially. Beads of sweat formed on his brow and upper lip. His hands quivered and tapped the steering wheel with greater intensity. Even his breathing became shallow, reduced to tight, wheezing gasps. She hated seeing him like this. It wasn't his fault. He'd been duped, programmed into false memories of a life he believed was real but that was riddled with fabrication. She wondered just how much of what he believed was actual fact.

"Where should we go now?" he asked in a voice fraught with anxiousness.

Sean had to be working for someone with phenomenal power and influence—but whom? And why had they asked him to escort her to Kauai as her bodyguard? She wrestled with a strange mix of emotions, tugged between feeling threatened and protected by the same individual. But if Sean was programmed to protect her, then she knew he would do everything in his power to make sure she was safe. If whoever was controlling him wanted her dead, she wouldn't have left the cabin alive.

"Most of the airplanes are over there," Erin said, pointing toward a row of corrugated metal hangars. "Let's go there and see what we find."

Sean nodded and hit the accelerator, visibly happy to be doing *something*.

Hangar five was at the end of the row. Erin was astounded at the plane that awaited them. Gleaming on the tarmac like a showroom model was a white Gulfstream G650. She remembered reading about the plane while traveling to a public health conference in Miami last year. It was the largest and fastest commercially available private jet on the market. But at nearly sixty million each, its price tag made it well beyond most company budgets. The photos she'd seen looked a little different than the plane standing before them.

"Nice ride," Erin said as they approached the plane. "Are you sure this is our flight?"

"No," he said before parking the Jeep beside the hangar.

A tall man in a black, Italian-cut suit and sunglasses approached the Jeep. Panic gripped Erin's chest, but she fought it back. Sean stepped out of the Jeep and placed his hand on the gun at the small of his back. The tall man stopped a few feet away and held up his hands in a truce.

"Who are you?" Sean demanded.

"*Meus cruor pro specialis. Meus corpus pro obsequium. Meus vita pro novus ordo seclorum,*" the man quoted.

Sean's head twitched a bit before his hand dropped from behind his back. The tall man then held out his fist, showing Sean the gnostic tattoos on his knuckles.

"*Meus vita pro novus ordo seclorum,*" Sean said evenly as he stepped up and touched his knuckles to the man's like two high-schoolers expressing camaraderie.

The man in the Italian suit then leaned into the Jeep. "Dr. Erin Cross?"

Erin felt the blood drain from her face. She nodded.

"My name is Timothy. Come with me, please," he said, turning and walking toward the private jet.

Erin slowly stepped out of the Jeep, surprised that her legs could support her. There was nothing between her and several cars in a parking lot a few yards away. She could run and scream for help. With the Jeep between her and the hit man, there was time. But she knew it would be a waste of energy. They had caught up with her. Sean was on their side. There was nothing she could do but obey.

She followed behind Sean as another man in black Armani unloaded their belongings from the Jeep and carried them to the jet. She ascended the retractable staircase numbly. For some macabre reason she pictured herself climbing the stairs to a gallows. Neither she nor Sean had to duck inside the spacious Gulfstream. It was opulent to an extreme. A generous seating area featured six wide seats: the four in front were able to swivel to face each other, the two in back also swiveling to face either forward or in toward the aisle. The back wall held a wet bar, a large flatscreen TV, and a door to the back portion of the plane. A very handsome flight steward greeted her and indicated the seat she was to occupy.

Sean sat across from her as she was buckled in by the attendant. "Too tight?" he asked very kindly.

Her lips formed the word *no*.

"Can I get you something to drink?"

She shook her head.

The young man stood and flashed a warm smile. "I'm John. If you change your mind or need anything, please don't hesitate to ask. If I'm in the back, just push that blue button on your armrest. Welcome aboard, Dr. Cross."

Erin tried to smile back. It felt like a grimace.

Sean seemed to be taking everything in stride. His face was impassive but not hypnotized. Timothy sat in the chair in front of hers. The man with the luggage stowed it in a closet then moved to the seat behind her. There was no one else on board. She assumed a captain and copilot were behind the paneled doors at the cockpit.

Steward John drew up the stairs and sealed the door then took a seat behind Sean's. The two jet engines whined to a high-pitched whistle. Timothy swiveled his seat so he was facing Erin. He removed his sunglasses and slipped them in a pocket. He was a good-looking man with a lean face and kind eyes. He leaned forward and clasped his hands together. Erin noticed he bore knuckle tattoos like Sean's.

"Dr. Cross. Let me first apologize about all the cloak-and-dagger proceedings. As soon as we are airborne, I will fill you in on everything. For now, let me assure you, you are in safe hands. We are not the men who have been trying to kill you."

"Who are you, then?" Erin asked, surprised that she'd found her voice.

The man smiled softly. "All in good time, Doctor. Please try to relax." He glanced out a window. "Ah, we are lining up for takeoff now."

Erin barely felt the motion as the plane taxied, so smooth was the ride. "Can you tell me where we are going?" she asked, already knowing.

"I promise to answer all your questions in just a moment," Timothy said. "This plane is modified for our unique needs. It has a very short takeoff and landing profile. It can be quite frightening or thrilling depending on your temperament. Now, lean back and enjoy the ride."

As Timothy spun back to facing forward, Erin saw he was wearing an earpiece to keep him in constant contact with others of his ilk. She could only guess who they might be. Still, the interior of the jet was comfortable and not unfriendly. So far, everyone on board had soft smiles, caring eyes, and gentle voices.

The engine whine rapidly increased, and she felt the fuselage tremor slightly. Suddenly she was pressed back into the seat as the plane shot forward with meteoric velocity. They were airborne in seconds and were heading skyward at an alarming angle.

After a few minutes of sheer terror, the plane leveled out, and she heard the soft conversations of the men behind her. Steward John left his seat to lower a narrow table from the wall next to Erin and placed two bottles of Italian water in the inset cup holders. He then set glasses of ice and cloth napkins beside the bottles, bowed, and did the same for Sean before backing away.

Timothy swiveled his seat around, opened his water bottle, and poured a portion in his glass. "Now," he said in way of a preamble, "where to begin?"

Chapter 55

THE MORNING'S FISHING WAS GOOD. Kapono caught four mahi-mahi, one of which weighed almost forty pounds. Jacob came back with a small sailfish and a yellowfin tuna. He had hooked a mahi-mahi but couldn't hold onto it—he didn't have the strength.

"*Mahi* mean 'strong' in da King's lingo," Kapono explained. "Dey fight so much we call 'em *very strong*: mahi-mahi. Dat why dey have so good meat, cha? Best-tastin' fish in da sea. Don' feel bad you loss yours, brah. Lotta *haole* can't land 'em. Dey 'bout as big a fight you can get oud here."

"What about a marlin?" Jacob asked.

"Yah yah yah, da marlin a good fight, too. But dey fight on da surface, cha? Da mahi-mahi fight from below. Dat make 'em harder to land, for sure."

They made it back to the small dock by two o'clock, and by then, Jacob was starving. Kapono had him haul a twenty-pound mahi-mahi and his tuna to his shack while he presented the other three mahi-mahi to the village elders. He insisted Jacob throw the sailfish back just after he landed it. Apparently it was some kind of deity to the people of Ni'ihau. He was in such a good mood, he didn't argue. Besides, the people of Ni'ihau would soon meet their deity anyway—as if such a thing existed.

Jacob placed the fish on a stone block next to Kapono's cook pit. He stepped back and stared at them. The tuna looked the same as when he pulled it in, but the mahi-mahi had turned a mottled, unappetizing color. When Kapono landed it, the fish was downright breathtaking.

The iridescent brilliance of its blue, yellow, and green scales reflected the sun in prismatic splendor. Within a few seconds, however, its shimmering body had begun to fade. By the time they got back to shore, most of the blue and green dazzle had muted to shades of gray. He assumed the flesh inside was still edible, yet he was hesitant to cut into it. He wasn't squeamish by any means; he simply didn't know how to gut a fish.

"You want me do dat?" a young voice asked.

Jacob jumped, issuing a high chirp of fright. Kaile'e stood directly behind him, wearing a bright-print muumuu and a wide smile.

"Don't you ever make any noise when you walk?" Jacob asked after he caught his breath.

"No. Kapono say I am *palu makani,* da soft wind."

"You mean you're like a breeze?" Jacob corrected.

"No. I am not *like* a breeze. I *am palu makani.* There be big diff'rence, ya know?" Not waiting for an answer, the little girl went into Kapono's hut and returned with a thin boning knife. She immediately set to work slitting the belly of each fish and placing the entrails on a broad leaf. "You should stir da coals. Get the fire breathin' again. These gotta be cooked right away."

Jacob used a stick to agitate the coals to life. He added some more wood from a nearby pile and coaxed a nice flame.

"Nah nah nah, Doc. You don't need dat big flame. We not sacrificin' nottin' ta Pele. We jus' cookin' da fish." She took the stick from Jacob's hand and pushed the larger chunks of burning wood to the side of the pit.

The scientist stepped back and watched the efficiency of the young Hawaiian girl. She breezed so effortlessly between her tasks . . . it was almost as if her feet never touched the ground. No wonder her brother called her a soft wind. It would be a shame to let that wind be a carrier of his deadly virus. While Kaile'e continued to prepare the meal, Jacob returned to the hut, stepped over Pegasus, and scrounged through his gear until he found the vial of Armageddon vaccine. He had plenty—just in case.

Jacob knew it had yet to be tested on children, but he didn't think that would be an issue. After all, they gave vaccines to infants all the time.

Why should his be any different? He'd even inoculated himself with no ill effects. He filled a syringe and returned to the cook pit.

"Kaile'e, I need to talk to you," he said in a tender yet serious tone. It surprised him how much his throat suddenly felt constricted with emotion.

"Say whad you wan' ta say, Doc." She kept her attention focused on preparing the fish, trimming the fins and heads.

"Something bad is going to happen soon that I want to protect you from."

She gave a light laugh. There was a musical lilt to it. "Lots of bad things happen, Doc. Life be boring widout dem, cha? You can't protect from every bad ting dat happen."

"True. But this bad thing *is* avoidable."

She paused from wrapping the fish in banana leaves and looked up. "Whad you talkin' about, Doc? You sound sad."

Jacob couldn't shake the image of Kimberly from his mind. "Everyone is going to get sick. Very sick. It's the mosquitoes, you see. They are carrying a very bad virus. They—"

Before Jacob knew what was happening, Kaile'e had her arms wrapped around his waist. "It's okay, doctor man, you here ta help my family and my people. Dat's all dat matter."

He reached down to stroke her hair. If speaking with the native girl was a misdemeanor crime, touching her was surely tantamount to a felony. He didn't care. Seeing only the top of her head, it was easy to imagine it was his daughter hugging him. Old emotions took over; he felt a wave of warmth radiate throughout his body, softening his heart. Calcified knots of bitterness over losing Kimberly dissolved in Kaile'e's embrace. Urges for revenge subsided—his resentful vows sweetening into gifts of forgiveness. It was a sign.

"It's okay, Kimberly. I won't let anything happen to you," he whispered. He kept one arm around the little girl as his free hand slipped into his pocket. His fingers coiled around the syringe and withdrew it.

"You always crackin', Docta Brown. You know my name is Kaile'e Kahuleula," she said, twisting slightly against his hold.

The clarity of her statement didn't pierce the transcendent euphoria he was in. "Kimberly, listen to me." His voice caught just shy of a sob.

He swallowed to clear it. "I love you so much, and I am so, so sorry about what happened last time."

Kaile'e squirmed. "Let me go, Docta Brown. I need to finish cooking da fish."

"No. You need to hold still," he said firmly. Using his teeth, he uncapped the syringe and poised it at her bare shoulder. "It'll hurt more if you keep moving."

Kaile'e was fighting now, trying to wedge her elbows between them to push away. "Let go me, Docta Brown. I don' know what you talk 'bout."

"I'm talking about saving your life, Kimberly. I'm sorry your family will die. It's necessary to prove the power of my virus. But you will live. I promise."

Kaile'e twisted violently. "Stop it!" she shouted.

Jacob struggled to hold her with one arm while lining up the needle with the other.

"Hold still, Kimberly. You're making me angry."

"Let go me!" she yelled. "I not Kimberly."

"Yes, you are. You're innocent and young, and I am here to save—"

"Whad's goin' on here?" Kapono's voice sounded a few feet behind him.

Quickly, he rammed the needle into Kaile'e's shoulder and depressed the plunger. The girl screamed. Jacob felt a powerful grip land on his shoulder and spin him around. Kaile'e collapsed in a heap.

"She's very sick," he said quickly. "I'm giving her something to make her better."

The fire in Kapono's eyes was unmistakable. His right arm was held slightly out and back, as if he was ready to slam his stonelike fist into Jacob's face.

"Please, help me get her into the hut. I need to . . . to check her vital signs." Jacob was making it up as he went, but he hoped the simple— *but large*—Hawaiian couldn't tell.

Kaile'e moaned and twisted on the ground. Kapono's eyes immediately softened. He picked her up and took her to his cot in the hut. Jacob was right behind. He grabbed a bottle from his kit and poured a generous amount into the wadded folds of an old rag.

"Hmm, that's odd," he said, holding it away from himself. "This doesn't seem like the right stuff."

Kapono drew near. "Whadsamadda, Doc?"

He handed the rag to the Hawaiian. "Here, take a deep sniff of this and tell me if it smells like chloroform to you."

Kapono complied without hesitation. He took a huge inhalation, winced, shook his head, and took a second. His head began to weave. A moment later a glassy vacancy filled his eyes. The rag fell to the ground—followed immediately by Kapono.

If you knew what chloroform is, you wouldn't have smelled it, Jacob thought with a sneer. *What a simpleton. You deserve what's coming.*

Chapter 56

The Global 5000 arrived in Honolulu just after two o'clock, Pacific Time. As the pilot saw to the refueling of his jet, Magnus got out to stretch his legs. Leaving the air-conditioned interior of his plane, he drew a quick breath as he hit a wall of humidity. Growing up on the East Coast, he figured he should be used to humidity. But he had grown so accustomed to the dry air of Utah that he'd forgotten how ambient mugginess made you feel like you were sweating even when you weren't. He gazed up at the lush, green mountains of Oahu and knew they owed part of their beauty to the humidity. So it wasn't all bad.

Captain Justin approached him with his hat in one hand and a clipboard in the other. "Excuse me, sir. Would you care to take in a restaurant while we wait?"

Magnus could tell his pilot was stalling. "Why? How long does it take to refuel the jet?"

"That takes less than an hour. It's just that the grade of jet fuel this Global uses is not readily available at HNL."

Incompetence! He was surrounded by incompetent people. That's why he had to micromanage everything. "Did you not call ahead to have the requisite fuel ready?"

The pilot bristled. "Of course I did, sir. But you did not schedule this flight with a proper notification window. As you know, all overseas flights require advanced logging of flight plans and proper documentation with the FAA and Homeland Security. We took off—"

"Do not lecture me!" Magnus yelled directly in the man's face. "I am well aware of the requirements for filing flight plans. It is *your* responsibility to see that they are done in the time frame *I* need. Are telling me you failed doing your job properly?"

Magnus could see the muscles flex in the man's jaw as he clenched his molars. "I know how to do my job, sir," he responded in an even tone. "As I said, the fuel is not readily available, but it is on the way. I secured the necessary amount from Pearl Harbor Naval Base. The tanker truck was supposed to be here when we arrived. When I learned that it wasn't, I immediately called the base. There was a hold on the paperwork until the authorization of credit went through. They said your corporate credit is—"

"I don't want a sob story, Captain. I want results!" Magnus didn't need to hear about his credit woes, especially from a subordinate. If his people would simply perform the way they were supposed to, he would not have so many problems. Magnus took a long, steadying breath and pressed his fingertips against his temples. "Just tell me when the gas will get here."

"Jet fuel, sir," the man said with continued evenness. "And they said it'll be here in under an hour."

Magnus nodded and gazed back at the verdant mountains, hoping to absorb some tranquility from them. "Thank you, Captain. I will be back in one hour."

"Very good, sir."

The Illuminate headed toward the private terminal reserved for executives and heads of state. On the way he checked his phone. Still no contact from that stupid scientist. For someone so smart, he sure was an insufferable idiot. But that would change before the day ended. He'd personally make sure of that.

Chapter 57

Erin glanced over at Sean several times during their flight over the Pacific. He was either extremely tired, or the water they served him was drugged. He had put on headphones, drunk half the bottle of water, and fallen asleep somewhere over the California coastline.

True to his word, mystery man Timothy didn't beat around the bush. He explained very plainly that they were agents of a secret brotherhood known as the Knights of Canterbury.

"As in Chaucer's *Canterbury Tales*?" she asked.

"Good heavens, no," the well-dressed man said. "We were formed from the original group of Gregorian missionaries sent to England around AD 600 at the request of Augustine of Canterbury."

Erin recognized the name but had heard they were mostly a defunct cult of would-be omniscients and hopeful omnipotents similar to the Illuminati. Tales of the ancient order were the fodder of conspiracy theorists worldwide.

"Yeah. I've seen conspiracy theory programs about you guys on the History Channel," she quipped glibly. "They list all sorts of anecdotal evidence and speculate till they're blue in the face, but they always end with the words, 'We may never know.'"

Timothy laughed warmly. "And that's precisely the way we like it. The world views conspiracy theorists as having a form of paranoid psychosis. The incredible thing is how close many of them come to the truth. You see, Augustine's missionaries were led by a man named Justus. He was selected by the archbishop because he possessed a unique collection of books and manuscripts that taught doctrines not found in Constantine's Bible. The St. Augustine Gospels is considered to be the only remaining Justinian manuscript and is now housed at Cambridge. In reality, all but one of the manuscripts still exists."

"Let me guess: they say you have a divine charge to rule the world."

Timothy frowned in a way that held more compassion than censure. "Our charge is as *guardians* of truth. We're not missionaries or mercenaries or even saviors. Let me explain. Throughout the ages, many secret groups have claimed to hold the complete truth when in reality they only had bits and pieces. You've heard their names: the Knights Templar, the Priory of Sion, the Illuminati. They are typically led by men who have deluded ideals and visions of ultimate power. As I said, such is not our purpose. We are merely here to *protect* higher knowledge and understanding. Whether you believe that or not is inconsequential, although we hope our actions will prove us out. You see, we have seen time and again instances where such delusional groups cause unspeakable damage and heartache. While we are not charged to prevent such atrocities, there are times when intervention is deemed prudent, especially when it comes to maintaining our anonymity." He paused and took a sip of water. "Do you understand thus far?"

"I think so," Erin said, disgusted by the quaver in her voice. "You assassinate people to remain secret."

Timothy's silent stare confirmed her statement, although the look in his eyes belied a surprising amount of chagrin.

Looking at Sean, Erin's frustration overpowered her fears. "So why trouble with the charade? Why taunt me with childish theatrics? Why don't you guys just kill me and get it over with?"

Timothy's expression changed to dismay. "That was not us, Dr. Cross. The threats you've been receiving have been from the other guys—one of the factions I mentioned—a brotherhood called Benjamin's Blood. I'll delineate their history if you like, but it is not germane to why they have targeted you. We're here to put an end to their efforts, hopefully before they succeed," he said with a wink.

She raised an eyebrow skeptically. "Funny. Isn't that exactly what the other guys would say about you?"

"Excellent point," he admitted. "You are a very brilliant scientist, Dr. Cross. I can see why the other faction has expressed such concern over you."

"But why me?"

"They are threatened by your intelligence, especially your research on viruses. More to the point, your inside knowledge of Dr. Jacob Krantz's research."

"Jacob Krantz? I thought as much."

"Yes. But this has little to do with your H1N1 research or your malaria vaccine."

Erin's jaw dropped.

Timothy laughed kindly. "Yes, we know about both areas of your work, Doctor. And we regard both as humanitarian and very noble. I believe the concern lies more with Dr. Krantz's other work. Are you aware of his spinoff project?"

"I've had my suspicions. And I have his notes," she confirmed, running a finger over the flash drive in her pocket.

"It is to be a doomsday weapon," Timothy said. "He calls it his 'Armageddon virus.'"

She thought hard for a moment, her confusion slowly clearing into comprehension. She stared at her empty hands as if searching for a resolution in her palms. But there were so many loose ends that didn't seem to have a purpose. How much did they know about her research and exactly who was involved?

As if reading her thoughts, Timothy continued. "Benjamin's Blood is not some crazed, ultrareligious group. They are a collection of highly educated, highly influential men. The Praefectus Magnus of Benjamin's Blood goes by the pseudonym 'Magnus.' You know him as Luther Mendenhall."

Erin's head snapped up. "Mendenhall? Tom's partner?"

Timothy nodded. "We feel strongly that Dr. Jenkins does not know of Mr. Mendenhall's alter ego. As far as we can tell, he has simply been a financial backer to Timpanogos Research Industries. He's had little influence on what you develop there . . . until recently. That's why he brought in Dr. Krantz to work with you specifically. Once he learned what he needed, as you know, he left."

Erin's mind was whirring, lining up one bit of information with another until they all joined in a contiguous stream. But there was still one huge factor that did not seem to fit anywhere.

"Then what does all this have to do with Sean?" she asked, nodding toward the unconscious man across the seating area.

Timothy rested his elbow on his knees and steepled his fingers. "Throughout history, the Knights of Canterbury have used special *envoys* to perform specific tasks. Anciently they were called 'Swords of Justice.' It used to be we called only the purest, most trustworthy volunteers for such assignments. Regrettably, times have changed. Now we, of necessity, are obliged to use individuals who otherwise would have no interest in the true mission of our organization. Some might call them assassins; others might consider them terrorists or spies." He paused, either for emphasis or so Erin could prepare herself. "Mr. Flannery is one of our Swords, but he is not a cold-blooded assassin. He was sent to Utah to follow and observe Magnus. Mr. Mendenhall. Wherever Magnus went, Mr. Flannery followed. Before long we learned of your place in their plans. So we had Mr. Flannery keep an eye on you, too. Frankly, we were curious to see if you'd join their Order. Happily, you never did. Mr. Flannery was our eyes and ears at the physical level. His main task is to observe and report . . . and only rarely to intervene. That's when he's at his best. Otherwise, he's just another citizen living day to day."

"Just observe and report, huh? So when he intervened at the deli, that was his own doing, not yours? He wasn't sent to protect me?"

"Correct."

"Okay," she said as if reaching a conclusion.

Bemusement crossed Timothy's face. "Knowing Mr. Flannery's true character does not surprise you?"

She scowled. "Oh, I'm surprised, all right. I'm surprised you can be so apathetic about messing up his mind, manipulating him, perhaps even brainwashing him to believe things that aren't real. Sometimes Sean's a very nice guy with a troubling past, trying to live a normal life as best he can. 'An ordinary citizen,' as you said. *That's* when he's at his best." Her voice was filled with equal parts animosity and sadness. "Other times he does things he doesn't remember later on. He's violent and uncaring and . . . and lethal. That's when he's at his *worst*. You may think what you're doing is illuminated, that you are saving the world one whacko at a time. But you're wrong. It's the vilest form of slavery

I've ever seen. You are degrading a human being to nothing more than an expendable robot!"

Timothy looked contrite and yet . . . what? Unchangeable? "I can see how it might appear that way. Perhaps I should tell you a little more about Mr. Flannery before you pass final judgment on us."

"I think you should tell me *everything* you know about him," Erin nearly spat.

Timothy pursed his lips and tapped his fingertips against them. "The Sean Flannery you know is fabrication. The Sean Flannery *he* knows is fabrication. We fabricated his past to save him, not to degrade him."

Chapter 58

The relatively low flight from Oahu to Kauai allowed Magnus to look down over the vast Pacific Ocean. He marveled at the grandeur of it. He wondered what mysteries dwelt under its azure surface—what curious creatures, what fantastic fish, what massive monsters, what unrealized riches. He smiled at his effortless alliterations. Okay, so that last one wasn't perfect—but it was close enough.

Normally, he was the kind of man to have everything planned to the minutest detail. Nothing escaped his vision, his understanding. Until now. The stupid scientist he'd recruited was a mistake—Magnus admitted that now. It was not something he was proud of, but fact was fact. Krantz had vision, sure. He seemed to have the mental capacity to see his ideas to fruition. Perhaps that was still true. But without constant contact and reports, Magnus could only assume he was proceeding as assigned. In the past, Jacob Krantz was an ideal adept in the Order. He had performed exactly as Magnus had expected, as he had hoped. But the greater the leash he'd given the scientist, the more license he took. Obviously, he did not have the same vision Magnus possessed. He wasn't ready for the greater illumination the Order offered. Benjamin's Blood was exceptional; therefore, all of its leaders needed to be exceptional too. Magnus had always sought out the brightest minds, the most influential movers, the wealthiest patrons. Krantz had such potential, but that's where it stayed, as simply a possibility of greatness. In reality, he was still a pawn, a minion. Yet because of his vast knowledge, he was also dangerous. To the Order he could be disastrous.

Pity, the Praefectus Magnus thought. He had held the same hopes for Dr. Erin Cross. Stumbling onto her was pure luck. No—not luck. He didn't believe in luck. He was captain of his own destiny, master of his own universe. Luck had little to do with it. And yet Dr. Cross had been the one to open the door to a means of fulfilling his ultimate goal. Without her, he doubted his scientist would have gotten this far.

Now Magnus could see his future as reality. It was within his reach—just inches away. But like a poet searching for that perfect fourteenth line to complete his sonnet, Magnus grappled with a reality he could see, touch, taste, smell, but could not quite grab hold of. That's why he was 10,000 feet over the Pacific, heading toward a speck of land inhabited by a simple people who, by their deaths, would unwittingly make him a god.

Yes, he would see this dream—this destiny—to fruition, without the unreliable Dr. Jacob Krantz.

Chapter 59

Erin Cross, Sean Flannery, and half a dozen subordinates from the Knights of Canterbury passed high over Honolulu International on their way to Ni'ihau.

Erin did not like what she had learned about Sean. There was no way to tell if Timothy had told the truth. It was one of those instances where it sounded so far-fetched it *had* to be true. Timothy assembled the pieces of the puzzle she'd been juggling into a seamless fit. The more he explained, the clearer it became. The final picture wasn't a pretty one.

After Timothy had laid out the facts, Erin withdrew into a sullen muse. She tried to unravel what she'd just learned—tried to find a flaw in the material presented—but the stitching was too tight. Why Luther Mendenhall—*Magnus*—wanted to kill her made sense. Even Sean's presence in the game made sense. But he wasn't a squeaky-clean player. Who he was and what he was capable of were not pleasant realities, but they confirmed the suspicions she'd formulated during their run from the bad guys. Who the bad guys were and what they were capable of also fit the scenario of the past few days.

"I appreciate the forensic dissection of everything to this point, but there are a few things that still don't make sense."

"For instance?" Timothy asked.

"For instance, what do you want with me?" she said harshly. "Also, if you knew about Mendenhall and Krantz's twisted schemes all along, why did you wait so long to do something about them? Why didn't you simply eliminate Krantz and Mendenhall in some well-coordinated 'accident'?"

Even as she asked her questions, she began to discern a possible answer. She leaned back and favored her captor with a knowing scowl. "You want me to find a way to stop the Armageddon virus, don't you," she stated.

"You are truly a bright individual, Dr. Cross," Timothy said with a satisfied expression. "The Grand Illuminate was correct when he said you were enlightened as well as intelligent."

"Gee, thanks," Erin scoffed. "So you expect me to just hop on this island and pull some kind of bug spray out of my back pocket that eradicates a biologically unique retrovirus?" She huffed. "Apparently your boss isn't as *illuminated* as you claim."

Timothy stood and extended his hand to help her up. "Come with me, Dr. Cross."

Ignoring the proffered hand, Erin stood and followed him through to the doorway at the back of their seating area. Opening the door, he said, "As you can see, we have converted the back half of this jet into a small lab, but the equipment is state-of-the-art, as are the chemicals and biologic agents. The computers are loaded with all the TRI research notes we could gather. We also have been able to retrieve all of Dr. Krantz's notes on how he developed Armageddon. That was surprisingly easy. Either he was unconcerned about others reading his material or he was simply not very computer savvy when it comes to security."

"Probably both," Erin said.

"Our thoughts exactly," Timothy confirmed. "As I mentioned, we normally let events such as this take their natural course. That's why we didn't intervene right away. But there are hundreds of lives in immediate jeopardy now, and potentially millions of lives in a matter of days. We do not believe Dr. Krantz has employed any means of preventing an unwarranted spread of the virus. It could become a global catastrophe within a few weeks. There is nothing natural about this scenario. It must be stopped—and we feel you are the only one capable of doing so."

"No pressure, right?" Erin said just under her breath.

"If you need anything else to complete your task, we can have it delivered in a matter of hours. Now," Timothy said, sliding his hands deep into his pockets, "while you are under no obligation to comply with our request, we can promise you that you won't regret doing so. We are at your mercy, Dr. Cross. The *world* is at your mercy. Will you help us?"

Erin felt curiously confident and unafraid. She knew she had the wherewithal to tackle a problem like this. It was the magnitude of the situation that left her speechless. "How much time do I have?"

"Our ETA on Ni'ihau is about one hour," Timothy said as if it were all the time in the world. "We'll land in a secluded location. While you work on the virus, we'll send a team in to collect Dr. Krantz."

"So I have a couple hours to catch up on years of research," she mumbled.

"Yes. But your training and expertise give you a huge head start," Timothy said by way of encouragement. He handed Erin a laptop. "This has all the files I mentioned. Good luck, Doctor."

She accepted the computer and walked slowly back to her seat. As she lowered herself into its comfortable embrace, she looked over at Sean's sleeping form. Reclined in the wide seat, he looked so peaceful—and yet she knew he battled a constant inner strife. He had done so much without ever knowing *why*.

But this time things were different. Well, as far as she was involved, they were different. When he had risked his life for hers, he'd done so of his own provocation. His response to her dilemma was out of true concern for *her*, not out of some brainwashed programming by this bizarre group of religious fanatics. He was trying to live his life without them—but he probably didn't even know who *they* were. He deserved to have a chance to be himself, to have his life returned to him, to become the man she knew he could be.

Looking up at Timothy, Erin said, "I'll do this on one condition."

Chapter 60

Steward John brought Sean into a seated position and gave him an injection. "It's a stimulant to counteract the sedative we gave him," he explained.

Erin fumed within. These people thought nothing of using Sean—and probably countless others—to play a dangerous game of chemical roulette. She didn't want to dwell on how many of their games had probably gone awry because of unforeseen metabolic issues in their Swords of Justice. She shook her head and fought to keep her rage from coming to full boil.

"I assure you it's perfectly safe, Dr. Cross," the steward said as if aware of her concerns. "These are fairly benign drugs that will have no lingering effects on his system."

"John is correct," Timothy chimed in, having returned to his own seat. "Having seen the medications Mr. Flannery takes—"

"Drugs," Erin interrupted bitterly. "*Medications* are for the benefit of the individual taking them; the *drugs* you're giving him benefit only your organization."

Timothy pursed his lips and looked at Erin with sharp focus. "Yes, I can see how it looks from your perspective. But remember our purpose. If we sought only personal gain, we would not risk exposure by helping bring this crisis to resolution."

"Yeah. I'm getting all warm and fuzzy over your humanitarian efforts."

Through a ceiling speaker, the pilot said to prepare for their landing. Timothy set about securing his safety belt and shoulder straps.

"I suggest you buckle in real tight. This plane is retrofitted with swivel-mounted thrusters that allow for very short landings. They tend to make touching down quite exhilarating," he added with a smile.

Remembering their NASA-esque takeoff, Erin promptly buckled in with a lap belt and shoulder restraints.

"Oh. Wow," Sean mumbled through a massive stretch. "How long was I asleep?"

"Only a few hours, Mr. Flannery. We're about to land on Ni'ihau," John said as he helped fasten his shoulder harnesses.

"Ni'ihau? Where's that?"

"It's a tiny island at the western tip of the Hawaiian archipelago," he explained. "It's privately owned, and there's no tourist trade there. In fact, there are no modern amenities to speak of at all: no public electricity, plumbing, or even roads. It's inhabited by a group of original islanders who stick to the traditions of their ancestors in an effort to preserve their culture."

"No roads? Does that mean no airport, too?" Erin asked.

"I'm afraid so, Doctor."

"Then . . . ?"

Small crinkles formed at the corners of Timothy's eyes. "There is a small U.S. Navy site at the southern point of the island. They use it for missile testing and as a radar relay point. It's very small and is ninety percent automated. It's usually only manned two or three weeks out of the year. They have a helicopter pad but no landing strip. What they *do* have is a fairly smooth dirt road leading a couple hundred yards along the edge of the cliff and eventually down to the beach."

"A dirt road . . . along a cliff," Erin mumbled. "This just keeps getting better."

"Our pilot was trained on Italian aircraft carriers, which typically have alarmingly small flight decks. He can land this plane in a football field if need be."

"I've landed on worse," Sean offered supportively, looking out his window. "We'll be fine."

"Great." Erin returned to her computer, where she'd already read nearly every file. They were mostly review. Her eidetic memory allowed for quick perusal of data she'd already studied. The new material comprised the notes and speculations and mindless wanderings of Jacob Krantz. There was no rhyme or reason to his musings. Worse, there was no definitive conclusion to his postulates. He would carry his thoughts so far then assume they would work without redundant analysis or confirmation. There was no telling what his Armageddon virus would do or his vaccine against it. It was H1N1 all over again. Erin felt sick to her stomach.

"Okay, time to lock down," Steward John announced. "The pilot says this will be bumpy."

* * *

The modified G650 landed violently but safely. Coming to a stop reminded Erin of the jerky conclusion of an amusement park ride. She wondered how well the makeshift lab had survived.

As soon as the plane came to a complete stop, Sean asked, "What's going on?" He wasn't fully lucid but was sharp enough to recognize where he was. Apparently, his trance had worn off. "Why are we on an island?"

Erin turned angrily to Timothy. "Yeah, so what *is* the plan? You gonna turn him into a robot again?" She still had not come to grips with what she'd learned from the pseudo-luminary.

"What's that supposed to mean?" Sean asked.

Ignoring him, Timothy said, "Yes. Mr. Flannery goes in, captures Dr. Krantz, and brings him here. In the meantime, we hope you'll find a way to correct the damage he's done. If not, we interrogate Dr. Krantz until we do."

In spite of her anger, Erin was thinking well ahead of their immediate actions. "Okay. So I find a cure, we save the good people of Ni'ihau, and all is well. What happens to Dr. Krantz? And to Luther Mendenhall?"

"Happily, that is not your concern," Timothy said without an edge to his voice.

"On the contrary, I believe it is. They are the ones trying to kill me, remember?"

"Trust me when I say they will never bother you again once this is over."

The implication landed on her like an anvil. "You're . . . you're not going to . . . ?"

Timothy favored her with a sympathetic look. "Do you really want me to answer that?"

"I think you just did."

"Wait—what's this all about?" Sean jumped in.

"It's okay, Sean. These aren't the guys after me," Erin said, gesturing toward the men sharing the cabin of the plane.

"I figured that one out on my own," he responded sharply. "Who are they, and what do they want?"

As Erin searched Sean's eyes, her heart filled with sadness. She turned to Timothy. "He really doesn't know, does he?"

"Know what?" Sean said, his voice rising in frustration.

Not answering him, she told Timothy, "I don't know that I want to be an accomplice to any of this. The police back home already think I'm the one who killed Harry Harriman."

"We've taken care of that," the luminary explained. "Your record is clean of all actions involving the Benjamin's Blood Order."

"Who's Benjamin's Blood—some street gang?" Sean asked heatedly.

Steward John stepped out of the cockpit. "Sir, it's time to go. We have a very narrow window. We jammed the radar so they are unaware of our presence. Their redundant systems will come online in roughly ten minutes, but they won't detect us until we fly out. The island's pretty quiet at night. We estimate you'll have just six hours to fulfill your mission before we have to leave."

"Right," Timothy said. "It'll be getting dark soon, so you better go."

Sean bolted to his feet and cocked his fists, ready for a fight. "No one is going anywhere until I get some answers."

Timothy looked at Erin with raised eyebrows. She sighed in resignation. She hated the thought of putting Sean in another trance. The whole concept was still repugnant to her. But she knew time was of the essence. She could—and *would*—explain everything later.

Looking Sean in the eyes—her own eyes misted with tears of

her hypocrisy—she said, "*Meus cruor pro specialis. Meus corpus pro obsequium. Meus vita pro novus ordo seclorum.*"

Sean blinked, his head twitching sharply a few times. He then held out his right hand, knuckles first. "*Meus vita pro novus ordo seclorum,*" he said.

Erin turned to Timothy. "I'm going with him. I need to see how Dr. Krantz set up his operation in order to shut it down. There's nothing I can do here without samples, anyway. No arguments, Tim. I'm going."

The knight simply nodded.

Chapter 61

MAGNUS HAD TO PAY AN exorbitant amount to get a helicopter pilot named Dutch to fly an uncharted route the seventeen miles from Lihue airport on Kauai to Halali'i Lake on Ni'ihau, but he deemed it necessary. He still had no clue what was happening over the tiny island, and the longer he remained in the dark, the more anxious and angry he became.

Dr. Jacob Krantz, expert in virology. Idiot.

"You realize this will be a dustoff," the pilot Dutch said over the headset.

"Meaning?"

"I gotta have clearance to land on Ni'ihau, which I ain't got. So before the skids even touch the ground, you're going to bail out. Got it?" It was hard enough understanding the pilot over the static-filled headset. The fact that he had a thick stub of cigar between his teeth made it even worse. "Just like back in 'Nam. Touchdown in the DMZ and you're hi-sto-ry. Instant SPAM in a can, son. I ain't losing my ticket just so's you can take a nature hike."

Magnus was appalled. After paying the man the offensive amount—in cash—you'd think he'd offer better service. Still, he'd be getting onto the island without anyone knowing. And a cash transaction with no paperwork meant there was no way to trace him to the flight.

"And the pickup?" Magnus asked.

Dutch handed him a compact walkie-talkie. "Keep it on channel two. Just click the button and say you need an extraction—you know, like you was calling a dentist. Cell phones don't work out here, so don't lose my walkie. We meet at the drop site exactly when I say, so you might wanna synchronize your watch to mine. You're not there when I show, and it's *hasta la pasta,* sorry I lost ya. Got it?"

Magnus frowned at his escort, wondering if the man was always so banal. "Yes, I got it."

"Roger that," he said as they lifted off.

They flew low to the surface of the ocean, much too low for Magnus's liking. But he didn't have much choice. They were flying under the radar. The pilot planned on coming in from the northeast, tucking in next to the hills of Pueo Point, and slipping in over Po'oneone Beach to Halali'i Lake. Magnus would "dust off" on the shoreline and check out the test site. If everything looked satisfactory, he'd call Dutch for a quick pick up. If not, he'd track down Krantz, give him a piece of his mind, collect all of the scientist's materials, and *then* call Dutch. He had a flashlight to signal his position should his foray last into the night.

The sun was already low on the horizon as they flew into the shadows of the rugged cliffs along the eastern shore of Ni'ihau. Passing low over the beach, they spotted the lake in a matter of minutes.

"Ain't much of a swimmin' hole, is it," Dutch scoffed as they skirted the rim of the nearly dry lake. "If you don't hurry, you're gonna get wet, anyway. Storm's comin' on pretty fast. I'm puttin' you down on that bare spot half a klick from the lake. I count to five and I'm gone. Got it?"

"Got it," Magnus said, securing his fanny pack around his waist and shucking an empty pack over his shoulder. The fanny pack contained everything he suspected he'd need: a flashlight, a can of DEET bug spray, the walkie-talkie, and a handgun with a silencer.

Chapter 62

SEAN MOVED LIKE A BREATH of wind between the trees and scrub of the arid island. The oncoming dusk lengthened shadows and darkened pockets. That was good. What wasn't good was his "partner." Normally he worked alone. He didn't mind team assaults but only if his team members were as highly trained and seasoned as he was. This woman was anything but.

When he received his orders, it seemed like a simple in-and-out job. Then his superior started adding qualifiers. He hated those—the little extras that slowed him down, that increased the likelihood of error and mission failure. He was to escort the woman into the "combat zone" to act as intelligence. Undoubtedly she was competent enough in that regard, but this was a *field* operation. It required a certain amount of physical conditioning. This woman looked soft, slightly overweight. And she wasn't dressed for such an operation . . . but neither was he. Her name was Dr. Erin Cross. He remembered her from previous assignments.

Spontaneous ops of this nature were extra risky because of a lack of analysis and planning. Still, his superior had explained it was an urgent situation. Expeditious action was paramount to success.

The terrain reminded Sean of parts of Spain and Northern Asia; semitropical with tendencies toward seasons of drought. The hills were low and regular, the vegetation heavy but not dense. Their objective was roughly twelve klicks from the rendezvous point. It was a small village of locals that had little in way of tactical defenses or armament. His target was nonindigenous—a Caucasian amidst a population of Polynesians. As backup, the woman would provide visual identification. The target was Dr. Jacob Krantz. His assignment was to capture Krantz and bring him back to the rendezvous point. Simple enough.

"We intercepted the transmissions arranging his stay," Timothy had explained. "He's operating under the guise of a WHO scientist studying West Nile virus. What he's really doing is developing another virus for bioterrorism purposes. He has a mandatory no-contact clause with all villagers except one, a young man named Kapono Kahuleula. Krantz is staying with him. We don't know where Kahuleula lives, but we assume it's on the outskirts of the village to lessen Krantz's contact with the other islanders."

He paused and looked at Erin. "You have anything to add, Doctor?"

"Yeah, Krantz is a jerk face moron."

Sean scowled. "Very helpful," he grumbled.

Timothy then said, "You take point, Flannery. Move out."

Sean turned to Erin. "Follow directly behind me. Try not to make any noise. The wind will help mask our approach. If it starts to rain, even better. We'll stick to the shadows. Let's move."

On their way to the target site, she kept remarkably silent. As always, stealth was crucial to success. At one point Sean thought he heard the steady thumping of helicopter rotors. The woman whispered that she was breathing too hard to hear anything. Sean nodded, fought not to roll his eyes in annoyance, and continued on.

Within four hours they spotted the village of Pu'uwai. The sun had slipped behind a thick bank of clouds on the horizon. A blanket of cirrus already obscured most of the stars. The steady wind tormented the treetops and brought with it the scent of rain. A storm was coming fast.

They moved catlike in a circuitous route to the outskirts of the village. A few huts were dispersed along the edge of the brush. One in particular caught Sean's attention because of its isolation from the others. He moved toward it in a crouch, paused, and scanned the area. His highly trained eyes picked up an encyclopedia of information in just a few seconds.

When Erin caught up, she whispered, "Is that the one?"

"Most likely. You stay here," he demanded. "I'm going in for a closer look and to make sure the rest of the village is secure before I neutralize the target."

* * *

Neutralize? Erin wanted to object, but she'd learned to trust Sean's instincts, even though she still hated to be ordered around, and even though he was acting more as a robot than Sean. It was that trust that had saved her life before. Hopefully, it would do so one more time.

Chapter 63

Kneeling in the darkness, Erin saw a man stagger into a small hut a few yards away. In the light issuing from the hut, she could tell he was wearing baggy pants and a ratty T-shirt. She also saw his narrow shoulders, white face, and greasy hair. It was Jacob Krantz.

Even though Sean had told her to stay put, he was nowhere in sight. And Krantz was *right there*. In a snap decision, Erin sprinted quietly to the hut. A goat tethered to the front stoop gave her pause. The bony animal wobbled to its feet and bleated. She moved quickly to the leash and untied it, allowing the animal to amble off into the night. Erin took a breath and stepped into the yellow light of the hut.

Krantz was leaning over a cot with his back to her.

"Hello, Jacob," she said evenly.

The scientist jumped and spun around. "What the—? Geez, you scared the—" He stopped and gawked at her. "Erin Cross? What are *you* doing here?"

"I'm here to put an end to your madness."

He forced a chuckle. "What madness are you talking about?"

"The Armageddon virus. Using mosquitoes as vectors. Need I go on?"

Krantz's skin, now pink with sunburn, went a shade whiter. When he held out his hands in a questioning gesture, Erin saw he was holding a syringe. It was only then that she saw there was someone lying on the cot behind him.

"What are you doing?" she hissed with raw anger.

He turned and glanced at the little girl behind him. "I—um . . . I'm trying to . . . she's very sick. I'm trying to help her," he stammered.

Erin marched over and pushed him aside. A beautiful little Hawaiian girl lay faceup. Her hair was wet with perspiration, her skin clammy with fever. Her breathing was coarse and shallow. One of her bare shoulders had a huge welt characteristic of a local infection. A pinpoint of blood identified a recent injection site.

Erin spun on Jacob. "What did you do to her?"

Krantz's expression was hollow, panic-stricken. "I was trying to save her, I swear. I didn't want her to die." He threw the syringe on the table as if he'd been holding a snake.

"What is that?" Erin asked with measured patience, eyeing the syringe.

"I didn't think she'd react like this. *I* felt fine after I had the injection. Maybe it's something else. Maybe she—"

"What injection?!" Erin shouted.

"A vaccine. My vaccine. The one I made to protect against Armageddon." His voice was high-pitched—terrified and a childlike. He'd been caught red-handed.

Erin took a breath to steady her angst and fury. "Is it the vaccine you labeled JK-1?"

Krantz flinched. "How—how do you know that?"

Not answering, she brushed past him to grab a rumpled T-shirt from the pile along the wall. It was then she saw a stout young man crumpled in the corner.

"Is he dead?" she asked as if she already knew the answer.

"Just unconscious," Krantz answered in a small voice.

Finding a gallon jug of water, Erin wet the tee and began wiping the sweat from the little girl's face and arms. The injection site on her shoulder was burning up. She groaned when Erin touched it.

"What's her name?" she asked in a harsh whisper.

"Kimber—I mean Kaile'e."

Erin glared at the cowering scientist. "I read your notes, Jacob. Never mind how I got them. You followed the genetic markers on your RNA virus to see where it divided to splice into the host DNA. Because it was the same RNA locus H1N1 used, you just modified your failed swine flu vaccine in hopes it would cover your new bug. But you never tested it, did you."

"Oh yes, I did," he cried defensively. "On myself."

"Really? Have you infected yourself with the Armageddon virus yet to see if the vaccine works?"

Krantz's eyes lowered from Erin's searing glare. "Well, no. But . . ."

"Of course not. Just like you didn't test your H1N1 vaccine."

His expression suddenly changed to one of accusation. "*My* vaccine? May I remind you that *you* were the one who developed it? That mess was your fault, not mine."

Erin's jaw clenched involuntarily. She returned to swabbing Kaile'e's face and neck, hoping to bring her fever down. The last thing she wanted was to get into an argument over ancient history when a little girl was dying right in front of them.

"Kaile'e, did you say? How much vaccine did you give her?" Erin asked a few decibels above a growl.

He hesitated. "I . . . I'm not sure."

"You're not sure? What is the concentration of your vaccine?"

"One thousand units per mL."

"And how much does she weigh?"

"I don't know."

"How old is she?"

"I don't know."

"Is she allergic to any medication or any excipient in your vaccine?"

"Oh, don't be stupid. How should I know?"

She spun on him. If a glare could cause spontaneous combustion, Krantz would be a bonfire. Trembling with rage, Erin returned to applying the cold cloth to Kaile'e's fevered body. "Jacob, could you come here for a sec? You need to see this."

He moved beside her and looked down at the little girl. As Erin withdrew her right hand from Kaile'e's forehead, her left fist arced in a powerful punch, hitting Jacob squarely in the face. She felt his nose collapse, heard the cartilage snap. He cried out, fell backward, and floundered on the plank floor in a maelstrom of pain. Erin shook out her bruised left while she continued to swab the little girl with her right hand. Her knuckles throbbed, but she was certain it was nothing compared to what Jacob was feeling. Behind her, he gagged and coughed on the blood pooling in his sinuses and throat. It was a very satisfying sound to Erin.

Then another sound filled the hut—the sound of applause. She looked at the silhouette filling the doorway, just out of reach of the pale light.

"Well done, Dr. Cross, well done. That's something I've wanted to do for a long time."

He was smaller in size than Sean, but the voice was familiar. It took a moment before she remembered when she'd heard it before.

"Luther Mendenhall," she said just above a whisper.

"I can't tell you what a fortuitous surprise it is to find you here," he said with a chuckle. When he stepped into the light, Erin saw he held a silenced handgun in one hand. "And I prefer the name Magnus, if you please."

Chapter 64

Erin was speechless, trying to sort out his presence. If Mendenhall was surprised to see *her,* it was nothing compared to her surprise. Krantz was still whimpering on the floor.

The CFO moved to the foot of the cot. "You're probably wondering about the name change. I will explain that later. Suffice it to say, Magnus is how I'm addressed in the intellectual circles I frequent."

Erin finally found her voice. "The only circle you'll ever frequent is one of Dante's."

He chuckled. "Only if you believe in hell, Doctor, which I do not. Right now you're undoubtedly questioning why I'm here—as is Dr. Krantz, if he can hear me. I'll be brief. I mean to accomplish three things: First, I need the materials Dr. Krantz brought with him. I brought an extra pack just in case," he said, tossing the large satchel to the ground. "That'd be all his paperwork, chemicals, vials, and so forth. The equipment can stay." To the bloodied man on the floor he said, "It will interest you to know I stopped by your test site, Dr. Krantz. I was greatly disappointed. I couldn't find anything in the way of scientific research being conducted. That is a pity. I also haven't received a single transmission from you the entire time you've been here. As that was part of your mandate, it too is a pity. You know the consequences of cheating the Order."

"But . . . the . . . experiment is . . . ongoing," Krantz choked through globs of mucus and blood. "And . . . I did . . . send an update."

"I saw no evidence of that!" Magnus bellowed. "And my patience is gone. This is not the first time you've screwed up, but it will be the last."

"What's that . . . supposed to . . . mean?" he replied as forcefully as he could.

In a much calmer voice, Magnus said, "It means you are no longer needed." And with that, he aimed his gun and squeezed the trigger. A muffled pop sounded at the same time the gun kicked a few millimeters. A 9mm brass casing hit the floor and rolled into a corner. Jacob grunted as a sudden hole appeared in his tee over his stomach. His eyes widened with shock. They widened even further as the pain set in. Erin covered her mouth to keep from screaming, but a wheeze of dismay escaped between her fingers. Kaile'e groaned and shifted on the narrow cot.

"Who is this?" Magnus asked.

It took a moment for Erin to feel like she could open her mouth without vomiting. "Jacob's last failure. Her name is Kaile'e."

He gave the little girl a cursory once-over. "Very pretty." Then, looking back at Erin, he said, "You're coming with me. I need you to help me carry this stuff."

"What about her?" Erin asked, nodding toward Kaile'e while keeping her eyes on the gun.

"What are her chances?" he asked in a tone that held little concern.

Erin felt her throat constrict. "Not good."

Magnus shrugged. "Pity. Now gather his notes and let's get going."

Erin was speechless. She stared at Tom's business partner, unable to fathom the implications of their association—let alone his apathy toward Kaile'e.

"Now," Magnus said, pointing the gun at her.

Erin shook her head. "She's terribly sick, Luther. If I can get her back to the plane, I might be able to save her."

Magnus's eyes narrowed. "What plane?"

"It belongs to the guys who brought me here to stop this insanity," she said gesturing to the piles of Krantz's research material.

Magnus tipped his head back and laughed. "You can't stop enlightenment, you can only add to it—and only then if you have *true* illumination. This discovery is groundbreaking. It will bring me wealth and power beyond anything you can imagine. There is no stopping it."

Erin glowered at him. "If it *was* enlightenment, this little girl wouldn't be dying!"

"Dr. Cross," he said in a condescending tone, "history is replete with times where a few lives are lost in pursuit of the greater good."

"Greater good? There is *nothing good* about this," she yelled, pointing at Kaile'e.

Magnus gave her a fatherly expression of tolerance before glancing at his watch. Erin wanted to punch him in his smug face even more than punching Jacob Krantz.

"Well, as delightful as this discussion is, it's time for us to be leaving," he said.

"Us?"

"Yes, of course. You're going to interpret all of these notes and data for me."

"You're not enlightened, you're hallucinating."

"No. I don't believe I am. The blood pouring from Dr. Krantz looks real enough." He pointed his gun at Erin. "Unless you want to add your blood to his, I suggest you do exactly as I say."

Erin looked down the barrel of the silencer. Her eyes drifted to Kaile'e.

"You need some incentive, Doctor?" Magnus asked. Without waiting for an answer, he pointed the gun at Kaile'e's chest. "Move now or I end her life."

Erin stopped breathing. She felt the blood drain from her face. The room began to sway. Even though the vile act would be more like mercy killing than murder, it was still the taking of an innocent life. Erin could not bring herself to call his bluff.

Numbly, she collected several stacks of papers and slid them into the satchel. She gathered the vials and syringes scattered about and rolled them in pieces of cloth before setting them in the bag. Kaile'e's raspy breathing sounded like two sheets of sandpaper rubbing together. If only she could give her some Tylenol for her fever and the pain.

"Stop stalling," Magnus barked as he rammed the gun barrel between Erin's shoulders. "We have precious little time."

* * *

Magnus led Erin through scrub brush and low trees to a hilltop that overlooked the lake valley. Cloud-dampened moonlight cast a milky pall over the vista, matching the feeling in Erin's heart. She carried the satchel filled with clinking vials and rustling papers. Magnus carried a second bag filled with more of Krantz's materials and his fanny pack. Before making the trek back to the extraction point, he had sprayed a generous amount of DEET on his exposed skin. It was a good thing he did. The mosquitoes were plentiful that evening. He had offered Erin some, but she had declined. Somehow it didn't seem right considering she'd had a part in this madness—even if it was fractional.

As she was packing, she had found a large bag of black licorice nibs. After all Jacob's claims about the protective properties of black licorice, it couldn't save him in the end. Then, like a light clicking on, Erin thought of a way it might save *her*.

Chapter 65

LIKE A SHADOW, SEAN PASSED through the village of Pu'uwai, checking on its citizens—watching them prepare evening meals, night fish on the beach, or work on various projects around their homes. He smelled the sharpness of Citronella candles and knew they were lit to ward off mosquitoes and biting flies. Stealth was his forte: blend in, observe, disappear in one place, reappear in another. The Sword had learned his skills in the military, honed them in Special Ops, and perfected them under the tutelage of the Grand Order.

When he wended his way back to where he'd left the woman, a movement to one side stopped him cold. He froze in a low crouch and listened. A variety of insects buzzed and chittered; the mosquitoes seemed to be thicker in the brush. The wind constantly rustled the trees and shrubbery, but he was able to distinguish between a natural scraping of one leaf against its neighbor and the forced contact of someone pushing through the vegetation. An animal scent wafted past him. He remained frozen while his eyes scanned back and forth. The scent became stronger. The crackling of dried leaves and snapping of twigs drew closer. He slowly turned his head and watched a scraggly goat wander by. He waited until it had meandered into the village before he moved again.

Deciding all was clear, he proceeded to the rendezvous point. As he approached, he heard the mournful wail of a young man. He was mumbling something in Hawaiian. And he was crying. Yellow light poured through the window and open doorway of the hut near where he'd left the woman. He rounded the hut and moved to the window at an angle. His gun was drawn. He knew the mosquito netting on the window would make seeing out difficult.

He saw two men. One lying face up on the floor, the other sitting on a cot, holding something close to his body. Sean drew closer.

The one on the floor was Caucasian, about forty. It was his target, Dr. Jacob Krantz. He matched the photo in his pocket. The doctor's face and belly were bloodied: his face from blunt trauma, his belly from gunshot wound. Sean reviewed the past few minutes in his mind but could not remember hearing a gun being fired. It must have been silenced. The amount of blood on the floor told him the doctor was not long for this world—if he wasn't dead already.

The second man was clearly Polynesian, maybe in his early twenties. He was the one crying. The remorseful sound touched Sean in ways he didn't think possible. He understood the man's anguish, commiserated with his sorrow, felt his pain. He was cradling a young girl. Her arms hung limply to the ground. Her face was pressed against the young man's chest. There was no movement in her limbs, no rise and fall of her chest.

He was crying into her silky black hair, rocking gently back and forth, endlessly repeating what Sean took to be her name: Kaile'e, Kaile'e, Kaile'e.

Chapter 66

Erin knew that the minute she unraveled the mess Jacob Krantz had left, her life would be forfeit. She doubted Luther Mendenhall would kill her before she completed the work, and yet if he detected she was stalling, he just might kill her, anyway. He was that unpredictable. Her one hope in all this was that Sean was out there in the darkness, heading her way, following the trail she'd left.

They walked past the first dry lake in the heavy darkness. The wind was steady, blowing from the north. The horizon was thick with coming rain. Out in the open, the harsh elements helped keep the mosquitoes to a minimum, for which she was grateful. She slowed her pace and let Luther put some distance between them as she regularly dropped licorice nibs.

"Keep up," he grumbled as he veered toward a clear patch near the larger lake. This lake still had some water. When he reached the spot, he dumped his bag and unzipped his fanny pack. "You can drop that stuff right there. We'll be out of here in a few minutes."

Erin wearily complied. She wasn't sure if her fatigue was from stress, remorse, or resignation.

"Sit down and don't move," he said brusquely. "And don't try any funny business. I don't want to be forced to tie you up or shoot you."

Erin did as she was told without comment. She watched him pull a small walkie-talkie from the fanny pack and distance himself from her. If only she had her phone, she'd send Sean a message with their exact location . . . if she could get service out there. She prayed he would find the licorice trail and recognize it for what is was.

Luther returned a few minutes later and sat next to her. He seemed happier. "This has proven to be quite an adventure, wouldn't you say?" he said, as if making small talk on a date.

Still battling violent efforts to claw her way out of a suffocating anxiety, Erin knew the more information she got from him, the better chance she'd have at finding a way out. So she needed to act calm and self-assured. Yet she was tired of playing games, tired of all the cloak and dagger, tired of running.

"It was you all along, wasn't it," she said without looking at him, already knowing the answer.

"Excuse me?"

"The threatening text messages. The silly games. The attempts on my life."

He gave a brief, closed-lip chuckle. "You were a threat to Dr. Krantz because he felt you could trace the origins of his virus back to your swine flu research. Additionally, he felt you were the only one with the know-how to stop his super bug—if that is possible. So to cover my investment, I went along and ordered your elimination."

"You mean murder."

"Again, it is not really murder if it's for a greater good. However, I can now see that my decision was a little premature. Dr. Krantz did not turn out to be the brilliant scientist he presented himself to be. In fact, I have a feeling he got most of his ideas from you in the first place. The text messages were my doing. Just a little fun I sometimes engage in to make things more interesting."

"So you ordered my *murder,* but now you find you need me."

He laughed as if his date had just made a joke. "Why, yes, dear lady. You are my new hope for finishing this great work. As you may readily surmise, I have strong connections in high places all over the world. I have politicians, bankers, even assassins who are subject to the same kind of mind controls as your friend Sean Flannery."

Erin finally looked up.

"Oh, yes, I know all about your hero friend."

I doubt that, she thought.

"He put forth a noble effort, but he can't protect you anymore. As you recall, I tried to warn you about him back in Cedar City."

Erin's eyes widened. Even in the darkness of the evening, there was enough light for Luther to notice her shock.

"Ah, I can see you do remember. But of course you do. It was no secret at TRI that you have a photographic memory. Well, if you'll search that wonderful memory of yours, you'll realize I've been trying to help you from the beginning. It was me that got you the funding to continue your virus research after the H1N1 fiasco. Tom wanted to pull all the plugs, but I knew you were onto something bigger."

"You're saying Tom was going to fire me?" she asked incredulously.

"Maybe not fire, but certainly booted out of the lead researcher chair. Nevertheless, all of that is history now. We're starting afresh as of tonight. And I can promise if you perfect the Armageddon virus, there will be no end to what you can ask for *and* receive." He smiled broadly and looked around. "You want this island, it's yours. Take the whole Hawaiian archipelago in fact. You've heard of the Australia's constellation the Southern Cross? I'll rename these islands the 'Northern Cross' in your honor."

Erin couldn't believe he was trying to recruit her to his twisted ways with material rewards. Just being within a few feet of him made her sick to her stomach. She rehearsed all the text messages she'd received a few days ago. *Had it only been a few days?* They had a certain childlike nature to them. In spite of his wealth and prestige, this man had never grown up.

"Why did you kill Harry Harriman?" she heard herself ask.

"Quite simply, he got in the way."

"And the innocent people in the deli?"

"Yes. That unfortunate business was purely the ineptitude of a new recruit—" He stopped short and looked to the eastern horizon.

She heard it, too. It was the same sound she'd come to fear in the mountains of Dixie National Forest. A helicopter.

"Ah, good. Our ride is almost here."

Chapter 67

SEAN FELT AN INEXPLICABLE BOND with the young man holding the dead girl. Whether the girl was the young man's daughter, sister, or friend, he couldn't tell. But the depth of the man's sorrow bespoke a boundless love and the pure anguish of loss. It reminded him of a similar loss . . . though he couldn't quite put his finger on it.

He felt nothing for Jacob Krantz. He was a target. He had developed a lethal virus to use against innocent people. His intent was to see if his virus could be transmitted using mosquitoes.

Sean recalled the swarms of mosquitoes he'd encountered on other assignments. The concept of using them as a bioweapon was terrifying. Since Krantz had been eliminated, his assignment was complete. He hadn't personally stopped the scientist . . . but perhaps he could help lessen his success. He couldn't run through the village warning people to take cover. That went against his mandate to remain covert. But the young man in the hut could.

Sean entered the hut and knelt next to Krantz to check his pulse.

"Who're you?" the Hawaiian said in a hoarse voice.

"It's better you don't know."

"Is he dead?"

"Yes."

"Good. He was nod a good man."

"I know," Sean said, standing. "Listen, we don't have much time. I came here to stop this man from completing his experiment. His mosquitoes carry a deadly virus. You need to warn your people to get indoors, secure all windows and doors, apply insect repellant, use every precaution available to avoid mosquito bites. I don't know how long this threat will last, but I will do all I can to make sure the virus doesn't spread." He paused and looked at the little girl. Sadness choked his voice. "I am honestly very sorry for your loss."

The Hawaiian silently looked down at the lifeless form in his arms but said nothing.

"It is best you pretend you never saw me," Sean said as he moved to the door. "Again, I'm very sorry for . . . for all of this. Now go!"

He exited the hut to return to the woman—but she was gone. *Where?* Two options: she had wandered off or she had been abducted. He slowly worked his way back toward the hut, meticulously searching for footprints or other clues, like . . . *there!* A shiny black object–just off to one side of the footpath. Occasional glimpses of moonlight acted as a spotlight that highlighted the inch-long piece of . . . what? He picked it up and held it to the light from the hut. It was a nib of black licorice. Very soft, fresh. There was very little dust on it, meaning the candy had just been dropped. He searched the ground and found another piece a few feet away. Then another one meter beyond that one and then another. It was a sign, a trail he was to follow. Did the woman leave it? He wasn't sure, but the licorice trail was undeniably intentional. The very fact that local rodents and birds—or the goat— hadn't yet consumed the treats attested to the freshness of the clues. A few footprints accompanied the licorice trail, leading away from the village.

Sean followed the trail at full speed.

He had just crested the ridge of the lake valley when he heard the thumping of helicopter blades. In the distance the machine's running lights were clear and bright. Commercial—not rigged for stealth. That's interesting. A flicker of light from the valley below caught his eye. He could see two figures: one brandished a flashlight without any thought to remaining covert, the other was seated next to what looked like two or three large duffel bags.

The helicopter drew closer, flying dangerously low. A commercial pilot would not fly that low, especially at night. Was it an extraction vehicle? Sean immediately began to move closer to the people on the lakeshore. He needed positive identification. The probability that Dr.

Cross was one of the two unknowns was high. But who was the second person? When he was within a hundred yards of the two, the helicopter crossed the beachhead and flew directly toward them. The flashlight bearer signaled their location. It *was* an extraction.

The helicopter began a touchdown descent about ten meters away. Its landing lights added to the illumination of the pickup point. Sean was close enough now to identify the people—and he blinked at what he saw. Luther Mendenhall, aka Magnus, and Dr. Erin Cross. He was to keep tabs on Magnus and was to protect Dr. Cross. Magnus wielded the flashlight in one hand and a gun in the other. *Move!*

Magnus pocketed his flashlight and grabbed a pack. He motioned for Cross to pick up the other two. The pilot rotated the bird so the passenger door faced the evacuees. High above, a clap of thunder announced the opening of the clouds. A deluge of heavy, fat raindrops instantly drenched the area.

As soon as their backs were turned, Sean sprinted forward. Buffeted by rotor wash and slickened by rain, Magnus struggled to open the passenger door. The noise also muffled Sean's approach. The door finally slid open. Magnus threw the packs inside. He helped Erin climb in—and saw Sean barreling toward them. With both feet on the landing skid, he yelled for the pilot to take off, which he did—but not before Sean leaped and grabbed the wet skid with both hands.

As the helicopter thumped into the night sky, Magnus tried to stomp on Sean's hands. They gained altitude quickly, ten feet, twenty, forty, seventy. Sean tried to avoid the slamming of Magnus's shoe, but he was only partially successful. His hands throbbed with pain. He was certain a couple of his metacarpals had fractured under the abuse. The whining of the engine and the whirl of the rotors distorted all sounds; the whipping rain and wind blurred all images. Magnus lurched backward into the cabin. Rain slashed at Sean's face, but he could see Magnus was now struggling with something else—the woman!

Sean took the brief respite to loop a leg over the skid and swing on top. They were now out to sea, some one hundred feet over the ocean. Below, blue-black water boiled and churned, whipped by the storm, spewing rabid flecks of white foam into the air. Inside the cabin, Erin wrestled with Magnus. He gripped her wrists, pinning her against the back bulkhead. The contest seemed evenly matched. She was not a particularly muscular woman, but the rage in her eyes bespoke an indomitable inner strength.

Sean went for his gun but paused. The pitch and roll of the helicopter made firing a round extremely dangerous, even at this close range. He reached in and yanked on Magnus's ankle. It unbalanced him enough for Erin to dislodge her right wrist. Magnus kicked at Sean's face while holding on to Erin's other wrist. The pilot turned and hollered something. Erin then yelled something at Magnus. He turned back to her, and she rammed her fist squarely into his nose. His head snapped back. Blood splattered everywhere. His grip on her left wrist faltered. As Erin yanked her hand free, Sean stood on the skid, leaned in, and grabbed Magnus's belt. With a powerful tug, Magnus was airborne. At the same time, Sean's footing slipped.

There was no handhold on the floor of the doorway. Sean's fingers scraped across the slick rubber matting. He heard Erin scream. His chest hit the skid, knocking the air from his lungs. He felt his body drop as he grappled for the landing skid. He managed to grab hold with one hand as his body dangled below. He heard Erin shouting to hold on. She was kneeling at the doorway, extending a hand to him. He swung his legs over the runners and reached for her hand. With surprising strength, she hoisted him to a point where he fell into the cabin.

In one fluid movement, Sean rolled to his knees, drew his gun, and pushed the barrel against the side of the pilot's head. The man jerked and froze. "Hey, I just work for a living," he cried.

Erin carefully leaned out and looked down for a few seconds. "He's gone. I can't see him," she shouted.

"Good. Shut the door," Sean hollered back.

She did, which greatly decreased the tumult of engine and storm. To the pilot, Sean ordered, "Turn this bird around."

He spit out the cigar butt from between his teeth. "Turn around?"

"You know the naval station, south end of the island?"

"Yes, sir," the pilot said quickly.

"Don't *sir* me. I'm just a grunt."

"Brother, me, too! Vietnam, two tours."

"Outstanding," Sean said, lowering the gun. "Then fly this bird like a Huey and get us there ASAP."

"Roger that," the pilot said, tilting the helicopter forward at full throttle.

Chapter 68

THE MODIFIED GULFSTREAM G650 TOOK off with the same thrill-ride trajectory it did the first time. Erin was too exhausted to experience either joy or terror.

"And you're sure Magnus is dead?" Timothy asked her once they leveled out.

"I'm not sure of anything," she said weakly. "I saw him fall out of the helicopter over the ocean. When I looked down, I couldn't see anything but choppy waves and whitecaps. We were pretty far out, so unless he's an excellent swimmer . . . yeah, he's dead."

Timothy nodded. "Thank you, Dr. Cross. I wish we could be more certain, but the odds are in our favor. I feel our anonymity is secure."

"What about the helicopter pilot. Is he now a dead man, too?"

"No, no. We paid him double the sum he got from Magnus. He's harmless," Timothy said. "Besides, who will believe him even if he does decide to talk?"

Erin gave an attempt at a smile that just wouldn't come.

"For a mission organized so quickly, the outcome was very good. You said you feel you got all of the materials Dr. Krantz used to develop his virus, and Mr. Flannery believes with acceptable certainty that Dr. Krantz is dead."

As is the beautiful, innocent Kaile'e, she thought bitterly.

She looked over at Sean's sleeping form. "And what about him? Is he going back to being one of your Swords?"

"No. We will hold true to our agreement. John will compile a list of the medications Mr. Flannery takes that make him respond to our keywords and commands. It is imperative you wean him off the drugs precisely as we prescribe. I cannot stress this enough. Sean is a strong man, physically and mentally. We are confident he will respond well to the cessation of the chemical influence. The part we are not sure of is how he will accept the facts of who he really is and what he's done for the past ten years."

"Ten? I thought it was only two or three."

"That was part of the program, part of his delusion. It will be removed along with everything else, as promised." Timothy looked at Erin with unquestionably serious eyes. "You must understand that we are putting an enormous amount of trust in you, Dr. Cross. Mr. Flannery may know he was part of a Special Ops team, but that will be the extent of his recollection. The final command we give him will involve a permanent subconscious block of his service for us. If he tries to delve into who we are and what we had him do, it will lead to a dead end and quite possibly deeper psychotic issues."

"And you're not going to simply jettison us somewhere over the Pacific?" Erin asked, only half-joking.

Timothy smiled. "Of course not. If we needed to kill either of you, we wouldn't be having this conversation."

She closed her eyes and leaned against the headrest. "How much *will* Sean remember?"

"He'll recall his childhood and his time in the military. Everything between his military discharge up to the incident at Giamboli's Deli will be blocked. As I said, that will take some getting used to for Mr. Flannery. Ten years of life is a significant amount of time to lose. We'll be more than happy to offer psychiatric counseling to help in this," Timothy said.

Erin scoffed. "Not likely. Sean doesn't care much for psychiatrists—for obvious reasons."

Timothy nodded. "We'll provide you with materials that will instruct you on the best ways to handle his recovery and reorientation to civilian life. We'll also provide a number by which you can reach us if you have no other recourse. It is a private, untraceable line. And believe me when I say we'll know if you try to use it against us."

"Believe me when I say I won't."

Chapter 69

THE TRIP BACK TO THE mainland was interrupted only by the need to get more fuel in Hilo, on the Big Island.

Erin distracted herself by running a few tests on the Armageddon virus in the aerial lab. Jacob Krantz had brought a vial of the virus along with the vaccine against it, and a variety of other chemicals and compounds. She'd already memorized his notes. There were no lab animals on which to test the virility of Krantz's super bug, but what she saw made her skin crawl. The mad scientist had almost created a global killer. She had no idea if either the virus or his vaccine would work. Krantz hadn't run conclusive tests on it. His notes indicated he had only injected himself with the vaccine. The bio-markers made sense on paper, but that didn't mean it would actually work that way in humans. Many times such things proved disastrous. It truly *was* H1N1 all over again.

As for the mosquitoes Krantz had brought to Ni'ihau, Erin demanded expedient measures be taken to kill them. Not surprisingly, the Grand Order had contacts with the Centers for Disease Control. Timothy assured Erin they'd order an immediate island-wide spraying of a mix of malathion and permethrin, potent insecticides with low human toxicity. As an added measure, she asked for an extra-dense application over Lakes Halulu and Halali'i. With the onset of winter storms, when the mosquito population was at its lowest, she hoped none of the Armageddon-carrying adults survived. Lamentably, only time would tell.

Erin felt wholly unprepared to do what had to be done next. Feelings of betrayal and forgiveness, hatred and compassion, conflict and resolve assaulted her. She was glad Sean would no longer be a puppet to these people. But what kind of life would he be left with? He had nothing to go back to. He'd been living a lie for the past ten years. *Ten years!* Erin had earned her PhD in less time. His road to normality would be difficult, almost impossible, and she prayed he'd be strong enough to traverse it.

* * *

Steward John gave Sean his stimulant injection and helped move him to a table in the lab. When he awoke, he was dizzy and disoriented. Erin rose from a chair and went to his side. At her request, they'd been left alone.

Gently touching his hand, she asked, "How are you feeling?"

"Like I've been hit by a cement truck," Sean mumbled. He sat up slowly and winced when he put pressure on his hand. "What happened here?" he asked, examining his bandages.

"The first, second, and third metacarpals are broken. They're clean breaks and should heal quickly. Your pain meds are causing most of your wooziness."

He rubbed his eyes with his good hand and vigorously shook his head. Mistake. His head pounded with a headache that threatened to split his skull. He grimaced and looked around. The lighting in the lab was bright but not so much as to cause excessive photosensitivity. He slid his legs off the table and stretched his arms over his head. He noted the tubular shape of the room and heard the rumbling whistle of the jets. "I assume we're still on the plane?"

"Yes," Erin said.

"Do I dare ask how I broke my hand?"

"Not yet."

Something about the hesitancy in her voice told him she was either hiding something, or she was about to divulge something that would be difficult to accept. Perhaps both. "Is everything okay?"

She nodded. "We confirmed who was after me—and we were right. It was Jacob Krantz and a man named Luther Mendenhall. Luther is my boss's business partner. Well, former business partner. He's dead. So is Krantz. They were trying to develop an apocalyptic bioweapon on the island of Ni'ihau. We were able to stop them."

"Seriously?" Sean was astounded by her news. They had suspected Krantz was involved in something sinister, but a bioweapon? Wow. Even more disconcerting were the words and tone in which Erin had delivered the news. "*We* stopped them?"

She nodded.

"So . . . why aren't *we* jumping for joy?"

Erin pulled a tissue from a pocket and clenched it in her fist. "Because in the process, I discovered something else—something that will be hard for you to stomach. But it's the truth, Sean. And before I tell you, you have to know it is the truth."

He saw the tremor in her hands, felt the angst in her voice. She was serious.

"Okay," he said, sliding from the table to stand.

"No, you'd better sit back down," she said without humor. "Please."

He frowned softly and complied. "You're the doctor."

She took a deep breath. Then another. "Sean, pretty much everything you know is not real," she blurted quickly.

With a questioning chuckle, he said, "What?"

Erin pushed on either side of her head and screwed her eyes closed. "Geez, this is so complex, it's hard to know where to start." Her throat closed with emotion. A shuddering wheeze turned to a plaintive whine before it slipped into a convulsive sob.

"Erin," Sean said quietly. "It's okay. Just start anywhere. I trust you."

She held the tissue to her eyes until she regained control of her emotions. "You remember that psychiatrist you saw at Beaumont Hospital?" she finally said. "The one who loaded you up on drugs? Well, he really wasn't with the hospital or the VA. He had an office there, but he was working for a group of men who are preparing the world—" She stopped cold and shook her head. "This sounds so insanely paranoid. I wouldn't believe it myself if I wasn't in the middle of it."

Sean remained silent. He knew she had to work through this in her own way. The intensity of her emotions was palpable. He wanted to put his arms around her to comfort and encourage her. She hadn't really revealed anything shocking, and yet the tears were already flowing.

"Okay, look," she forced from herself. "You were in Special Ops, right? You sometimes did things 'off the record,' because sometimes it was the only way to not clue in your target, right? Or sometimes it was just better for the public not to know. Well, this group does things like that, only on a much bigger scale. And they've been doing it for . . . for centuries. They are not bad men . . . but they're not good either. They . . . oh, I don't know. We'll discuss how I feel about them later. But you know all the pills you take? You don't like them because they make you feel weird, like you're not yourself? Well, that's precisely what they do. When you take them, you're *not* yourself. You become someone else."

Sean stood again and began pacing back and forth in front of the table. He needed the blood circulation to help him concentrate. "You mean like a schizophrenic?"

"Yes . . . and no. They *created* an alter ego, one that's not naturally within you, but it's one *they* can manipulate."

He snorted. "Now you do sound paranoid." He couldn't believe it—like he was part of some lame spy movie from the sixties.

She wiped her eyes with her sodden tissue. "I know. I wouldn't have believed it either. But it's true, Sean. I can't believe I'm even saying this, but I don't have an option. And it gets worse."

"Great."

Erin went to a computer and pulled up a file. "Take a look at this."

Sean moved to the computer and began to read an article dated ten years earlier. It told of a recently discharged Special Ops Marine who was receiving treatment for PTSD when his wife and daughter were killed in a traffic accident. The man suffered a nervous breakdown the next day. He went into lockdown to control his psychoses and suicidal tendencies. He became so despondent they had to feed him intravenously and keep him in restraints. One evening, he managed to escape, leaving two unconscious guards in his wake. A weeklong manhunt ended in finding his partial remains in a swamp—apparently the victim of an alligator attack. Or a gruesome suicide. He had a closed-casket military funeral. The man's name was John Ferguson. He was Sean's age—his tours of service were the same dates Sean had served. A black-and-white snapshot showed a young man in Marine Corps dress. It was Sean.

Sean swallowed what felt like a fist-sized rock. He read the article again. The implications were gut-wrenching. His mind refused to accept such an impossible reality. He was Sean Flannery, not John Ferguson. His wife was alive and living with a dermatologist in Florida. He'd never suffered a nervous breakdown, but he felt as if one was coming on. *My daughter . . .* He sucked in a hung breath. Bile churned at the base of his throat, threatening to rise. *My daughter . . . no! Britt was* not *dead. She* couldn't *be dead. It's impossible.* He texted her weekly. E-mail, too. He looked at Erin as her words came back to haunt him, not as accusation but as confirmation.

When was the last time you talked to her? Not texted, not e-mailed, talked?

When was the last time you actually heard her voice?

When was the last time you told *her you love her?*

He couldn't answer any of those questions because he couldn't remember. Why couldn't he remember? Was it because it never happened? Impossible! But . . . was it?

He staggered back and collapsed in a chair. Erin was immediately at his side.

"I'm so sorry, Sean," she said, very near a sob.

Sean looked at her and saw pure concern, pure love in her eyes. She was there for him—there was no question of that. No fabrication.

"I . . . I don't understand," he managed to whisper. To him it felt like he was yelling. He wanted to yell—to scream at the top of his lungs. The more he thought about his life, his odd relationship with his daughter—or whoever it was—the quirkiness of his life compared to others', the more the clues fell into place. They began slowly, one at a time, then rapidly dropped in succession, like a long line of dominoes that once started could not be stopped until it reached the end.

He tried to stand but had no strength in his legs. He sensed Erin's arms around his shoulders, her mouth to his ear, but he couldn't feel her touch. He heard her whispering. Words like "sorry," "unfair," and "terrible." Yes, this truth—if it *was* the truth—was the most terrible thing he'd ever experienced.

He gritted his teeth and forced his mind to stop its frenzied twirling. He shucked her embrace and leaned forward. He knew he still couldn't stand—didn't even want to try. He heard himself speak. His voice sounded half-animal.

"You're saying I am not who I think I am? That my daughter died ten years ago? That my whole life is not real?"

"I'm so sorry, Sean," Erin repeated. "What they've done is despicable, unforgiveable. It's downright inhumane. You have every right to be angry. But before you do anything, please hear me out."

It took a while for her words to register in his mind. Still, he had questions. Thousands of questions. Millions. He didn't want to hear anyone out. Yet he needed answers!

"The article said I was eaten by an alligator. So who was in the casket?"

"I don't know."

"Then why would the paper say it was me?"

"It was falsified so they could . . . use you." Her voice ached with remorse.

"They. Who are 'they'?"

She hung her head. "That's where it gets *really* bizarre. Have you ever heard of the Knights of Canterbury?"

"Yeah, I think so."

"Well, I won't go into the history lesson right now, but suffice it to say they are still around. I'm still not clear on what their exact mission is, but they have been using you as a spy of sorts."

"A former Special Ops Marine," he huffed. "Right up my alley."

"I despise what they did to you, Sean, but at the same time, I realize they first saved you from self-destruction. I've read all the hospital records. They gave you a new life—one with minimal sorrow or heartache or remorse."

"And one that is totally fake!" Sean yelled. He couldn't believe she was defending the people who had deceived him for so many years. His hands trembled with fury. He wanted to hit something—to tear something apart—but he still didn't have the strength to even stand. "One without Britt," he said, his throat constricting his voice to a husky wheeze.

Erin moved in front of him and wrapped her arms around his neck—but he didn't want to be touched, to be held. He wanted to lash out, to hurt someone with the same anguish he was experiencing. But Erin's tender embrace had a magical effect. It made him feel important even though he was nobody. It made him feel loved in spite of his past. It made him feel like an individual in the face of proof to the contrary.

Slowly, Sean put his arms around her back. He rested his arms against her, hesitantly at first, not sure if he deserved her compassion. When Erin didn't let go, he held her tighter, returning her embrace. Then his emotional wall crumbled. He clung to her and sobbed into her shoulder.

* * *

Sean didn't know how many minutes or hours had passed, but when he opened his eyes, he was lying on the table again. Only this time, Erin was sitting next to him on a drafting stool, holding his hand. Her head drooped to his chest, her breathing slow and steady.

"Hey," he whispered. "You okay?"

Erin stirred and lifted her head. Her eyes were puffy and her face drawn. But Sean had never seen anyone more beautiful. She offered a feeble smile. "Yeah. How about you?"

"I think I'll live. I'm just not sure how." He wasn't trying to be sarcastic or morose. He was stating a fact as plainly as he could.

She took his good hand in both of hers. "Tell me how I can help."

Sean sat up, careful not to release their bond. "Let's get Timothy in here. I want to know everything from the beginning."

Erin's look was unsure, fearful.

"It's okay," Sean said. "I want you right next to me to tell me what's true and what isn't."

"And what if I don't know?"

"Then we'll figure it out together."

Chapter 70

The Gulfstream G650 landed at McCarren International around five in the morning. Timothy had covered everything, from the drugs they used to the procedures for deprogramming a Sword. Sean asked some very pointed questions: He had been married. They did have a daughter named Britt Ferguson. He was hospitalized for PTSD. They'd never moved to Colorado. His wife did have an affair with a doctor in North Carolina and moved with him and Britt to Florida. They were killed in a traffic accident shortly afterward. Sean did have a complete nervous breakdown. And that's where the Knights of Canterbury took over. Using snippets from his past, they were able to create a volume of very convincing memories.

"After you saved Dr. Cross the first time, we kept close tabs on you," Timothy divulged. "We knew you had taken Dr. Cross to your cabin in Dixie National Forest. We deemed it a very smart move and decided to let you lie low for a time."

"That explains the stealth helicopter we saw pass over us that night."

"Yes. But it was only a couple days later that we needed you and Dr. Cross to accompany us to Ni'ihau to help stop Dr. Krantz's poorly executed experiment. You'll be happy to know the Dixie search and rescue team never found your cabin. It's still a secret."

"As are you," Erin said with a small barb of animosity. She wouldn't *ever* get used to the idea of being used against her will.

Timothy smiled. "Yes, Doctor. As are we."

Thunderheads billowed across the expanse of the Las Vegas valley, but no rain had fallen. The sky remained steely and dark. Erin noted that it matched the look in Sean's eyes.

The private jet taxied to a secured hangar where Sean's Jeep awaited.

"We took the liberty of bringing your vehicle to Las Vegas while you were away," a subordinate explained. "It has a full tank of gas, and we've included a cooler with drinks and snacks for your trip home."

"What about the APBs on us?" Sean asked Timothy.

"As I mentioned, those have been cleared. Unless you do something foolish, you should not have any delays from local law enforcement."

Timothy extended his hand. Erin hesitated. "I still don't know whether to shake it or punch you in the face."

The hand retracted. "No hard feelings on my end, I can assure you," he said. "You are a truly brilliant scientist, Dr. Cross. You have a very bright future ahead of you. We feel your malaria vaccine is the result of pure illumination. The world will benefit from what you have done."

"Thank you," she said in honest appreciation.

"So now that I don't have a life. What do you suggest I do?" Sean asked the luminary.

"You do have a life, Mr. Flannery. You are a writer of children's books."

"That was in my false life."

"Only part of it. You actually have penned a number of stories. I am no expert on children's literature, but I thought they were quite good. I particularly like the story of the snail and his slimy trail. We couldn't let you actually publish them, because it would weaken your covert nature with too much popularity. You will find all of your writing still in your computer in your apartment. It's up to you what to do with your work, but I highly recommend you seek out a reputable agent and continue writing. You have talent, Mr. Flannery."

"How will I subsist until I start earning a paycheck?" he asked.

"Your apartment lease is paid through next year. The title to your Jeep is in your desk. Your debit card is assigned to a bank account with a balance of two million U.S. dollars. Consider it a small payment for services rendered. Your social security number and driver's license are valid. In effect, your life is the same as it was—only you'll be on your own."

"No, he won't," Erin chimed in.

* * *

The drive along I-15 from Vegas to St. George was wonderfully cool and calm. The clouds kept the Nevada heat at bay, and knowledge that no one was after them kept their anxiety to a minimum. They were safe for a time—hopefully a very long time.

By the time they reached Cedar City, they had received word that the spraying of insecticide on Ni'ihau was completed. A pair of legitimate scientists had accompanied the mosquito abatement team from the CDC to check on all aspects of mosquito life on the island. Halali'i Lake had no mosquito larvae or pupae in its waters. Only a few adults appeared to have survived the spraying; those caught in traps proved to be indigenous to the island. There was no sign of Krantz's mosquitoes.

Erin prayed the deadly Armageddon virus was no more. To be sure, she was determined to develop a vaccine against it—just in case. She called Tom Jenkins and filled him in on the information she was allowed to share. She didn't dare try and expose everything. Although Tom promised his line was secure, she knew the Order was listening in. They would be the rest of her life. Strangely, it was creepy and comforting at the same time.

"It turns out Luther had his hands in several under-the-table transactions," Erin explained on speaker phone so Sean could listen in. "You know he had his own investment company, right? Well, they found out he was borrowing money in seven-figure amounts from arms dealers in Saudi Arabia."

"What?" Tom gasped, disbelieving.

"It's true, Tom. We discovered this on the island. The people associated with his lenders are the ones who really put a stop to everything. Hopefully, we won't be hearing from them ever again." Erin knew it was a lie, but it was the safest explanation. "And, sorry to break this to you, but Luther shot and killed Dr. Krantz."

"I know. It's all over the news wires," Tom confirmed. "Have they found Luther yet?"

"No." This time it wasn't a lie. "I guess they'll keep looking for a while. The good news is that Krantz's experiment amounted to nothing."

"Just like when he worked here."

If you only knew!

"Pretty much." She paused, struggling to keep her emotions in check. "Hey, Tom?"

"Yeah?"

"Thanks."

"For what?"

"For everything. It was comforting to know there was someone I could trust."

This time it was Tom who paused. "What about this Flannery guy?"

Erin looked at Sean as he concentrated on the highway. "Oh, him? Yeah. I trust him with my life."

Sean smiled.

After disconnecting, Erin sat in a melancholy funk watching the barren landscape speed by. She felt she should be happier with the way everything turned out. They were both safe and free of guilt. She still had her malaria vaccine to perfect. And then there was the Armageddon antiviral med to create. But her biggest challenge was one her science background would have very little influence on.

She reached over and placed a hand on Sean's knee. "Have I thanked you yet today?"

He chuckled. "Um, I think only about eleven times."

"Let's make it an even dozen." She scooted over and kissed his cheek. "Thank you, Sean."

"You're welcome." He gave her a quick glance filled with uncertainty. "Have I asked you if you're sure about taking me on as your next project?"

"Not that I can remember," she lied. He'd already asked that question at least a dozen times, too. "But I honestly don't mind."

"Well, thank you, Erin. This is something I may never be able to repay."

"Don't worry, Sean. I'll bill you."

He gave her that adorable lopsided smile. He probably had no idea what that did to her.

"Just one thing," he said in a more serious tone.

"Yes?"

About the Author

GREGG LUKE WAS BORN IN Bakersfield, California, but spent the majority of his childhood and young adult life in Santa Barbara, California. He served an LDS mission to Wisconsin then pursued his education in biological sciences at SBCC, UCSB, BYU, and subsequently graduated from the University of Utah College of Pharmacy. His biggest loves are family, reading, writing, music, science, and nature. You can visit Gregg at www.greggluke.com.

Gregg has traveled to mosquito endemic areas for research on this book and has extensively studied parasitology and blood-borne diseases, including traveling to the Yucatan peninsula during the H1N1 pandemic of 2009.

"No more Latin?"
She laughed. "Or black licorice."
He laid his hand on top of hers. "Deal."